PRAISE FOR THE
STEEL BROTHERS SAGA

"Hold onto the reins:
this red-hot Steel story is one wild ride."
~ A Love So True

"A spellbinding read from a
New York Times *bestselling author!"*
~ BookBub

"I'm in complete awe of this author. She has gone and delivered an epic, all-consuming, addicting, insanely intense story that's had me holding my breath, my heart pounding and my mind reeling."
~ The Sassy Nerd

"Absolutely UNPUTDOWNABLE!"
~ Bookalicious Babes

BLAZE

BLAZE

STEEL BROTHERS SAGA
BOOK TWENTY-ONE

HELEN HARDT

This book is an original publication of Waterhouse Press.

Cover Design by Waterhouse Press, LLC
Cover Photographs: Shutterstock

ISBN: 978-1-64263-296-5

For Dean

PROLOGUE

Callie

The door of the bank opens then, and a woman wearing jeans and a red T-shirt walks through. The shirt reads *Karen's Locks*.

Rory and I abruptly stand.

"You're the locksmith?" Rory asks.

"Yes, I am. I'm here to see Michael Keats."

Mr. Keats approaches us quickly. "Karen Bates?"

"Yes, I'm sorry I'm late."

"Wait a minute," Rory says. "Is the baby okay? The one who was locked in the car?"

Karen smiles. "She's fine. She slept through the whole thing. The poor mother cried like a baby, but the little one was just fine."

Rory lets out a relieved sigh. "Thank goodness."

Yes, my sister will be a hell of a mother. I hope she gets that chance.

"Come on back, all of you," Mr. Keats says.

I inhale a deep breath, gathering all my courage.

In a moment, we'll find out.

We'll find out if our property was stolen.

And if it was . . . I don't know what we'll do.

The four of us—Keats, Karen, Rory, and I—crowd into the room. The walls are lined with locked boxes of various sizes. I cast a glance around. Which one of these is Donny's? My gaze falls on Box 451.

That's it. That's the number that was on the key inside the glasses case. Funny that I only now remember. How did I think, for one minute, that Donny had taken our key?

Karen opens up her toolkit and pulls out a drill. Keats nods to a plug on the wall. Several minutes pass while Karen readies her tools. The boxes on the wall seem to move in closer. The room is shrinking, closing in on us.

Then the piercing shriek as she drills into the lock.

CHAPTER ONE

Callie

The girls' restroom on Monday following homecoming is a veritable gossip fest. Makes it hard for me to stay invisible. I walk in. All the stalls are occupied, so I get to wait.

Several girls huddle around the sinks, their backs toward me.

"I heard she almost died," one of them says.

"I know. It's scary," says another.

"How much of it did she drink?"

"No one really knows. She went to the hospital later, after the bonfire."

I'm never one to force myself into a conversation, but I saw how sick Rory got Friday night after drinking a cup of the hairy buffalo spiked punch. I force myself out of my comfort zone to insert myself and approach the girls.

"Who are you talking about?" I ask.

"You haven't heard, Callie?" It's Sarah Harger, a B-lister.

"Would I be asking if I had?"

I don't really know these girls. I mean, I know their names. Snow Creek High School is a small school.

"Diana Steel," the second girl says. Her name is Mary. I think her last name is McCullough.

"What about her?"

"She's in the hospital." From Sarah.

My jaw drops. "Is she all right?"

"We don't know," a third girl, Lavinia Ross, says. "No one's heard. They say she has alcohol poisoning or something."

"From what?"

"No one seems to know," Sarah says. "Probably from that stuff Friday night at the bonfire. Didn't you have any?"

I shake my head. "I didn't, but Rory and Carmen did."

"I did too," Sarah says. "I've never been so trashed."

I don't add anything, but I do remember Carmen looking really pale. Of course, she's fair and redhaired anyway, but something was different about her. She was out of it. And Rory? Rory is always outgoing and boisterous. She's a singer. A performer. Her personality has always been flamboyant. Plus she was just crowned homecoming queen and was on top of the world as the most beautiful and popular girl in school. She drank a whole cup of the punch.

"Wow, Callie," she said after downing it. "That is the sweetest stuff I've ever put in my mouth."

I was pretty close to tasting it myself... until I saw Carmen acting like—no lie—she was about to walk right into the bonfire. I nudged her away from the fire and kept one eye on her the rest of the evening until her cousin picked her up and drove her home. I also made Rory promise not to drink any more of it.

And now... Diana Steel. The sweetheart of the Steel family and the freshman class homecoming attendant. In the hospital? With alcohol poisoning?

"Do you know when Diana went to the hospital?" I ask.

"No," Sarah says, "just that it was sometime after she went home. But haven't you heard? The Steels are offering a reward for anyone who can tell them who spiked the hairy buffalo."

"Could have been anyone," I say.

"But they want to know," Lavinia says, "because it wasn't spiked with just alcohol."

I resist the urge to widen my eyes. Lavinia's words are surprising yet not surprising. I saw how that stuff affected Carmen and Rory.

"You think someone drugged it," I say.

"No one knows." Mary applies a stroke of blush to one of her cheekbones.

Except the Steels know. If Diana is in the hospital, she probably had her blood tested.

"How much are the Steels offering for this information?"

"I don't know for sure," Sarah says. "I heard it was ten thousand dollars."

Again I resist the urge to widen my eyes. Ten thousand dollars? Wow. We Pikes sure could use ten thousand dollars.

But anyone could have spiked the punch. The punch at bonfires is almost always spiked. We're all disappointed when it isn't. Usually it's just alcohol, though, and never enough to cause any significant damage. Finding out who did it this time will be near impossible because usually no one cares.

"Let me know if you hear anything else," I say.

"Oh, sure thing, Callie." Lavinia offers a saccharine smile.

I'm used to saccharine smiles from B-listers—the A-list wannabes. They're nice to me because I'm Rory's sister. Jordan's cousin. I'm related to A-listers, though I don't make the cut myself.

They won't tell me what they hear. Why should they? I wouldn't either. If I find out who's responsible, I'll go running to the Steels to capture that reward.

And I plan to do exactly that.

★ ★ ★

The shriek... The horrific shriek of Karen's drill.

It won't be long now. Within seconds, Rory and I will know if our evidence is still in this safe-deposit box.

Images float through my head. After that conversation in the bathroom, when ten thousand dollars clouded my brain and I was determined to find out who was behind the hairy buffalo. I prepared to investigate, but I needn't have bothered.

The investigation came to me.

★ ★ ★

Being invisible has its perks.

Perks I put to good use.

Sure, I was on the homecoming court, but by Monday morning, I was plain old Callie Pike again. Snow Creek is a small town, and I'm the kind of person who listens. Who observes. Another perk of being invisible. No one sees me, but I see everything. I hear everything.

And I've got all my senses on alert for ten grand.

I didn't see who spiked the hairy buffalo Friday night at the bonfire. But there is one group at Snow Creek High School who tends to be responsible for all the crap.

The FLMC—short for the future lawmakers' club. It's a newer club. Rory says they started it her freshman year, so it's only three years old. It's supposedly for people who want to go into law enforcement or into law. Except it's not. Not at all.

The law has always been my calling, so last year, when I was a freshman, I attended a meeting of the FLMC. We didn't talk about law at all. We talked about how to stick it to the man.

I wasn't interested in sticking it to anyone, so I never went to another meeting. Soon after that, the club became invite only, but it's not an exclusive club—not by a long shot. Anyone can get an invite, but you have to prove you're willing to stick it to the man. *What this entails, I don't know, and I don't want to know.*

FLMC takes credit for a lot of the crap that goes on at Snow Creek High. I don't even know who all the members are, but I'm willing to bet I'll find the culprit among that group.

Except I don't need to research the FLMC, because the answer comes to me.

Yes, being invisible has its perks.

After school later in the week, I'm still sitting in my algebra classroom, going through my backpack, which is a mess. Mr. Frost, the algebra teacher, has left the room and so has everyone else. Algebra is my last class of the day, so the halls are bustling with people checking their lockers and then leaving the school grounds.

That's when I hear the voices.

"Yeah, we need to keep it under wraps."

"I don't know, man. The Steels… They can find out anything."

"Why the hell did you let her drink that shit?"

"Hey, man, I thought it was just alcohol."

"Bullshit. What was that stuff, Lamone?"

My ears perk. Pat Lamone. The male homecoming attendant for the junior class, who's been trying to date Rory for months.

A short pause, and then, "The dude told me it was angel dust."

"What the fuck?" another voice says. "You could get in some deep shit."

"I won't, and you won't, as long as we don't tell anyone."

"Right, Jimmy."

Jimmy Dawson? My escort? Who couldn't keep his eyes off Diana's ass?

"We've got to keep it under wraps. No texting about it. No talking on the phone. Who knows what kind of surveillance the Steels have?"

"In fact," the first voice says, "this is the last time we speak of this. Ever."

Hustling and bustling gets softer and softer, and when I'm sure they're gone, I finally peek out of the algebra classroom. The halls are empty. Rory is probably outside chatting with her friends as usual and waiting for me, also as usual. She'll drive us home.

This was almost too easy. I was ready to move about quietly and observe everything, but the information came to me instead.

Yes, being invisible definitely has its perks.

The only problem? Lamone and the others will deny it. I'll have to get proof. And I know just the one person who can help me.

Rory. My sister. The homecoming queen and the most beautiful girl in school.

She can get anyone to say anything.

CHAPTER TWO

Donny

After prosecuting two speeding tickets and a jaywalker, I'm back in the office and trying not to think of Callie. She's still in Denver, having her safe-deposit box drilled open.

I don't know what's bothering her. She wanted to tell me Saturday before I left, but I shushed her. I already know I have to let her go, so I didn't want to drag something out of her that she wasn't ready to talk about anyway.

Now I wonder if that was a mistake. If I knew, I could fix it for her. I can't be with her. I can't have a relationship with her, but I can at least take care of her past.

I've already decided to funnel money to her family somehow. I just haven't figured out how to do it yet.

"You're a dick," I say out loud, staring at my closed door.

Here I am, trying to fix everything with my money. Maybe it will work. Maybe Callie doesn't love me as much as I love her. Maybe the money will be enough.

I scoff. I know that's not true. I know Callie feels the same way I do. Not solely by her words, but by her actions. By the way she comforts and cares for me.

Damn her. She probably won't take the money. Neither will her family.

They're too proud.

My thoughts turn to Pat Lamone, who told me the Pikes were gold diggers.

And I can't help but wonder…

Why did he say that? And is he part of the reason Callie is so troubled? She seemed fine until we ran into him at the hotel that night.

She'll be home tonight, and she'll have to come by to bring me the car.

My phone buzzes. My mother. I say a frantic hello.

"Hi, sweetie. I have good news."

A swooshing sigh of relief leaves me. "Thank God. I could use some."

"Dad's being released today. We're coming home, Donny."

"That's great." Despite the fact that I'm happy with this news, my tone sounds anything but. My mom will no doubt call me on it.

"It certainly is. But you sound kind of…"

Yup. There she goes. "Everything is fine, Mom. I had a good morning in court. Everything's under control."

It's not a lie. Everything *is* under control at the office. Of course, the city of Snow Creek could probably run itself, but I won't say that to my mother. She takes her job very seriously.

"I'm glad to hear that. I knew you would be a great assistant city attorney. In fact, I have a lot to talk to you about."

"What?"

"Let's leave it until we get home. We'll talk after we get Dad settled back in."

"Sure, Mom."

Just as well. As much as I would love a distraction from everything else that's going on, I'm not sure I can handle anything new my mom is going to throw at me. She certainly sounds like it's good news. Or she's just happy that my father is finally being released from the hospital. Probably both. I'm pretty good at reading my mom. If it were something bad, I'd be able to tell.

"I'll see you tomorrow. I'm sure looking forward to getting back home," she says.

"It'll be great to have you both home," I say.

"I hear Dale and Ashley are almost moved out."

"They're working on it."

"I'm sure you'll be happy not to be living with your parents."

"You know I don't mind that. In fact, I'm happy to stay longer if you need help with Dad."

"That's so kind of you, Donny. You're sweet to suggest it, but we're going to have a live-in nurse for a while until he's completely recovered."

"All right. If you're sure."

So much else weighs on my mind, none of which I want to burden my mother with. Especially since some of it may concern her, my father, and the rest of the family. How much have they been hiding from us over the years?

"Yes, I'm sure. I can't rely on you for everything. You need to have your own life too. Dad and I have been talking, and it's time for you to choose your plot of land on the property. I can't expect you to live in the guesthouse forever."

"Wow. I guess I hadn't even thought of that. But since I'm back in town for the duration now, I suppose I should have my own place."

"Of course you should. You're the second oldest of all your siblings and cousins. Now that Dale's is almost complete, it's time for you to think about yours."

Except I don't want to think about it. Building a home means preparing for a family. I won't be doing that because I have to let Callie—the only woman I've ever considered having a family with—go.

But I can't let Mom think I'm having any reservations.

"I'll get on it."

"Good. And don't forget the big party this weekend to celebrate your dad's homecoming."

"Of course."

I love a good Steel party as much as anyone, but boy, am I *not* in the partying mood.

"I'll talk to you soon, Donny. And I'll see you soon."

"Right, Mom. So glad to hear everything is going well."

After ending the call, I stare at my computer. I haven't heard from Callie, so I don't know if she's on her way back to the western slope yet. Dad's coming home. Big party this weekend.

Plus...

Who opened a safe-deposit box in my name and left me those GPS coordinates and the ring?

Who trashed Brendan Murphy's place?

Most importantly... Who shot my father? Then tried to poison him? And why?

All this crap on my plate, plus...

I have to find the strength to break up with Callie.

God help me.

CHAPTER THREE

Callie

My heart thuds, pounding against my sternum, and as I look down, I swear I can see it—the quick movement of my chest.

I must be imagining things.

At least the shrieking is gone. But that brings us closer, closer, closer . . . to the truth.

While Karen puts away her tools, Mr. Keats pulls out the small metal container—Rory's safe-deposit box.

"Ms. Bates and I will leave you to it," Keats says.

"Sure," Rory says. "Thank you. How much do we owe you for the locksmith?"

"You'll be billed at your address on file." Mr. Keats flattens his lips into a straight line.

I'd love to punch his smug face. We didn't lose the damn key. It was stolen.

I inhale deeply and let it out. No time for me to get nasty.

"Thank you, Ms. Bates," Rory says. "And thank you very much for rescuing the baby this morning."

"All in a day's work." Karen smiles and hands Rory a business card. "If you ever need my services again."

"Thank you. We don't live in the area, but I'll keep it anyway." Rory shoves the card in her purse and smiles.

How is she staying so calm?

Being a performer does have its perks.

Just like being invisible has its perks.

That was my mantra in high school.

And the past displays itself before me once more.

★ ★ ★

"Are you serious?" Rory's pretty brown eyes widen into near circles.

"I swear to God I heard it. It was Pat Lamone. Someone named Jimmy. It could have been Jimmy Dawson, but we do have a couple Jimmys here at school."

"But only one Lamone," Rory says.

"Right. I suppose you've heard about Diana Steel."

"I've heard the whispers," my sister says. "And the whispers about the reward."

"Yeah, I got that scoop from a couple girls in the bathroom earlier today. I was getting all ready to do some snooping of my own—starting with the future lawmakers—when this information landed in my lap."

"None of them looked in the classroom to see if anyone was in there?"

I shake my head. "I've told you before. Being invisible has its perks."

"You're not invisible, Callie. I hate it when you say that. You were on the homecoming court, for God's sake."

"And you and I both know why. Because I'm your sister. Jordan's cousin. The sister of the amazing Jesse Pike, Snow Creek's greatest quarterback of all time."

"You're beautiful, Callie. You're the only one who doesn't see it."

"Cut it out, will you? I'm not here to debate which one of us is prettier." Besides, we all know who that is. *"We need to figure this out. We can get the ten grand from the Steels if we can prove Lamone is the one who spiked that punch with angel dust."*

"Angel dust… Man… No wonder I was flying high."

"And I'm damned glad I told you not to drink any more of it."

"Honestly, Callie, I would have. The flavor was unreal. But I've never broken a promise to you yet in my short life, and I'm glad I didn't."

"Me too. I'm glad Carmen is okay too. She looked like a mess. Like she was under some kind of spell. Totally freaked me out."

"It's a wonder more people aren't hospitalized from it."

"You're telling me." I inhale a breath and let it out slowly. Time to tell my sister my plan. "So I figure we need to get Lamone to admit what he did."

"How do you expect to do that?" Rory asks.

"I can't do anything. Pat Lamone has never given me a look. But…"

Queasiness meanders its way up my throat. I'm seriously thinking about pimping out my older sister to get information that will lead to money. Lamone needs to pay for what he did to Diana, and unfortunately, I can't think of another way.

Rory narrows her eyes. "Oh no. No way."

"It's the only way, Rory. We know he has a crush on you. It's become pretty near to stalking."

"A few phone calls and notes in my locker are hardly stalking."

"They are when you've told him to back off."

"And that's my point. I've told him in no uncertain terms

that I'm not interested. So he's going to believe I am now?"

"He's a seventeen-year-old guy," I say. "Whether he believes it isn't really the issue. If he thinks he's going to get some, he'll say whatever you want him to say."

"He's a seventeen-year-old guy," Rory says, "not an idiot."

"Same freaking difference."

That gets a laugh out of Rory. "I suppose you have a point. We can play on his testosterone."

"Exactly. Act like you're interested, maybe even take off a few items of clothing, and he'll be singing like a mockingbird."

Rory curls her lips into a grimace. "One problem, Cal. I can't stand Pat Lamone, and I don't want to get anywhere close to naked with him."

"Ten grand..."

"You want me to whore myself out for ten grand?"

The queasiness is back, but I force myself to work through it. "You're not whoring yourself out, Rory. You're doing an investigation. It's not like you're selling your body for ten grand. You're selling information that you obtain for the Steels for ten grand."

"Information that I obtain by whoring myself out."

"No. It's not like that. You're not going to actually do *anything with him. You're going to use your feminine wiles to get what you want. Women have been doing it for years."*

"And it still sucks."

I nod. "You're not wrong. I don't love the idea either, but what else do we have? He needs to pay for this crime... and Ror, we could sure use ten grand."

Rory pauses a moment, twists her lips. She's thinking. That's the Rory thinking pose.

"All right. But we're going to need help with this."

"Carmen. Carmen and Jordan. They'll help us."

"Can we trust them?"

"Jordan's our cousin. Of course we can trust her, and you and Carmen are friends. Besides, she drank that shit too, and I swear it nearly obliterated her."

"All right. We'll bring them in." Rory rolls her eyes. "Do you really think I can pull this off?"

"Rory, you've starred in every school musical since you were in the sixth grade. You're an actress by nature. Of course you can pull it off. Plus, you're Rory Pike. You're the only person who can."

"I hope you're right, Cal. Because this is the freaking role of a lifetime."

★ ★ ★

Keats and Karen leave the room, and Rory and I stare at the closed box sitting on the table in front of us.

"Now or never," Rory says.

"Just open the damned thing."

She rests her fingers on the lid. "I'm frightened, Callie."

"Either it's there or it isn't. We have to know, Rory. We have to, so we know how to approach this."

"I can't believe this is all coming back to bite us in the ass."

"Well, it is. So open the damned thing, will you?"

Rory bites her lower lip. "Do you ever wish you could go back and relive a certain time in your life?"

"Ror . . ."

"Screw it all. All right." She lifts the lid of the metal box.

CHAPTER FOUR

Donny

I head over to Ava's for lunch. As soon as I open the door, though, I wish I'd chosen something else.

Brendan Murphy, his long ginger hair pulled into a low ponytail, sits at one of the small tables in the bakery, and Ava stands next to his table, her black apron smudged with flour and her pink hair piled into a hair net, talking to him.

"Shit," I mutter under my breath.

Ava looks up when the bells on the door tinkle. "Hey, Donny!"

"Hey, cuz. Brendan."

Brendan meets my gaze, his blue eyes glaring. He's not happy, though of course I don't expect him to be. How much of his attitude am I projecting onto him because I'm upset at myself for putting all this shit in motion?

But it is what it is, and I have to deal with the fallout.

"Any news?" Brendan asks.

"Not really. I did check in with the energy board on Friday. All the paperwork has been updated about the error with regard to the potential gas leak on your property."

"Yeah, I'm not talking about that. I'm talking about any news on who trashed my place."

"I was in Denver on Friday, and it's noon on Monday.

I don't have any new news on that. Have you checked with Hardy?"

"Yes, I've checked with Hardy."

"And . . . ?"

"Nothing. Freaking nothing."

"This happened three days ago. Investigations take time, Brendan."

"I know." He sighs.

"Brendan, we all understand," Ava says. "What happened to you is horrible."

"Yeah, it is. But I'll deal."

The scuttlebutt from Callie is that Brendan has a major crush on my cousin. Clearly he's trying to be strong for her, to act like this doesn't matter in the grand scheme of things.

But he's still pissed. I can see it in those menacing blue eyes.

And I don't blame him one bit.

"Your sandwich is on the house today," Ava says.

"That's sweet of you," Brendan says, "but totally not necessary. I always pay my way."

"Not today you don't." Ava wipes her flour-covered fingers on her apron. "This is non-negotiable." Then she walks back behind the counter and into the kitchen.

"I guess she told you," I say.

"I refuse to be a Steel charity case." Brendan's lips turn into a flat line.

I sit down across from him without being invited. "You need to understand Ava. She doesn't take Steel charity either. You probably know this story already, but she opened this place on her own. She makes her own money, pays her employees, and doesn't touch her parents' money. So if she's not a Steel charity case, you certainly won't be either by taking a free sandwich. Take it for what it is. A gift. Because she cares."

Brendan gazes down at the table. "You're right. I don't know why I said that."

"Because you're angry. And you have every reason to be. You think none of us have ever been there?"

He raises his head and meets my gaze, his blue eyes glaring again. "You're a fucking Steel, Donny."

I clear my throat but then stay quiet as Maya brings us two glasses of ice water.

"What will it be, Don?" she asks.

"The Donny. Turkey and avocado. You know the drill." I smile.

She blushes. "Yours will be out in a minute, Brendan."

Once Maya is back at the counter, Brendan opens his mouth, but I raise my hand to stop him.

"You're not going to get a free pass with me today. Yes, I'm a Steel. But I wasn't always a Steel. You know that."

His fair cheeks pink a little. "Look, I don't want to get into some big knock-down, drag-out with you. I'm just fucking pissed. That's what this comes down to."

"All right. I'll take you at your word."

I force myself to simmer down. He's angry, and he has every right to be. My early childhood is not his fault, and I'm sure as hell not about to tell Brendan Murphy how Dale and I came to be Steels. It's none of his damned business, and I don't want it getting to Ava or anyone else. It's bad enough that Ashley knows. And Brock.

"What are your plans?" he asks.

"For your case? I've got Troy on it. I'll probably put Callie on it too."

Callie's name crossed my lips before I had a chance to even think about it. I have to let her go. Does that mean I have to let her go from the office as well? It'll be hell to see her every day but not be able to touch her. Still, I can't take her job away from her on top of everything else.

"How long does an investigation usually take?"

"There's no easy answer to that question. First of all, I'm new to this. Second, every case is different. From what I saw when I walked through your place the other day, whoever trashed it didn't leave any clues at all. Now granted, I gave it only a cursory look. I imagine Hardy and his guys will go in there and bag evidence, and I'll send Troy over as well. He's a competent investigator."

"In the meantime...where the hell am I supposed to live?"

"That's where I can give you some good news. The energy board has agreed to reimburse you for a stay at the Snow Creek Inn."

He lifts his eyebrows. "I have to tell you. I'm surprised."

"I pulled a few strings. Cashed in a few favors."

I hate lying. In fact, the person footing the bill will be me. The least I can do.

"I appreciate it. I really do."

I smile—totally forced—and take a drink of my ice water.

I feel like a complete asshole. This is all my fault. I may not have trashed Brendan's place, but it's because of my shenanigans that he wasn't home at the time.

Maya comes by with Brendan's sandwich. "A few more minutes on yours," she says to me.

"Not a problem."

Brendan takes a bite of sandwich, chews, swallows. "I've

been thinking, and I have no idea who would do this."

"You mean other than some member of my family."

"Well . . . yeah. Your words, not mine."

"They were *your* words, Brendan. On Thursday, when you came storming into my office."

"I'm not accusing you, Don, or any member of your immediate family. But don't you think it's strange that the place got trashed *after* I uncovered documents pertaining to the Steels?"

"I'm not going to lie to you. Yes, the thought has occurred to me. My family is not without its enemies. That's for sure. And the more I learn about our history . . ."

"What?"

I sigh. "I just don't know enough to make any comment, to be honest. Suffice it to say that Dale and I are looking into a lot of things."

"Can I help?"

"I'm afraid you can't. It's a family mess, and family needs to take care of it."

"Yeah, but your family mess may have invaded its way into my life."

"I get it. But if you were uncovering things about your own family, you wouldn't want any other family involved."

He cocks his head and then finally nods. "Point taken."

My sandwich appears in front of me, and I mumble a thank you to Maya.

I take a bite, chew, swallow.

Brendan and I don't say much after that.

CHAPTER FIVE

Callie

I nearly faint with relief when Rory pulls out the thumb drive.

"Thank God," she says, her voice more of a sigh than actual words.

I hold out my palm. "Let me touch it. I need to feel that it's real."

She drops it into my open hand. Yes, the thumb drive. The only copy of Pat Lamone's confession. We have our leverage.

The statute of limitations has passed. He can't be arrested. So what? We can still ruin him. And once the Steels find out . . .

Oh, God . . . Nausea crawls up my throat.

The Steels.

We kept this information from them when they wanted it. Granted, we had our reasons, and we didn't know the Steels very well back then. Sure, we live on a ranch adjacent to theirs, but they're a powerful family.

Now that I know the Steels better—and now that I'm involved with Donny—I realize we could have gone to them. They would have protected us.

But we were kids. Sure, Rory was technically an adult, but only an eighteen-year-old girl. I wasn't quite sixteen.

Still, holding the thumb drive in my palm, feeling its shape and weight, gives me relief.

"Whoever got the key," Rory says, "didn't get here."

"They couldn't have. Not unless they had your ID. And if it *was* Pat Lamone, I doubt he could have convinced anyone he was a woman named Aurora Pike."

"We don't even know for sure it was him."

"Who else could it be? The only other person who knows where we hid it is Jordan. Unless someone else followed us and she didn't notice."

"I know." Rory wrings her hands together. "I think we have to consider the possibility that someone else saw us back then."

"Or that Jordan . . ."

Rory shakes her head. "Don't go there, Cal. She's our cousin."

I nod. I want to believe Jordan wouldn't be behind any of this. I want to so badly. But what if . . .

Jordan's parents live on our land, help us with the ranching and winemaking. At least we have ownership of the property. They don't even have that.

If someone offered her money . . .

"I see those cogs in your brain turning," Rory says. "She didn't do it."

"I know."

But the truth is that I *don't* know. My brain works differently than Rory's. She's a performer, an artist. She works on emotion.

My mind is analytical. I look at all the facts, discard all the emotion, and then hypothesize theories.

And frankly, the fact is that Jordan is the only other person who knows where we buried that key.

★ ★ ★

"How well do you know him?" I ask Jordan.

"He came on to me. But then again, he comes on to everyone. I didn't particularly want him to be my escort for the homecoming procession, but it's not like I had a choice. He was voted onto the court."

"Why is that again? He's not a football player." Rory cocks her head.

"Yeah, but he's a star baseball player, and he hangs out with the football team."

"You know he's been stalking Rory, right?" I say.

Jordan's eyes widen. "He has?"

"Geez, Callie."

"Hey, I'm just trying to get information on the guy. He freaking poisoned that punch at the homecoming bonfire. A girl is in the hospital because of him."

"Yeah, and the two of you want to get the Steel reward." Jordan's tone is dry.

"Well... duh!" I drop my mouth open. "Don't you want your cut?"

"Sure. But I'm not sure how I can help you."

"You're helping right now by telling us what you know about the guy."

"And what are you going to do with that information?"

"We're going to get him to confess," I say.

Jordan's jaw drops. "No way. He never will."

"We have some tricks in our arsenal." I gesture to Rory.

"Please tell me you're not going to—"

"I don't like the idea any more than you do," Rory says, "but we have to try. Not just for the ten grand, but for Diana's sake."

"Diana is going to be fine," Jordan says. "Haven't you heard? She's already been released from the hospital."

"I haven't seen her back in school," I say.

"She's probably taking a few days off. Or maybe the Steels will be putting her in private school." Jordan shrugs. "I'm not sure why all of them aren't in private school, to be honest. They're richer than God."

I bite my bottom lip, my mind whirling. How can we pull this off? It's going to take more than just Rory and her sexual prowess.

The two of them need to be contained.

We need something like—

"Can you get Cage's van?" I ask Jordan.

Jordan narrows her eyes. "Why do we need his van?"

"We need a closed-in space. Where we can monitor what goes on."

"You want me to lock myself in the back of a van with Pat Lamone?" Rory raises an eyebrow.

"We have to keep the whole thing contained," I tell her. "We need to be able to stay close enough that we can get an accurate recording. Plus, we need to be able to stay close enough that we can come in in case something goes wrong."

"Nothing will go wrong," Rory says. "I can handle Pat Lamone."

"I don't doubt that you can. But we don't know much about him. What if he gets violent?"

"What if I slip him a little something?" Rory's lips curve slightly upward.

I'm not sure if it's a smile or a . . . Yeah, I'm not sure.

"Then we're no better than he is," Jordan says.

"True. I can't help but agree." I rub my forehead. "But

maybe . . . Maybe there's something we can slip him that isn't . . . illegal."

*"We're all under twenty-one," Rory says. "*Everything *is illegal for us."*

"Not everything. What about a big dose of antihistamine?"

"What if he's allergic?" Jordan asks.

"Who the hell is allergic to Benadryl? It's meant to counteract allergies."

"I want him to talk," Rory says, "not fall asleep."

"There's that alpha place between asleep and awake," I say. "That's when you'll be able to get him to talk."

Jordan frowns. "I don't know, guys. I still think that makes us no better than he is."

"Jordan," I say, "there is a huge *difference between spiking punch that the entire school is going to drink with an illegal drug like angel dust and spiking* one *guy's drink with Benadryl."*

"Which is not illegal." Rory nods. "We can buy it at the pharmacy."

Jordan's expression is unreadable for a few seconds, until—

"Okay. I'll talk to Cage."

I smile. "Then it's settled. Jordan, get the van. Rory and I will take care of the rest."

CHAPTER SIX

Donny

In the office, midafternoon, my phone buzzes with a text from Callie.

We're about fifteen minutes out.
Do you want Rory and me to drop
the car at the office?

The text is basic, but still, it heats my skin just knowing Callie sent it.

I text her back.

Don't worry about that. Just
go ahead home, and I'll pick up
the car at your place later.

Are you sure? I can put in an hour
or two of work once we get there.

Such a work ethic. Callie Pike is something else.

No, that's okay. But would you
like to have dinner tonight?

I hit send, and then I realize that Mom and Dad will be home by dinnertime. Crap. That's okay. We'll drive into Grand Junction and have dinner.

Sure. I have a lot to tell you.

Right. She's going to tell me what's been bothering her and how it has something to do with the safe-deposit box that she and Rory lost the key to.

As curious as I am, and as much as I want to help her, is it really fair of me to take that information when I'm going to break up with her?

If only . . .

I can't believe I'm even thinking this, but if Mom and Dad weren't coming home tonight, I could have one last night with Callie.

How can I exist knowing I'll never make love to her again?

And honestly? It isn't even the making love that's important. It's Callie herself. Her presence in my life. The happiness she brings me.

How can I live without that?

You don't have to let her go, you know, the little voice inside me says. *Dale brought Ashley into all of this, and she's doing fine.*

All true. But Dale brought Ashley in before we knew of these developments, and God only knows what they will lead to.

I haven't spoken to Dale because he's been busy moving into his new house. He said he was going to check out those GPS coordinates, but I never heard whether he did. Instead of checking in with him yesterday, I stayed at home. I had a big pity party for myself. No matter how hard I tried, I couldn't get comfortable with the fact that I had to let Callie go.

Maybe I need to talk to Dale now.

He'll tell me to not let her go.

And perhaps that's what I need to hear.

I text Callie back quickly, telling her I'll let her know when I'll pick her up for dinner, and then I call Dale.

He doesn't answer. I get ready to leave a voicemail, when he blips, interrupting my message.

"Hey," I say.

"Sorry. I left the phone on the counter of the new house, and I was upstairs. I heard it ring and ran down, but I was too late. What's up?"

"I should have checked in with you yesterday. Any luck on figuring out the GPS coordinates?"

"Yeah. I drove out and took a look at all of them. They're just standard points. One is even on our own property."

I widen my eyes. "It is?"

"Yeah, our property is pretty vast. This is way north, almost on the Wyoming border."

"Is it property that we use?"

"There are some old buildings, but no, we don't use them. I'm surprised we don't have squatters, to tell you the truth."

"Did you find anything in those buildings?"

"No. I didn't go inside any of them because I was due back at the winery. I figured you and I would go back together to do the thorough checking."

"What about the other GPS coordinates?"

"Just outside our property."

"Who owns that part of the land?"

"I don't know, Don. That's where you come in. You'll need

to check all the databases."

"Right. I suppose I can do that this afternoon. I'm not sure why I didn't think of it before."

Except that I know exactly why I didn't think of it before. I've been ruminating on Callie and the fact that I have to let her go.

"I know this is a big mess," Dale says. "Neither one of us has really been acting like ourselves."

"You noticed, huh?"

"Yeah. I have to tell you, Ashley is keeping me very grounded. I'm glad I shared what's going on with her."

I say nothing.

"Don?"

"Yeah?"

"How are things with Callie? Is she back from Denver?"

"Almost. I just got a text from her. She's about fifteen minutes out."

"Good. I think you need a heavy dose of Callie Pike."

"Funny you should mention that..."

"What?"

I sigh. "Dale, I have to let her go."

"What?" My brother's voice is almost shrill. He doesn't sound like himself at all.

"You heard me. And I know you understand why."

"No, I don't understand. And I'll tell you the reason why I don't understand. Because a few weeks ago, I was exactly where you are now. I almost let the best thing in my life go, and it would have been the biggest mistake I ever made."

"Dale, you and I have a hell of a lot of baggage. But now with these new developments—"

"So we have more baggage. So what? You have a woman

who loves you and who you love in return. Don't let all this baggage—"

I can almost see my brother's air quotes.

"—lead you into making a bad decision."

"I'm only thinking about her."

"I get that. I've been there, like I said. Do I need to come over and pound some sense into you?"

I scoff. "I'd like to see you try."

"Hey, I work out. I have a taekwondo *dojang* in my basement. You sit at a desk all day."

My brother is not wrong, and he also has way more of a temper than I do. Still, we're pretty evenly matched body-wise.

"Dale," I say, "this is different."

"How is it different?"

"This is some major family drama we're uncovering. It could affect our finances. It could affect everything."

"So?"

"This isn't just my own personal baggage. That's what you were struggling with when you were deciding whether to keep Ashley in your life. And you know that you and I handle that differently."

"Don't give me that. Don't tell me it affected me more than it affected you."

"Maybe it did. We're two different people."

I hate the words as soon as they leave my mouth. They're not untrue. Dale and I *are* two very different people. But I'm not unaffected by my past. I just don't allow myself to think about it.

"Don, I'm done. I'm done feeling guilty that I couldn't save you."

"That's not what I'm getting at."

"But it is. You think this affected me more than it affected you. In some ways, I'm sure it did. But you were younger. You were seven years old. Don't tell me our past hasn't shaped you into the man you are today."

"It hasn't."

"Maybe I didn't say that right. Of course it hasn't. But everything that we've been through has had an effect on who we became. Our lives here on the ranch with Mom and Dad. Our successes and our failures. And . . . those two months."

"You think that's the reason I want to cut things off with Callie?"

"I think you need to consider that it might have more to do with it than you think it does."

This is my brother. If anyone else said these words to me, even Mom or Dad, I would probably say they're barking up the wrong tree. But Dale . . . Dale, who went through it with me. Who in some ways suffered so much more than I did.

Could he be right?

Sure, I don't let this affect my life. At least I don't think I do. But I *have* been thinking about it more often than I normally do. That feeling . . . That horrendous feeling of being caged in . . . Of having no control over anything.

Sure, I was a child. A mere seven-year-old. But children should not be caged.

And the feelings I've had lately as things have piled on my shoulders more and more and more—Dad's shooting, my near breach of my own ethics, the documents Brendan uncovered in his place, the safe-deposit box someone opened for me . . .

All of it . . . All of it is making me feel *very* caged in.

"Don? You still there?"

"Yeah."

"Don't give her up," Dale says. "Needing someone in your life doesn't make you weaker. It makes you stronger."

I consider his words. I *have* felt less strong since Callie came into my life, but it's not because of her. It's because of all the other shit that came along for the ride.

"I'm not worried about my own weakness or strength. I'm worried about *her*."

"Believe me, brother. I understand that. But what I'm telling you is that you'll hurt her more by cutting her loose."

"I'm not sure that's true. Callie is going through some of her own stuff right now that I don't even know about. Maybe dealing with me and my baggage is just too much for her."

"What's she going through?"

"I don't know. She was going to tell me when we were in Denver, but I told her not to. I just wanted to hold her. I wanted to relish the time we had left because I knew the end was coming."

"Don't make that mistake. Please. I'm your brother, and I love you. And I think Callie Pike is the best thing that has ever happened to you, Donny."

Again, I consider his words.

And I wonder…

Is it even *my* decision to make? Maybe I should give Callie the choice. She may choose to walk, and that's her prerogative.

"I'll think about all of it. She and I are going to dinner tonight. I think we'll drive into Grand Junction and maybe go check out that new steakhouse, the Fortnight. That'll give Mom and Dad a chance to get settled back home without me being underfoot."

"Just a warning… the sommelier there, Idris, is a big-ass flirt."

"Idris?"

"Yeah, and he has some snooty French last name, which escapes me at the moment. He couldn't take his eyes off Ashley."

I laugh. And it feels damned good to laugh. "Anyone is a big-ass flirt to you, Dale. You don't have the first *clue* how to flirt."

This gets a chuckle out of my brother. "Touché, little bro. Touché. I never claimed to. Thankfully, my wife seems to like me anyway."

"Who knows why?" I scoff.

Good. We're back to normal now. Giving each other crap and laughing.

"I'll think about it." I return to the subject at hand. "I do love her, man."

"I know you do. I'm happy for you. Don't fuck it up, all right?"

"I'll talk to you soon. After you're settled in the new house, you and I have a date to check out those GPS coordinates."

"Nice subject change. But good enough. You're my brother, and I love you, and I know you'll do the right thing—for both Callie and yourself."

I set my phone back down on the desk. Within a minute though, I've picked it up again. I quickly make reservations for two at Fortnight and then text Callie the details.

Tonight…

Tonight the future of Donny Steel and Callie Pike will be decided.

CHAPTER SEVEN

Callie

Cage is Jesse's age, and he uses his van to transport the musical instruments and other equipment for their band. Which means... when the equipment isn't in there, the back of the van is completely available. Somehow, Jordan managed to get him to agree to let us borrow it.

"What did you tell him?" Rory asks as the three of us chat behind the high school football stadium.

"I said we were helping the football team and cheerleaders move equipment."

I nod. "Nice. Since the season is over after homecoming, that makes perfect sense."

"I do have a brain in my head, Callie." My cousin scoffs. "Quit thinking you're the only smart one in this family."

"I don't think that."

"Oh, come on, Callie," Rory says.

"I don't. I think I have a different kind of brain. Analytical as opposed to emotional."

They both roll their eyes at me. No biggie. I'm used to it.

"What about all the equipment they store in the van?" I ask, intentionally steering off the subject of my brain.

"We'll have to use the van sometime while they're rehearsing. That way the equipment will be out."

"Nice," I say.

The back of the van is big enough for a queen-size mattress.

How to get the mattress is a problem. Mom and Dad will notice if either Rory or I move our mattress out of the house. So that's out.

"Are you sure about this, Rory?" Jordan says.

My sister nods. "I don't know of an alternative. Don't worry. I'll take care of myself."

"And you and I won't be far away," I tell Jordan.

"Are you sure you can keep the record on your phone?" Jordan asks.

"Yeah," Rory says. "I'll just set it down next to the bed. Trust me. He won't notice."

"And the line will be open," I say, "so while she's recording, I'll also be listening."

"Good." Jordan nods. "Now… where do we find a queen-size mattress?"

"I can help you out."

The three of us drop our jaws in near unison.

Carmen Murphy and two others stand about ten feet away from us.

"Damn," Rory says. "Where the hell did you guys come from?"

"We were walking by and noticed you guys in a thick conversation."

"Yeah, well, this is private," I say.

"We only want to help," Carmen says. "We know Lamone was behind that hairy buffalo. And we'd like to see him get his due."

"How do you know?" I ask.

"Because Lamone is such a dickhead that he spouts off his

mouth. I heard him talking to Jimmy Dawson and DeShawn Phillips behind the equipment shed yesterday afternoon.

"So it was *Jimmy," I say. So much for "this is the last time we speak of this. Ever."*

"Yeah. Although from what I heard, Jimmy and DeShawn didn't have anything to do with the actual spiking. That was all Pat."

Rory nods. "Figures."

"So you need a mattress, huh?" Carmen says.

"We do." I nod.

"I don't even want to think about what you're planning to do with it," one of the other girls says.

"I'm sure you can imagine." Rory tugs at a strand of hair that has come loose from her ponytail.

"Are you sure about this?" Carmen asks.

"I'm sure."

"So you're going after the Steel reward money," Carmen says.

"And now I suppose you're going to want to split that six ways," I say.

Carmen nods. "I think that's only fair, Callie."

"I suppose you're right. It's still a lot of money."

"All right, then." Carmen smiles. "Jenna has a queen-size mattress in her shed."

I nod to Jenna. "Good. When can we pick it up?"

★ ★ ★

Donny and I don't talk much on the way to Grand Junction. He seems preoccupied. When we reach the restaurant, we're seated quickly, and Donny orders us a couple of margaritas. I don't have the heart to tell him I'd prefer a Diet Coke.

"How's your dad looking?" I ask.

"Good. A little weak, but good. They'd only been home for about a half hour when I left to pick you up."

"Didn't you want to stay home tonight? Be with them?"

"I thought about it, but I figured it would be better for me to get out of there so he could get settled back in."

I nod. "Yeah, that makes sense."

Our margaritas arrive, and I take a sip. A little too sweet for me, but I smile. "I have a lot to tell you."

"I know. But Callie . . . It's up to you. If you're not ready . . ."

Am I ready? Admittedly, I'm feeling a lot better about the situation now that I know we still have our evidence against Pat Lamone. But we were hardly innocent back then.

If we still have our evidence . . .

He most likely still has his as well.

And his evidence can make our lives pretty miserable.

"A lot of it is high school drama. Some drama that we let get out of hand."

"*We?*"

"Rory and me. And Jordan. And Carmen, Jenna McKnight, and Letitia Hayes."

"Oh?"

"I don't want you to be angry with me."

"Callie, I promise I won't be angry with you for something you did in high school. High school doesn't define a person."

"I know that."

"But I mean it. If you're not ready to talk about it—"

I hold up a hand to stop him. "I have to, Donny. I *want* to."

He takes a long sip of his margarita then. "Before you do . . ." He takes another sip. "I should give you a choice."

I wrinkle my forehead. "What kind of choice are you talking about?"

He clears his throat. "There's a lot going on right now in my family."

"I know. I wish there were something I could do to help."

He inhales sharply and shakes his head. "None of it is your problem."

My heart jumps a little. Where is he going with this?

"I guess what I'm trying to say is…" He rubs at his temples. "Damn it."

My heart is doing a freaking chicken dance. "Donny, what is it?"

"I just… So much. My dad. I need to find out who tried to kill him. I need to find out who trashed Brendan's place. It's all my fault, Callie. If I hadn't worked with the energy board to…" He says no more. It's almost like he can't bear to say the words.

"Donny, you can't bear the burden for all of this."

"I put it into motion."

"Maybe the whole thing with regard to Brendan's place being vandalized. I'll give you that. But your dad getting shot. All the new information about your family… That's not on you."

"What if it is? You don't know my history, Callie."

I feel like I'm back in a damned cage.

Those words that Donny uttered only days ago have haunted me since.

What did Donny go through before he became a Steel? Do I even want to know? Can I stomach it?

"We all have a history, Donny. We've all done things we regret."

His face takes on a distressed look, as if something is trapped inside him, gnawing at him from the inside out. I can almost see his mind churning, taking him back to something he never thinks about.

I know, because I've seen that look on my own face lately whenever I stare into a mirror.

I never thought about this Pat Lamone stuff. For ten years, it lay dormant inside me.

Until he came back to town.

"Donny… Please. Let me help you."

"No one can help me, Callie. You can't help me. You can only help yourself." He inhales, lets it out slowly, and then tilts his neck up and stares at the ceiling. "And the best thing you might be able to do for yourself is to walk away from me."

CHAPTER EIGHT

Donny

A cage doesn't have to have bars.

My cage is a concrete room. A bucket and a roll of toilet paper sit in the corner where we poop and pee. It's gross, and the smell made my eyes water at first, but I don't smell it anymore.

Maybe it stopped stinking. We don't get much to eat, so we don't go that often anyway.

Dale says we just got used to the smell. That's why we can't smell it anymore.

But I prefer to think that it stopped stinking.

It hurts down there. I'm not even sure what they did to me.

It's not something I ever thought about. Ever. I didn't even know something like that could happen.

Dale tried to explain it to me once, after the first time.

They had done it to him a couple of times before they took me. And he tried. He tried so hard to get them to take him instead of me.

I didn't understand.

Until I saw it happen.

I saw them do it to Dale right in front of me.

The times before they had taken him out of the room.

That's when I realized a cage isn't protection.

I'm not safe here.

Not when they can come in and do those awful things that hurt me so badly.

Are the lions in cages at the zoo to protect them? Or to protect us?

Or are they just slaves, being used?

Things instead of beings.

I know one thing.

If I ever get out of here, I'll never go to a zoo again.

★ ★ ★

Callie's lips tremble. Her eyes glaze over with a transparent sheen.

I wait for her to say something. Anything.

But she stays silent.

"I love you," I say.

She meets my gaze then, and a tear slides out of her right eye. "Then why do you want me to leave you?"

"Damn it, Callie, I *don't* want you to leave. I'm giving you a choice. An out. My life has suddenly become an unbearable mess, and I don't want to drag you into it."

"What if I want to get dragged into it?"

"Then… I guess that's your choice."

"Is it? *My* choice? The fact that you even gave me this choice means that you don't feel the way I do. You're not willing to walk through fire for this."

Fire. The fact that she chose that particular word isn't lost on me. Fire destroyed her chance for law school, but I have no doubt she'd face the highest flames in the world for me, as I would for her.

"That's not true. I want you more than anything. I'm giving you an—"

She stands then with such force that she knocks her margarita over, and it spills onto the table, leaving a lime-green splotch on the stark white fabric of the tablecloth. "I reject your choice. You want to get rid of me? You're going to have to tell me to leave."

"I..."

"Do it, Donny. If you want to get rid of me, then get rid of me."

"I love you."

"I love you too, damn it. And I don't care that your life is in the toilet right now. I'll do anything I can to help."

"Callie..."

"Would it help," she says, "if I tell you what's going on with me?"

"I already said, if you don't want to—"

"I *do* want to. And you know what? Once you hear what *I* did, you may no longer give me the choice. *You* may choose to end things."

Already I know she's wrong. Short of murder, I don't think there's anything she could have ever done that would get rid of me. That would make me feel any differently about her.

"All right, Callie. Tell me."

She sits back down as a server finally comes to clean up the margarita mess.

"Would you like another drink, ma'am?" he asks.

"No, thank you. A Diet Coke, please."

"Right away." The server dashes away.

"Ten years ago," Callie says, "your sister was hospitalized with alcohol poisoning."

I cock my head. "Boy, I haven't thought about that in ages. Right after homecoming."

"Yeah. You and Jesse were announcing the game. Rory was the homecoming queen. I was the attendant for the sophomore class."

"Right. And Diana was the attendant for the freshman class."

She nods. "Someone spiked the hairy buffalo at the bonfire that night. Your family offered a reward for any information regarding who had done it."

"Did we? I'm sure my parents probably did."

"Yes. Ten thousand dollars. But no one ever came forward."

"Not surprising."

She clears her throat then. Pauses a moment. Her eyes are still glassy, and she sniffles. "I found out who spiked the punch that night."

I widen my eyes. "You know who did that to my sister?"

She sighs, nodding. "I do."

"Who the hell was it? Why didn't you say anything?"

"Because . . ." She swallows. "The person who did it tried to destroy Rory and me."

CHAPTER NINE

Callie

Donny's cheeks turn red, and the anger flows off him in waves.

Yes. This will definitely test his love for me. The Steels are all about family, and I could have helped them avenge one of their own.

But I didn't. I didn't because to do so would have dragged my sister and me, and consequently our entire family, through the mud.

★ ★ ★

After doing some research, I borrowed my mother's mortar and pestle and ground up just enough Benadryl tablets to get Pat Lamone in a sleepy state but not harm him.

"You're going to have a window of about fifteen minutes," I tell Rory, "until he falls asleep."

"Got it. I know how to handle a man, Callie."

I nod. My sister does. I certainly don't. Probably never will. Being the ugly duckling of the family and all. Still, being invisible has its perks.

"After you're done, we'll let him sleep it off. Between you, me, and Jordan, we should be able to drive him somewhere and then let him wake up on his own. He may not even realize what happened."

"And then... we give the evidence to the Steels, and ka-ching," Rory says.

I nod. "It's a good plan. He deserves to be caught."

"If it weren't for the reward money, would you two still be doing this?" Jordan asks.

"I don't know if we'd actually be doing this*," Rory says. "But we'd definitely go to the Steel family with what we know."*

"The problem is," I say, "it would just be hearsay at that point. It's something I heard Pat Lamone say. He would deny it. We may not get the reward money unless it's clear and cohesive evidence."

Jordan scoffs. "I swear to God, Callie. Were you born with law books in your head?"

Though I know my cousin doesn't mean the statement as a compliment, I take it as such. "One day... One day I'll be the best fucking lawyer in the free world."

★ ★ ★

Those words come back to me so clearly. Funny. Here I am, age twenty-six, and no closer to that goal than I was then.

"I'm waiting," Donny says.

"We didn't have any evidence at first," I say. "I heard the person who did it bragging about it the next week when I was hanging around in the algebra room after school."

"And you didn't go to anyone?"

"He would have just denied it. You wouldn't have had any evidence."

"We're the Steels. We would have *gotten* the evidence."

I widen my eyes. Yes, the Steels. They get what they want because they pay for it.

I'm learning more and more about the Steel family. I love their son. I love this man across from me more than I love the air that I breathe.

But the Steels . . .

They do have skeletons in their closet.

Some of which are coming to the surface now, which is why Donny is giving me this choice in the first place.

Perhaps I should take him up on it. Perhaps that would be less painful than to have him dump me—and he may very well dump me—when he finds out I actually *had* evidence all those years ago.

But Donny is not his family. Just like I'm not my family.

"I was a kid. I wasn't quite sixteen, and Rory was barely eighteen. We knew your family wouldn't pay for hearsay evidence, so we set out to get actual evidence."

"And you weren't successful?"

"Actually . . . we were."

Donny's cheeks redden. "Then why the hell didn't you give it to us? We would have paid handsomely. Surely you could have used the money."

"Yes, we could have. That was our original intent. To claim the reward money when we gave you the actual evidence."

"Why didn't you?"

"We couldn't. Not without destroying ourselves and our family."

Donny sucks in a breath and holds it for what seems like longer than he should, and then he finally lets it out in a whooshing sigh.

"I'm sorry," he says. "You were just a kid. You and Rory both. This is what you've been trying to tell me, isn't it?"

I nod. "I've wanted to tell you, but I've been afraid."

"Afraid that I would react exactly as I did."

"Well . . . yeah."

"I'm sure you had a good reason why you didn't give us the evidence at the time."

"I do, although, looking back, it seems like an immature reason."

"You *were* immature. You were fifteen years old."

"Please." I look down at my lap. "Please don't try to make this easy for me. I don't deserve that."

"You didn't deserve my anger either."

"Maybe I did. Maybe I do. Maybe I do deserve your anger, and maybe, Donny, you deserve mine. If we truly love each other, none of this should be an issue. We all have backstories. Things we can't change but wish we could."

He shakes his head then. "Callie, you have no idea."

I feel like I'm back in a damned cage.

Again those words haunt me. So much I don't know.

"I'd like to level with you," I say. "I thought this part of my life was over, but when Pat Lamone showed back up in town—"

"Pat Lamone? He has something to do with this?"

I nod. "It was him, Donny. He's the one who spiked the hairy buffalo that night. And I do have the evidence, although it's too late to do anything about it because I researched the statute of limitations. He can't be held accountable at this point."

"Want to bet?"

"Don't go all vigilante on me. Please."

"That's not me. That's Dale. That's Brock. That's Uncle Joe. Me? I'm a little more subtle."

"I still have the evidence. That's what was in the safe-deposit box in Denver."

He lifts his eyebrows. "I see. Why did you have to drill the lock open?"

"Because someone stole our key. We buried it ten years ago, and when Rory and I went to dig it up a couple of days ago, it was gone."

"And you think Pat Lamone . . ."

"Who else? He leaves town ten years ago and now he's back? He's telling you lies about me? And that's not all. He got to Raine too. Told the same lies about Rory that he told you."

Donny rakes his fingers through his hair, making it stand up so that he looks wild.

I glance around the restaurant. "Maybe we should go."

He nods. "I can't eat right now anyway."

"Neither can I."

"My mom and dad are at home. I assume yours are as well."

"Yeah."

"Then we'll go to a hotel. I'll book us a room so we can have privacy. If we get hungry later, we can order room service. But for now, Callie, we need to talk."

CHAPTER TEN

Donny

Homecoming night ten years ago . . .

I haven't thought about it in . . . Well . . . in ten years . . .

Diana recovered quickly, and we were all so glad that we didn't take a lot of time or much of our own resources researching who was responsible.

At least not that I know of. I went back to Denver after the weekend.

Back to law school.

Honestly I never thought I would return to the western slope. My life wasn't here. It was in Denver, at a high-powered firm.

But things change.

As I drive from the restaurant to the hotel, Callie sitting silently beside me in the passenger seat, I think about that homecoming game.

About the bonfire afterward.

★ ★ ★

Jesse Pike and I aren't friends. We've never been friends. We're rivals, despite the fact that we played for the same team four years ago in high school. He never got over the fact that I was chosen as MVP that year when he was the quarterback.

As far as raw talent goes? I might actually have to give him the edge. Of course, I'm the one who scored all those touchdowns. He just threw the passes.

My little sister Diana is a freshman this year, and of course, being the beauty that she is, she will be representing the freshman class on the homecoming court. Jesse's sister Rory has been named homecoming queen, and his other sister Callie sophomore attendant.

So the school invited both of us back to announce the homecoming game.

Jesse is a rocker now. His dark hair is long and pulled back into a low ponytail. He has a dragon tattoo on his left upper arm. And his ears are pierced. He wears small diamond studs. Actually, they're probably cubic zirconia.

We tolerated each other during the announcing of the game. In fact, I think we did pretty well. We joked, as if we were old friends.

Even though we're not.

His sisters are both gorgeous, of course. The Pikes are as good-looking as the Steels. Good genes, obviously. It's his sister Rory, the queen herself, who begs us to come to the bonfire.

"Come on, Jess. It'll be fun."

"Don and I aren't in high school anymore."

"So what? Come on."

I agree to go, if only to keep a close eye on my little sister. I remember the Snow Creek High School bonfires. They can get pretty wild.

So Jesse and I go, but we don't stay long.

Later that evening, I regretted my choice. I followed Dad in my car as he rushed Diana to the hospital in Grand Junction.

Alcohol poisoning. Except that it wasn't just alcohol. The shit everyone was drinking that night had been laced with at least two other substances. PCP. Street name angel dust. And crystal meth.

That's what the blood work showed.

How much had Diana drunk? No one seemed to know. Mom called all her friends, waking them up, asking.

Only one drink.

Maybe a full cup.

Two cups.

Diana didn't drink at all.

All answers that Mom got.

Once Diana came to, she couldn't remember. Whatever had affected her had given her retrograde amnesia, and she didn't even remember being at the bonfire.

I should have stayed.

I should have taken care of her. That night I failed as a brother.

⋆ ⋆ ⋆

The Carlton doesn't have any suites available, so Callie and I check into a deluxe room with two king-size beds.

I do love this woman, and just looking at her and a king-size bed makes me think of all the luscious ways those two things go together.

But I'm determined to be strong. We need to talk this out.

I open the minibar and pull out a Diet Coke for her.

"Thanks," she mumbles, unscrewing the lid and taking a deep sip.

I take a water for myself and drain it halfway. I'm not sure where this thirst came from, but it's begging to be sated.

Callie sighs and sits down on one of the beds. "There's a lot more to my story."

"I know."

"But Rory and I were wondering… Do you know what was in that punch? I heard Pat say it was angel dust. I don't know anything about angel dust or any drug, but I watched both Rory and Carmen get completely stoned on it."

"Neither of them ended up in the hospital."

"No, they did not. I'm so sorry for what happened to Diana. But I heard the next Monday that she had already been released."

I nod. "She recovered quickly. She was young and healthy."

"Still… she should have never had to go through that."

"True enough." I take another drink of the water, draining the bottle.

"So… are you going to answer my question?"

"Sorry. What question?"

"Did you ever find out what was in the punch?"

"Yeah. It *was* PCP. Angel dust. But there was also some crystal meth in it."

"Methamphetamine?"

"Yes. Diana showed traces of meth in her blood as well as PCP and alcohol."

"Oh my God."

"You know," I say, "I went to that school. I knew what the bonfires were like. Someone always spiked the damned punch. But this went beyond spiking. Somebody *drugged* this punch. That's why we were offering a reward for information."

"I get it. Diana could have died."

"Yes, she could have. Many others could have as well."

She nods. What else can she do? "A lot of people probably

got very lucky."

"We could have prosecuted Pat Lamone," I say.

She nods again. "I know that."

"I know you, Callie. And I love you. So I'm hoping you have a damned good reason why you didn't come forward with this evidence."

"I have what I thought was a good reason at the time. What Rory and I *both* thought was a good reason at the time. In retrospect, I can't say I would have made a different decision. I was a high school kid, Donny."

"I know that. I'm going to give you the benefit of the doubt. But Callie, you have to tell me why you didn't go public with that information."

"First I have to tell you what I did to get the information that's on that thumb drive."

"Did you break any laws?"

She shakes her head vehemently. "We did not. Rory and I were very careful about that."

"So Rory was in on it with you, along with Jordan, Carmen, and the others."

"Yes." She clears her throat.

"Fuck." I thread my fingers through my already screwed-up hair.

"We had to get him to admit what he did. So we got him into a compromising situation with Rory, and she got him to admit it."

"Then she *did*—"

"Oh my God, no! He was lying, Donny. She never slept with him."

"You're sure?"

"Of course I'm sure. Rory never would have done that.

Besides, I witnessed the whole thing."

My jaw drops. "You *watched* them?"

"No, no no no. I was listening. We recorded him."

"So Rory seduced the information out of him?"

"Yes. It was the only way. But she didn't do anything."

"Not *anything*?"

Callie's eyes narrow. "Just kissing and a little over the blouse action. She let him touch her boobs."

A sick feeling of dread wells inside me. Rory Pike. The homecoming queen. "Why didn't you just come to me? With the hearsay? We would have gotten him to admit it."

"Donny, we didn't even know you guys. You were the Steels. Untouchable. There was no way we were going to just come to you with this."

I bite my lower lip. The rumors. The rumors that the Steels owned the town. Then of course there was Jesse's and my rivalry. His assertion that he was passed over for MVP because we funded the football team. There was no love lost between the Pikes and the Steels during those years.

Of course Callie wasn't going to come to us for help. She and Rory were going to get the evidence they needed by themselves and then collect the reward money.

I can't resent her for that. In her mind, it made perfect sense, and I understand the logic that was driving her.

"I'm sorry," I say.

"What for?"

"I'm sorry you didn't feel you could come to any of us. I'm sorry..."

"Donny..."

"You've seen the evidence. You've seen what the property titles show. Apparently the Steels *do* own this town. Of course you couldn't come to us. Of course you had to be sure."

She swallows. "Thank you for understanding."

"You don't deserve my anger, Callie. My family does."

"Donny, I—"

"Damn it, Callie." I advance on her, pull her off the bed, into my body, and crush my lips to hers.

It's an angry kiss, but she is not the object of my anger. Perhaps she should be, but she's not.

How do you hold a high school girl responsible for a decision made based on her knowledge of who my family was?

You don't.

And I can't.

I kiss her. I kiss her hard, and I kiss her with raw passion and anger. I kiss her with a little bit of remorse as well.

My baby sister was drugged. Poisoned.

And I went back to Denver once she had recovered. I went back to Denver to live my own life.

I should have stayed on the western slope. I should have uncovered the untruths about my family. Some of which, it turns out, appear not to be untrue after all.

I melt into Callie, taking her with this kiss. I devour her mouth, and I know, before this night is over, I will also devour her body.

Why she covered up the evidence no longer matters to me.

None of this is her fault.

It's mine.

It's mine for deserting my family. For deserting my sister. For thinking I could find a life outside the western slope.

I should have been here.

I never should have left.

I rip my mouth from hers and push her—not gently—onto the bed.

"Undress," I say calmly.

She widens her eyes, parts her lips.

"Undress," I say again, this time a bit more forcefully.

She kicks off her shoes and then removes her socks. "Donny . . ."

"No talking. I don't want to talk anymore right now."

"But there's more . . ."

"Yeah, I've got a lot more too, but we'll deal with it later. Now, undress." This time I say it through clenched teeth.

"Are you going to . . . ?"

"Callie, I swear to God, if you don't undress right now, I'm going to turn you over my knee and spank that pretty little ass of yours."

Her cheeks redden.

"Donny . . ."

"Get. Un. Dressed."

She stands then and swiftly unbuttons her blouse. She shimmies out of it and tosses it onto the other bed. Then she unclasps her bra, and her beautiful breasts fall gently against her chest. The bra joins the blouse on the other bed. Now only her skinny black pants separate her from being naked.

My groin tightens. I'm already hard, but damn it, I get harder.

"The rest of it, Callie. Now."

CHAPTER ELEVEN

Callie

My body erupts in a fiery blaze.

And in a split second, I see the blaze of the bonfire all those years ago.

The bonfire that led to where I am today.

★ ★ ★

Jordan and I wait.

Rory is running late. She was supposed to have the van—and Pat Lamone—here five minutes ago. The parking lot behind the library. That's where everyone goes to park, and the police turn a blind eye unless someone complains.

We're in Jordan's car. Or rather Uncle Scott and Aunt Lena's car that she borrowed for the evening under the pretense of us going into town for ice cream. Meeting some friends.

I don't dare text Rory. Phones are off-limits tonight so that Pat doesn't have any chance to spy at hers. I have to wait at least half an hour before I check in with her.

"Shit," Jordan says. "You think she couldn't get him in the van?"

"Not a chance. Pat Lamone has been trying to get into Rory's pants for months."

"I know, but maybe he'll realize something's up."

"Maybe, but his small head will overrule his big one. Trust me."

I make myself sound more confident than I am. I believe in my sister, but that doesn't mean something can't go wrong.

"Look!" Jordan points.

Finally! The van rolls into the parking lot.

"Here comes the call." I hit the green button, turn on the speaker, and hit mute so Jordan and I can listen in and know if Rory has any trouble.

"Not too many cars here tonight," Rory says.

"Just as well." Pat Lamone's voice. "No one to bother us."

"I know. I've been looking forward to this."

I want to gag. Damn, Rory is a good actress. She'll make it in performing. No doubt. With her gorgeous singing voice and acting ability, the world is her stage.

"God, you look hot." Rory's voice again.

"Not as hot as you, baby."

Ugh. Gag again. Jordan is starting to look a little green, even in the dark. We can't speak. We have to stay very quiet even with the mute button on. It's important that we hear every word so we know if Rory needs us.

Did she get him to drink the Coke laced with Benadryl? She was supposed to do that before they got to the parking lot.

"Tell me something," Rory says.

"What?"

"I'm dying to find out what was in that hairy buffalo homecoming night. I've never had such an amazing high."

"Probably just some Everclear," Lamone says.

"No, it was more than that. I've drunk my share of Everclear."

"God, you're fucking hot."

"So are you." Rory giggles.

Yeah, upchuck city.

Rustling of clothes. A few moans. God, they're kissing.

"Getting tired?" Rory asks.

"A little. But believe me, I have enough energy to make you happy."

Then a pause. Is that a yawn? Hard to tell.

If Pat is yawning, that's a good sign.

"You can't stop looking at my tits, can you?"

"Baby, no one can stop looking at your tits."

"Here."

Pause. What is she doing? Letting him touch her? My God, I'm going to puke.

"I want to suck on them, baby. I want to pinch them until they're red."

"Easy. We'll get there, stud."

Another pause.

Then Rory's voice. "Come on. Lie down here with me."

More rustling. A pause. Then—

"I wish I knew who spiked the punch. Then I could find out what they put in it. Get some more of that for myself."

"I can get you some stuff."

"Can you? Wow, that would be great. So you know what was in the punch then?

"Sure, I do, baby. After all, I'm the one who fucking spiked it."

A smile splits my face.

Gotcha, Pat Lamone.

★ ★ ★

I slide my pants off my hips and legs. Then my underwear.

I'm naked. Naked while Donny is still fully clothed.

And I'm fucking hot. So damned hot.

Donny sucks in a breath. "God, you're beautiful."

"Am I?"

It's not like me to be coy. I've been thinking so much about the past. About how I never felt I was beautiful. In fact, I was invisible.

What makes a person invisible? Is it the lack of beauty?

Or is it the lack of self-love?

I always thought I had a terrible acne problem, but in reality, I had maybe one or two blemishes at a time. I knew people who had real problems. Whose faces are scarred in adulthood because of it.

My breasts aren't as big as Rory's, Maddie's, or my mother's. But does that mean a lack of beauty? All those years, I thought it did.

But Donny loves my breasts. Loves them just the way they are.

You don't need big breasts to be beautiful.

Beauty is in the eye of the beholder, my mother used to say.

I always scoffed at her. Easy to say when you were born beautiful like she was. Like Rory and Maddie were.

What was the core difference between Rory and me?

Personality. She was flamboyant and outgoing. The classic performer's personality.

I was introverted and withdrawn.

It was a self-fulfilling prophecy.

I made my*self* invisible.

I'm no longer invisible. Donny Steel sees me. Donny Steel, who I love so much. And who . . .

Who I deserve. No matter what mistakes I made in the past.

Although . . .

He mentioned he was going to turn me over his lap and spank me. I can't deny the idea turns me on.

When he spanked me previously, I loved it. Every minute of it. And I wonder . . . Why now? Why now, when I've never had the desire to be spanked before? Am I punishing myself? Punishing myself for the mess ten years ago that is now coming back to haunt me?

Or is it a kink I enjoy that I just never realized before?

Does it really matter?

And I know. I know what I'm going to do.

I turn around and push him down into the sitting position on the bed. Then I lie across his lap.

"Spank me, Donny. Spank me hard."

CHAPTER TWELVE

Donny

Slap!

I bring my hand down on her ass so hard my palm stings.

Slap! Slap! Slap!

Her ass turns a lovely light red, as the tiny blood vessels burst underneath her milky skin and spread the blush over the firm cheeks of her ass.

"Is this what you want? You want a spanking, Callie?"

"Yes." The word comes out on a glorious moan. "Please."

"Do you want it because it turns you on? Or do you want it to punish yourself?"

She doesn't respond.

"Tell me, Callie. Tell me, or I won't spank you again."

"Donny, I . . ."

"What? Tell me. Is this for passion? Or is it for punishment?"

"I think it's for . . . I think it's for both."

I raise my hand then, ready to bring it down on her ass once more, but I stop. My hand hovers about three inches from her beautiful flushed skin.

I can't deny that spanking her turns me on. I'm a man, after all. I've engaged in spanking many times.

But never as punishment. I have no desire to punish a

woman. Especially not a woman that I love.

I gently move her off my lap until she's lying on the bed. Still fully clothed, I lie down next to her and take her in my arms.

"I think you want to punish yourself for something that happened ten years ago." I kiss the top of her head.

"So what if I do?"

"Callie, I'm not going to be your judge in this. I'm not here to dole out punishment."

"But I don't know for sure that it's punishment. I also really like it."

"I like it too. I love how beautiful your ass is under my hand. But as long as there's some part of you that thinks you deserve punishment, and who sees the spanking as punishment, I'm not going to be the one to give it out."

"You know… Most men wouldn't have this issue. Most men would take any chance to spank a woman."

Most men haven't been caged and beaten, either, but I can't tell Callie that part of my life. Not now.

At least not yet.

"I've never been most men."

She smiles then. "I know. And I love you for it."

"So you understand, then?"

"I do. I won't say I no longer desire the spanking, but I understand your thought process. You're happy to give it to me if it's sexual in nature, but if I see it as punishment, you won't do it."

"Good."

"When I think about everything objectively, I don't want to punish myself. I realize I was just a kid, and even though technically she was an adult, Rory was pretty much just a kid too. We did what we thought we should at the time."

"I know. And I know I got angry with you at first, but I do get it. Though I have to ask, Callie… What happened? Why didn't you bring us the evidence once you obtained it?"

She doesn't respond right away. I kiss the top of her head, hoping that I'm showing her that I love her no matter what.

There must be a good reason.

They got the evidence. In fact, they still have it, even though it's too late to prosecute Pat Lamone.

Several moments pass. Finally, "Callie?"

"It's not a pretty story," she says.

"I didn't expect that it would be. Obviously there was a good reason for you and Rory not to turn the evidence over to us."

"He vowed to destroy us," she says.

"We would have—"

I stop abruptly. *We would have protected you.* Those were the words on the tip of my tongue.

But Callie had no way of knowing this back then. She didn't know us. She thought we owned the town. She didn't know what we would do.

"What?" she asks.

"Never mind." I brush my lips over her hair again. "It doesn't matter."

She moves away from me then, props her head up on her hand, and meets my gaze. "All of it *does* matter, Donny. It all matters because it's brought us here today. Perhaps I'm not the woman you thought I was."

"I've told you. I don't resent you for things you did when you were a kid."

"I know that. Is it yourself you're resenting?"

I sigh. "In many ways, yes. I should have stayed. Especially after Diana was hospitalized. But no… I couldn't wait to get back to Denver, back to my first year of law school. I never thought I'd return, Callie."

"So you had a different life in mind for yourself. There's no crime in that. It's the life I want too. I want law school. A career. I just haven't been able to get it."

"No, you've stayed here to help your family. That's the difference. I left. I should have been here. Not just for Diana, but for my mother and father. For Dale. For my aunts, uncles, and cousins. The Steel family has given me so much, and what did I give back? I left as soon as I could—to follow my *own* dreams."

"Donny, you can't compare yourself to me. I stayed because I had no choice. I didn't have the money for law school, and once I finally had it, the fire happened."

"But so much else was going on, and it was right in front of our noses the whole time. Our parents have been lying to us. Not just to Dale and me, but to all our cousins. And I'm wondering… I'm wondering if the Steels maybe *aren't* the pillars of society that we've been led to believe."

Those words.

Finally I've said them out loud.

There's something in our history that our parents have tried to bury.

And frankly, it scares the hell out of me.

Who are the Steels, *really*?

How did we become billionaires when our business is in ranching, fruit growing, and winemaking? Sure, we have investments. Lots of investments, domestically and overseas.

But the money had to come from somewhere to begin with.

"Donny, whatever is going on is not your fault."

"I know that. But if I had stayed... If I had stayed, maybe I could have unearthed this sooner. Or at least I should have come back here after law school. But no. It was more important for me to have some powerful position in Denver. Why? I didn't need the money. I'm set for the next five lifetimes. Why was it so important to me to leave my family?"

"It's not such a horrible thing to want to make it on your own," she says. "I think it's kind of admirable."

"Thank you, Callie. Thank you for saying that."

I do appreciate her sentiment.

But she's wrong.

What I did was *not* admirable.

I abandoned my little sister. I abandoned my family.

My brother, to whom I owe everything.

And my parents, to whom I also owe everything.

And who, I'm finding out, may not be the people I thought they were.

CHAPTER THIRTEEN

Callie

I hand one thumb drive with Pat Lamone's confession to Rory. The other I place in my purse. Rory and I have plans to drive to Denver this weekend and open up a safe-deposit box in a downtown bank. The confession will be safe there.

"I can't believe we pulled this off," Rory says.

"I can't believe you let that piece of shit kiss you without gagging," I retort.

"Believe me, it was difficult. I guess I'm a better actress than I ever thought I was."

"Are you kidding? You're a great actress. And a great vocalist. You're going to make it, Ror."

"I hope you're right. I wish I could make this my audition." She laughs. Sort of. More like a nervous giggle.

"I know you feel pretty dirty about the whole thing. But don't. We're going to be ten thousand dollars richer pretty quick."

"You mean thirty-three hundred dollars richer. Between the two of us. We have to split it with all the others."

"Yeah, that does kind of suck. Oh, well. Thirty-three hundred sure is a lot better than zero."

"True that. So we'll go to the Steels after we make sure this one is safely deposited in Denver?"

"Or we go now. What do you think?"

"I don't trust Pat Lamone. Or any of the other guys who know about this. I want to make sure the evidence is secure before we go to the Steels."

I nod. "Good enough." Then my phone buzzes.

I have more information for you about
Pat Lamone. Under the bleachers. Noon.

I widen my eyes as my heart starts beating rapidly. I shove my phone under Rory's nose. "What do you make of this?"

She pulls her own phone out of her purse. "I have the same text. My phone is still on silent from the other night."

"What do you think? Do we go?"

"I don't know. We already have the evidence. How can there be any more?"

"I don't know. Maybe one of us goes, and the other stands watch."

"Sounds good. I'm the older sister. I should go."

"You've already done enough, Ror."

"I know, but no offense, Cal. I'm a senior and the homecoming queen. People are going to be more apt to talk to me."

I ruminate a moment. She's probably right.

"Okay. You go, and I'll stay out of sight, ready to intervene if necessary."

She nods. "It's a plan."

The campus is quiet on a Saturday. But at noon, Rory and I head toward the stadium. I'm armed with binoculars so I can see what's going on.

Good. It's a couple of girls who are waiting for Rory. Juniors.

I should have told Rory to turn on her phone so I could hear what was going on.

I watch, staying hidden.

After all, being invisible has its perks.

Until—

Rory crumples to the ground.

"Shit." Now what? I don't think. I run. Run toward my sister. One of the girls turns toward me. Pulls out what looks like—

"No!" I scream.

Then I crumple to the ground as well.

★ ★ ★

Donny is quiet.

I'm quite aware of my nakedness. I'm also aware that his cock is straining against his pants. He still wants me, and I still want him.

Still, those images from ten years ago are seared into my brain.

The day Pat Lamone got the best of us. Of Rory and me, and the day he threatened to destroy us.

We never found out what he had tranquilized us with. We guessed it was a simple veterinary tranquilizer dart because one of the girls he roped into helping him, Brittany Sheraton, was the daughter of the town vet.

By the time Rory and I woke up in the shed behind the baseball field, we were fully clothed, and several photos were strewn about us.

Photos of both of us. Naked. In very compromising positions.

Our eyes were closed. We were clearly unconscious. But

to someone who didn't know, we could have easily been there out of our own accord.

Then the texts came.

We meet tomorrow at noon, same place.
We exchange evidence. Otherwise, those
photos will be plastered on social media.
The homecoming queen will be ruined.
And so will her ugly duckling sister.

If I hadn't yet considered every part of me invisible by that point, I did then.

The few blemishes—normal for any teenager—I suffered from became a terrible case of acne.

My well-proportioned breasts became small compared to Rory's and Maddie's.

It was a self-fulfilling prophecy.

I became the ugly duckling.

And it wasn't until Donny Steel that I truly believed that was never me.

"Donny?"

"Yeah, baby?"

"I want to tell you everything. I want to tell you why we didn't come to you with the evidence."

"It doesn't matter now."

"I want to tell you anyway. You opened up to me about something that was bothering you. What you tried to do with the energy board. I know how difficult that was for you, and I'm so glad you were able to stop it."

"Yeah, but not before Brendan's place was trashed."

"I know, and that's a horrible thing. But you did the right

thing in the end, and I want you to know why Rory and I did not."

"All right."

"First of all, if something really terrible had happened to Diana, I'm sure we would have done the right thing."

"We're all very lucky that she was fine."

"I know that. I also want you to know that we got the evidence because we were being mercenaries. We wanted the reward money."

He swallows audibly.

Probably not my finest moment, but I want him to know the truth.

"I hope you don't think less of me for that."

"Callie, we offer rewards for a reason. Because people need money. Money gets results. It's not a crime to want to collect on a reward."

"Thank you for understanding. Anyway… We got the evidence, as you know. But then…"

"It's okay."

"Pat got two girls from the junior class to help him. One of them was Brittany Sheraton."

"Dr. Sheraton's daughter?"

"The veterinarian. Yeah."

"Go on."

"Somehow, Pat found out what we did to him. We're not sure how. But he found out that we had his confession, so Brittany and her friend Kayla sent us a text saying they had extra information."

"And you went?"

"Yeah, but we had backup. Rory went, and I stayed hidden, to make sure she was okay."

“But she wasn’t okay.”

I get up. “No. They tranquilized her with something, I watched her fall to the ground, and then, when I ran after her, they zapped me as well. The next thing we remember is we woke up in the shed behind the baseball field. We were still dressed, but…”

Donny’s jaw clenches. “Damn it! What the hell did they do to you? Are you all right?”

“We’re fine. Neither of us showed any evidence that we had been assaulted in any way. Other than being tranquilized. I was a virgin at that point, and I didn’t have any pain or any blood. Rory wasn’t a virgin, but there was no evidence that anyone had raped her. However, there were”—I gulp down a surge of stomach acid—“photos left with us. Full-color photos of the two of us naked, our eyes closed.”

“I’ll fucking kill him.”

“The photos didn’t show anyone touching us. Pat wasn’t even in the photos. Our eyes were closed, but our legs were spread, and we looked ready and willing.”

Donny stands then and leaves the bed in a rush. “I’m going to kill that fucking bastard. First he poisons my sister and then—”

“Donny, that’s not the end of the story.”

“Fuck. What the hell else happened?”

“We were told we had to meet him and hand over our evidence, and then he would hand over the photos. We both had to promise that we didn’t keep copies of either.”

“But you said you have the thumb drive?”

“We do. We kept a copy just in case he screwed us over. Which makes me think… He probably kept his evidence as well. And now he’s back. Back in Snow Creek when he knows he can't be prosecuted for his crimes."

"Drugging my sister and the two of you. Fuck. Fucking statute of limitations."

"Yeah. I researched them myself. He's free and clear now."

"And he doesn't have anything on you?"

I shake my head. "We fed him Benadryl, but it's not a controlled substance. Not our finest hour, but technically, we didn't break any laws."

"But *he* did, the motherfucker."

"Yeah, he did. Quite a few of them."

"Whatever happened to him? Why did he leave town?"

"No one really knows for sure, but it happened pretty soon after this whole ordeal. Rory and I like to say that we chased him out of town, but in reality, it probably had nothing to do with us. His dad probably got a job somewhere else. Could be anything."

"Still . . . he left town . . . and now he's back."

"I'm not sure why, though," I say. "We still have the evidence against him. So if he still has the photos, we still have our leverage."

Donny wrinkles his forehead. "I'm not so sure."

"But the thumb drive was there."

"Callie, have either you or Rory *looked* on the thumb drive?"

My jaw drops. "Oh my God."

"Someone took the key to your safe-deposit box. Don't you think it's a little weird that the thumb drive is still there? And Pat Lamone is back in town?"

"I do now."

He pulls me off the bed and into his arms. "I swear to God, I will protect you. Pat Lamone will be sorry he ever tried to fuck with the people I love."

"He tried telling you his lies. He tried telling Raine his lies. Neither of those worked. So my guess is he's going to bring out the photos, assuming he still has them. And he knows you have money, Donny."

"Callie, I'll spend my entire fortune protecting you if I have to."

Anger rises in me. "I don't want you to give him a damned nickel, Donny. Do not give that son of a bitch one cent of your money."

"The money means nothing to me. I'd gladly spend millions to protect you, and I'll still have plenty."

"Don't you see? If he truly still has the photos, plus he's absconded with our evidence, he'll never stop. Once he runs out of the money you give him, he'll come back for more. Is that what you want?"

"None of this is what I want, but I won't have you in danger. And I sure as hell won't have your beautiful body on display for everybody else to salivate over."

"Wait!" A moment of truth hits me with the force of an avalanche. "I was underage at that time. If he makes those photos public, we can get him on child porn charges. Why didn't I think of this before?"

A smile splits Donny's face. "Because you were stressed. But you're a genius. You're going to be a great lawyer, Cal."

I frown then—a big frown that brings acid crawling up my throat like the tiny feet of a centipede. "But Rory… She was eighteen. Legal. We have to protect her, Donny. We have to."

CHAPTER FOURTEEN

Donny

I sit up in bed then. The beautiful woman before me is still naked. Her skin is flushed, her lips trembling. She's frightened—not for herself, but for her sister.

"I promise you, Callie." I touch her cheek, trail my finger over her still-trembling lips. "Nothing will happen to you or Rory on my watch."

She closes her eyes, sighs softly. "Thank you. Thank you so much."

I lean down then and brush my lips against hers, thinking she needs a gentle kiss, a gentle hand.

But she pulls me close, forces her tongue between my lips, and kisses me hard.

Hard. I'm hard all over, especially in my groin.

We got derailed earlier, when I chose to interrogate Callie about her need for spanking. Now, I'd like to turn her over my knee and continue the assault on her gorgeous ass.

No. Not as long as she feels it's punishment.

I can still make love to her, though. Fuck her hard and fast too.

My clothes are binding me, but having her naked while I'm still fully clothed is a big turn-on as well. We kiss and we kiss and we kiss, until finally I have to break the suction to inhale a much-needed breath.

Her beautiful breasts beckon me. They're rosy and flushed, her dark-pink nipples hard and sticking out like red currants.

I kiss her neck, the top of her chest, sprinkle a few kisses around one areola, and then I suck one of her nipples into my mouth. Hard.

She groans beneath me. "God, yes. Feels so good."

I suck harder and then bite her gently. She gasps in a breath.

I take the other nipple between my fingers, pull on it, tug it, twist it.

"God, Donny. God. Feels so damned good."

She's telling *me*. The texture of her nipple in my mouth is like velvet over a hard nob. I want to suck on it all day, all night.

My other hand goes searching for different treasures. I let her nipple go, slide over her soft belly to her mound.

And then between her legs.

I groan. God, she's wet. Slick as the caramel coating a Fuji apple, and so much sweeter. I slide my fingers through her pussy and dip one finger shallowly into her channel.

"Yes, please, Donny. Please."

I drill into her this time with two fingers. Find that spongy spot and give it a good massage.

And still I'm sucking on her nipple. Her delicious, silky nipple.

"Too many clothes, Donny. Too many freaking clothes."

I agree. I want my clothes gone, but I don't want to leave her nipple or remove my fingers from her pussy.

She's holding me spellbound. Spellbound by her beautiful body, by her responsiveness to my every touch.

"Inside me. Please. Inside me."

That plea does it for me. I let her nipple drop from my lips, and I remove my fingers from her warm, sweet pussy. Then I undress. I undress so quickly I'm sure I've set a new record. I throw my clothes on the other bed where hers lie, and then, naked, my cock hard and shooting straight out, I return to my beautiful love.

"Spread those legs, baby," I say. "I'm going to eat that pussy."

Her response is a groan as she obeys, fanning out her legs and exposing her most private parts to my loving gaze so I have a bird's-eye view of her beautiful treasures. She's pink and swollen and glistening with cream.

"My God. You're so beautiful, Callie."

Her eyes are closed, her hands scrunched into fists, her hips raised.

She doesn't respond, except with body language.

And I know what she wants.

I go straight for her clit, sucking it hard between my lips as I jam those two fingers back inside her pussy.

I drill into her, massage her G-spot, bring her to the brink, and just when I know she's ready to explode, I let go of her clit.

"Please," she begs. "Please."

I regard her from between her legs. Her beautiful lips are parted, her breasts are rosy, her nipples tight and hard.

I slowly move my fingers in and out of her, scissoring them, touching the anterior and then the posterior of her cunt.

She wriggles beneath me.

I know what she's feeling. She's almost there, and if I just—

I swipe my tongue over her clit and then suck on it gently.

And she shatters beneath me.

My cock pulses in time with the contractions of her pussy as she comes around my fingers.

She's so beautiful, and she tastes so good.

How did I ever think I could let her go?

We'll get through this together. Both her issues and mine. We give each other strength, and we help each other see that our vulnerabilities are not a lack of strength but simply more strength in a different guise.

I crawl atop her, thrust my cock inside her heat.

She's still coming, and her pussy vibrates around me as I thrust.

She gloves me so completely, her suction so perfect around me. I pump and I pump and I pump, and then I capture her lips with mine, kissing her hard.

The kiss is urgent and passionate, and as I continue to fuck her, with each thrust, my love for her grows.

We've learned something new about each other. Neither of us is perfect, and we've both made mistakes.

But together . . .

Together, Callie and I are stronger.

We complement each other.

We complete each other.

We will find the answers we're searching for.

We will protect each other.

We will love each other.

Forever.

★ ★ ★

"Are you hungry?" I ask as we lie in our afterglow. "I didn't feed you."

"You know? Now that I've talked about this with you, I do think I could eat."

"What sounds good? Room service has a full menu."

"I don't know. Salmon maybe?"

"Sounds great." I get on the phone and order two salmon dinners and a couple of Diet Cokes. "Should be here in about a half hour. Now what could we do between now and then?"

She giggles. "I love you, Donny, but I'm not sure I'm up for anything more until I find out for sure whether that thumb drive is empty."

"You can call Rory."

"What time is it?"

"About eight thirty."

"Great. Not too late. I think I will give her a call."

"All right. I'll give you some privacy. I'll use the facilities."

She smiles and nods, though her eyes still have a far-off, haunted look.

"It doesn't matter, Callie. Whatever happens, we *will* get through this together. I will protect you."

"I know you can protect me. I'm more worried about Rory. She was legal age when those photos were taken."

"Callie, I promise you that I will die before I let any harm come to you or to Rory."

I head to the bathroom then, secure in those words that I mean with every ounce of my being.

CHAPTER FIFTEEN

Callie

My breath catches as I call Rory.

"Hey, Cal," she says into my ear. Her voice cracks a little.

She's freaked too.

Uh-oh.

"Hey. Don't tell me . . . You listened to the thumb drive."

"I did."

"And it's blank, right?"

"Actually, it's not."

Relief surges through me. "Thank God. So his confession is still there?"

"Not exactly. Everything is still there . . . up to the point where he confessed. So basically, it just makes *me* look bad."

That relief I just felt? It's morphed into full-fledged panic.

"He turned it against *us*, Cal. He made it into something that harms us instead of helps us."

"Damn it. Thank God we at least listened to it before we started trying to negotiate with him."

She sighs. "Yeah. I wanted to wait for you, but I couldn't. I had to know."

"Donny and I were talking, and he actually came up with the idea that it might be a fake. I mean, the dude stole our key. I'm not sure why we didn't think of it in the first place." I rub at my now throbbing temples. "Except I do know why. We were both so relieved that it was still there."

"I know. We need to keep our emotions at bay through this and focus on facts and logic. And before you say it, yes, I know I sound just like you. How did he get into the safe-deposit box to make the switch? He would have needed to show ID that he was me."

"Easy enough. He took a woman with him who had a fake ID."

"So someone is out there masquerading as me."

"Probably not. Probably just for that particular thing."

"So? I don't fucking care. Someone's got my name and social security number and used it to fabricate an ID."

"Have you noticed any weird charges on your credit cards or anything?"

"No, but I haven't exactly been looking."

"Fire up your computer right now, while we're on the phone. Tell me if anything looks amiss."

"Yeah, okay. Where are you anyway?"

"I'm in Grand Junction with Donny."

"Will you be back tonight?"

I look down at the ruffled bed. "Probably not. Honestly, I don't know."

It could go either way. Though since Donny's dad just got home, he'll probably want to be home in the morning.

"Nothing wrong on my Visa so far," Rory says. "I recognize all the charges. Let me look at my checking and savings accounts." She taps furiously on her keys, so loud that I can hear it over the phone. "Thank God." She heaves a sigh so loud I'm almost sure I can feel it through the phone. "Nothing seems out of the ordinary."

"Just in case, you should probably get some identity theft protection right now. Someone obviously has your information."

"I beat you to it, sis," she says. "I'm already checking out the Norton website."

"I'll do the same once I get home," I say.

"Good idea."

"Rory… I told Donny. I told him everything."

My sister is silent for a moment. Then, "Okay."

"He doesn't blame us. For anything. He was a little upset when he first found out we kept the information from him about who poisoned Diana, but he understood when I explained the whole thing."

"You've got a great guy there, Callie. Don't screw it up."

"I almost did. *He* almost did. He gave me the choice to walk away—to walk away from everything he's dealing with right now. That's why I felt I had to tell him."

"Yeah, at least no one in our family has been shot. Man, this is screwed up."

"He's going to help us, Rory."

"So he knows everything? About the photos…"

"Yeah… and we have some leverage. For me at least. I was underage when those photos were taken. If Lamone tries to make them public, we can bring him up on child pornography charges."

"There's no statute of limitations on that?"

"No, it's illegal for him to be in possession of nude pictures of any underage person. Since I was underage at that time, it counts."

Silence for another moment. "But it won't help me."

"It may. You were barely eighteen. We could tell him that

you were underage. Scare the shit out of him."

"Why didn't we think of this back then?"

"Because we were kids, Rory. We were faced with our lives being ruined in this small town. We didn't stop to think about any other laws he might be breaking. He had already broken a big one by drugging people."

"Man, we had him on everything. A minor in possession. Possession of illegal substance. Drugging the punch, resulting in Diana's hospitalization, and then drugging us with whatever the hell was in that tranquilizer gun. Then assault and battery for removing our clothes and taking those damned photos."

"I know. Perhaps we made the wrong decision back then, but we can't play that game, Rory. We did what we thought we had to do at the time."

"I know. Honest to God, Callie? I'm glad Raine isn't here. I wouldn't want her to see me go through this."

"She's not the person you thought she was," I say. "You're better off without her. You'll find the one, Rory. If I can, anyone can."

"I'm not sure I will. We can keep Pat Lamone from distributing your pictures online, but what can we do about *mine*?"

"First, we don't even know he still has them. Our agreement was to destroy the evidence."

"Callie, you know as well as I do that he has them. He didn't trust us any more than we trusted him. We kept a copy of *our* evidence."

I say nothing. What can I say? My sister is undoubtedly right. Pat Lamone may not be the brightest bulb in the basket, but he's not the stupidest either.

He's back for one reason. To take us down because he

knows we can't take him down with us. He destroyed our evidence.

"Let me talk to Donny," I say. "He'll know what to do. If we have to, we can break into Pat's place, find the photos, and—"

"Callie, the solution to our problems isn't more breaking of the law."

"Let me remind you that we never broke the law. *He* did."

"I'm sure he could find a way to spin the Benadryl thing."

"Rory, he doesn't even *know* about the Benadryl. All he knows is that you gave him a Coke. He doesn't know there was anything in it. He just knows he got kind of tired and passed out."

"He'll say I spiked the Coke or something, and since I was under twenty-one at the time, it was a crime for me to have alcohol."

"Yeah, but there's no evidence. It's just his word. He can try to say the thumb drive shows you were together, but who in his right mind is going to believe that you wanted to hook up with Pat Lamone? Plus, we can't test his blood from ten years ago. And even if he did have evidence, the statute of limitations applies to you as well as to him."

"I know . . ." Rory sighs heavily. Again. "This is all so fucked up. I can't believe we got so complacent. I totally thought this was over. I haven't given it a thought in . . . I don't know how long."

"I know. I haven't either. But we *will* get through this. And I swear, I will not allow Pat freaking Lamone to destroy your life."

"Here's another thing, Callie. What if he says the pictures are recent? I mean, you don't look that much different than you did then."

My heart falls. "I didn't think of that. Neither of us look a lot different. I had a few more zits back then."

"For God's sake, you've never had an acne problem. Get over yourself already."

She's right. Just because Pat Lamone called me the ugly duckling sister doesn't mean I *am* the ugly duckling sister. Pat Lamone is an idiot.

"Sorry. And you know what? We'll get Brittany Sheraton or Kayla whatever the fuck her name was to come forward and admit when the pictures were taken. Admit what they did to us. Donny will pay them off if we have to."

"Yeah, okay."

"You don't sound too excited about that plan."

"I just wish we could handle this ourselves. I hate that other people even have to know about it."

"I agree. But there's no shame in taking help from people who want to help us."

"Lamone told Donny and Raine that we're gold diggers." Rory sighs. "So what do we do now? We take help from the Steels, which equates to taking their money."

An epiphany shoots through me. "We were after the reward money ten years ago. That's why we needed the evidence, and that's where Lamone got the idea that we were gold diggers. Damn. But why would he lie about you sleeping with him and me being next in line?"

"Hell if I know, but he has evidence, after all. Naked photos of both of us."

"That proves nothing," I say.

"True, if you want to get technical, but naked photos are easily spun."

My sister's far from wrong, but what if there's something

much more sinister behind all of this? Why, after ten years, would Pat Lamone come back here and stir all this up again? We've pretty much determined he's not here to dredge up the past. He's here to mess with the present and the future.

But why?

What on earth does he have to gain?

Hush money from the Steels, sure. But is he only a mercenary? Or is there something larger at work?

I draw in a deep breath. Best to stick with the issue at hand. "Donny wants to help us. And I want to help him with things he's going through."

"What the hell is Donny going through? He's a fucking Steel."

"I think we've had the wrong idea about the Steels all this time. Yeah, they seem golden on the outside, but they harbor just as many secrets and issues as any other family."

"They do?"

"They do. I'll ask Donny how much I can tell you."

"No, please don't. This may sound selfish, but I don't want to get in the middle of anybody else's drama right now."

"Fair enough. In the meantime, we do need to check out Pat Lamone. I have the sinking feeling that all the crap that's gone down in our lives isn't just a coincidence. I mean your breakup with Raine. We already know he played a hand in it."

"Raine and I were already over. She didn't believe his lies."

"I know that. But Pat Lamone certainly didn't help the situation. He tried the same thing with Donny and me. And I'm wondering… That fire… Our winery and vineyards get destroyed, and all of a sudden Pat Lamone is back in town? Having stolen our evidence?"

Rory stays silent.

"Rory?" I say.

"Sorry. Just thinking. Why? Why would he come back ten years later, just to destroy us? All we did was get evidence of him saying that he drugged the punch that poisoned Diana Steel. That's it, and we didn't even hand over the evidence, because he blackmailed us with the photos. So why? Why now?"

"He probably got wind of the fact that I'm dating Donny Steel and thought he could make a buck. That's the only thing I can think of on the surface. But there's more. I feel it."

"You weren't dating him when the fire struck."

"That's true. Though we were pretty cozy at the Steels' wedding reception for Dale and Ashley."

"But Lamone wasn't there."

"No, he wasn't. Not that I saw anyway. But this is a small town, and news travels fast."

"He's back, and he wants something," Rory says. "If it's money, why would he go to all the trouble of starting a fire?"

"I don't know. Just call it a hunch. I've had that feeling since he surfaced. He tried to destroy us once, and he failed. How best to destroy us than to take away our family's ability to make a living?"

"You think it's not just money? But some sort of twisted revenge?"

"I don't know. Like I said, call it a hunch. And since I've been with Donny, I've learned one thing. He never ignores his hunches, and I don't think I should either."

CHAPTER SIXTEEN

Donny

"What's your hunch?" I ask Callie as she ends the call with her sister.

She turns quickly, nearly dropping her phone.

"I'm sorry," I say. "I didn't mean to eavesdrop. But I couldn't help hearing that you told Rory you had a hunch and that you had decided not to ignore your hunches."

"I learned from the best." She gives me a nervous smile.

"Tell me. What's your hunch? Maybe I'll have some insight."

She clears her throat. And I stare at her. She's still naked, of course, as am I. I'm already hardening at the sight of her. We won't be leaving this room anytime soon.

"I'm not sure it makes a lot of sense, especially since you and I weren't together at the time of the fire, but here we are . . . and Pat Lamone is back in town. Do you happen to know when he returned?"

"I don't. I saw him at the same time you did, at the Snow Creek Inn that night."

"Yeah. Maybe we should find out when he first came back. Because I was thinking . . . What if he started that fire, Donny?"

"Interesting. But if he's trying to get money out of me . . ."

"You and I both know that our property took the brunt of that fire. Dale's Syrah vineyards were an unfortunate side effect."

I wrinkle my forehead. "I don't want to discount your hunch, but it would be really hard to control where a fire goes. It depends on the wind, the humidity in the air, so many other factors that an arsonist wouldn't have any control over."

"Really? Any good meteorologist could have given him the information he needs."

Callie is looking to blame someone for the fact that her family has suffered such a loss. For the fact that her law school has been put on hold. I don't blame her. Pointing the finger, although it doesn't change anything, can at least give you someone to blame. Someone other than the weather. Someone other than God and his random acts.

"I don't know," I tell her. "But I can tell you this. The fire marshal *does* think the fire was started by a campfire. Dale is wringing his hands over that, of course, because he was camping in the area at that time."

Her hand flies to her mouth. "Dale thinks *he* started the fire?"

"My brother is always very careful when he camps. It's doubtful that he started it, but I know him. If he thinks there's a reason he can blame himself for it, he will. The truth of the matter is, Callie, that we'll never actually know. If it was started by a campfire, Dale was hardly the only person out there during that time."

"And as you said, Dale is always very careful."

"Yeah. He really is. He's been going up into those mountains for years to camp. He's a loner. Always has been as you know, and sometimes he seeks solace, and he finds it in nature."

"That makes sense. And for what it's worth, I don't believe for one minute that Dale was the cause of that fire."

"Truthfully? I don't either. I've told my brother that. He's not blaming himself anymore. He seems to have his head on a little bit straighter now that Ashley has come into his life."

Callie smiles. "Well, a good woman can do that for a man."

I rake my gaze over her beautiful body. "Oh, yes. She can."

"You have a one-track mind, Donovan Steel."

"Yes, I do, when it comes to you, Caroline Pike."

"I promised you a good time. But first... Do you think my hunch has any merit? Or am I just really wanting to blame Pat Lamone for all my troubles?"

"I think it would be easy to blame him for all your troubles. After all, he's the source of a lot of them. Whether he's the source of the fire, we may never know. We'd have to put him in the area at the time, and we don't even know when he got back into town."

"Yeah." She rubs her forehead. "And if he went into the woods alone, we can't prove anything."

"But... if it will make you feel better, I have the resources. I'm going to be putting a tail on Lamone anyway, so why not check out when he got here and where he's been?"

"You would do that for me?"

I advance toward her, caress her silky cheek. "Isn't it clear by now? I'll do *anything* for you, Callie." I bring my lips down on hers in a forceful kiss.

She opens for me instantly, and our tongues tangle in passion. It's not as raw as it was previously, but still, it's passionate and euphoric.

To my surprise, though, she breaks the kiss and walks backward.

I lift my eyebrows.

"Sorry. I just… I need to think this through. I want you. I always want you. But I—"

I hold up my hand to stop her from speaking. "You don't have to explain anything. I get it. Believe me."

She sits down on the bed. "I just need to know. Rory is beside herself. Someone clearly got into our safe-deposit box, which means they had to have Rory's ID."

"I know. The good news is… I happen to have access to all the databases in the state of Colorado. And so do you."

A smile spreads slowly over her face. "Which means we can find out when a new ID was issued in the name of Aurora Pike. Except… what if it's a completely fake ID? Then it wouldn't be in the databases."

"Good point. However, someone at the bank took the ID. It obviously wasn't the manager you and Rory saw, or he would have remembered."

"Would he have?"

"Most likely, if it was recent. We need to question the other managers at the bank who would have access to the safe-deposit boxes."

"Right. But Donny, what if this happened a long time ago? What if he found out where we buried the key, dug it up back then, and did all of this ten years ago?"

"When you and Rory went to dig up the key, did the land look disturbed?"

"Honestly, I don't know. Neither one of us gave it much of a thought."

"Then it probably didn't look disturbed. You would have taken note if it had."

"Yeah, maybe."

"Still, that doesn't mean he wasn't there recently. Anyone worth his salt would know how to make it look like he hadn't been there."

"I never thought Pat Lamone was that much of a genius, but perhaps I've underestimated him." She shakes her head.

"It's best to never underestimate your enemies," I tell her. "But don't blame yourself. You thought this was over."

"That was my first mistake."

"Trust me, I know where you're coming from. Things seem to be popping up from the past to bite both our asses at the moment."

"I'm sorry, because what you're going through is so much worse than what I'm going through."

"Don't say that. No one has naked pictures of me. Not that I know of, anyway." I let out a short laugh.

"I feel so ridiculous. How did I let any of this happen?"

"Don't go back there. You were a kid. You and Rory handled it far better than most people your age would have. You got him to go away. And you did it without breaking any laws when he broke several."

"I feel like he planned this from the beginning, though," she says. "And then he waited. Waited until the statute of limitations had run out so that he'd be spared, and now he's back. Back to make our lives hell."

"Remember, he was a kid as well. He likely didn't think this through at the time."

"He thought it through enough that he kept his evidence."

"We don't know that, Callie. Sure, you and Rory kept yours, and he stole it. You don't know for sure that he still has those pictures."

"Come on, Donny."

"The two of you had him dead to rights. Neither of you broke a law. You weren't going to prison, but he was. Sure, he could have screwed you over by posting naked pictures on the internet, and then he would have been arrested for child pornography. Something none of you thought about at the time."

"You're right. Still . . ."

"We can't get inside his head. In fact, I'm not sure either of us really want to. Obviously, he's a nutcase. But if he had anything to do with setting that fire, I promise you I will prove it."

"And if he didn't?"

"We'll still get rid of him. If he has those pictures, it is illegal for him to possess them, and *that* we can easily prove."

"And if he doesn't have them?"

"Then why is he here?"

"To screw Rory and me over. He couldn't do it ten years ago, and he's back to do it now."

I can't fault her logic. She may well be right. Pat Lamone wouldn't be the first person to hold a grudge for ten years, even though he was completely in the wrong. Makes me think of people in my own family. And it makes me think about others—others who have a grudge against the Steel family and who have waited God knows how long for their revenge.

"And that's it?" I ask.

She bites her lip. "Maybe not. Maybe not at all. I was telling Rory that I think this may go deeper, but for the life of me, I don't know why I think that. It's a hunch."

"Another hunch." I smile. "You may well be right, but I'm not sure it has anything to do with the fire."

In fact, I'm wondering if what Callie and I are both going

through could all be intermingled somehow.

But that would be improbable at best.

Still . . .

My mind whirls with possibilities, none of which I can prove.

No. I need something else now. Something real and pure and alive.

I need to lose myself—lose myself in the beauty and passion that is Callie Pike.

I pull her up from the bed, drag her to me, my cock hard and ready, and crush my mouth to hers.

She responds this time, and she doesn't stop the kiss. Good thing, because I'm not sure I'd be able to.

I need her. I need to lose myself in her beautiful body. I need to stop thinking about all this shit.

Tomorrow.

Tomorrow we will continue our search for the truth.

Tonight, though . . .

Tonight, I'm going to escape.

Expel the demons.

And only the woman I love can help me do that.

CHAPTER SEVENTEEN

Callie

I melt into his kiss. I relish his lips sliding around mine, his tongue battling with mine, openmouthed and glorious. I let him drug me with this kiss.

Even though, all those years ago, Pat Lamone drugged our high school, right now I want to be drugged more than anything.

By Donny Steel.

I want to escape in his body, and I want him to escape in mine.

We fall onto the bed. Still kissing him, I slide my hands over the hard globes of his perfect butt. Up the side of him, over his shoulders, and I thread my fingers in his silky hair.

His hands, too, are everywhere. Cupping my breast, the cheek of my ass, trailing over my hips, settling between my legs.

He toys with my clit as we still kiss, and I reach between his legs, grasp his firm length.

I work him, and he works me.

And still we kiss, our mouths glued together, our tongues in a constant battle for control.

I moan into his mouth, he moans into mine, and we work each other, until—

I rip my mouth from his and shriek when an orgasm

explodes through my body.

I'm not expecting it, and it takes me, pulses through me, in a different way than it ever has before.

My body quakes, and though I don't want to, I let go of his dick. I roll onto my back, and simply shudder as the euphoria surges through me.

My eyes are closed, and words leave my lips. I can't know what they are.

He's inside me then, thrusting. I open my eyes, my orgasm still reeling, and meet his hazel eyes staring at me. Burning. Blazing.

His hair is pasted to his hairline with sweat, and his lips are parted, red and swollen from our kiss.

He thrusts. He thrusts. He thrusts.

He fills me, tunnels through me, easing the empty ache as my orgasm finally begins to slow. He's so large, and he burns into me, leaving a blazing trail of embers in his wake. I cup both his cheeks, holding him steady, never letting my gaze waver from his.

He closes his eyes then, grits his teeth, and thrusts into me hard.

I feel every spasm of his cock as he empties into me.

And I know…

I know…

Together we will figure everything out.

Because that's what we do.

That's what you do when you love another person.

★ ★ ★

Two hours later, I'm home. Donny was willing to stay, but

I insisted that he go home as well. In the end, he agreed. He should be home in the morning so he can see his mother and father.

It's late. After midnight. But I knock softly on Rory's door.

"Yeah?" she says through the door.

"It's me. I'm home."

"Come on in."

My sister is in bed, and the light is off, but I knew she wouldn't be asleep. I walk in, closing the door behind me, and sit down on her bed.

"Hey," I say. "I convinced Donny that he needed to be home in the morning since his parents are home. They're going to want to spend some time with him."

She nods.

"We're going to figure this out, Ror. First thing is to figure out when Pat Lamone came back in town. I'll go over to the inn tomorrow and ask when he started working there."

"What if he's there?"

"Then I'll tell him to have the owner call me."

"Why don't you just call *him*?"

"Good idea. I will. First thing tomorrow when I get into the office."

Rory nods again. "I wish there were more I could do."

"You can."

"Oh, yeah? What? I have students tomorrow. I'm a musician, Callie. I don't have any expertise in any of this crap."

"Go see Doc Sheraton."

"What for? I don't have a pet. I'm supposed to just walk in and say, 'Hey, where's Brittany?'"

"Actually . . ."

"What?"

"Let's get a dog. We live on a ranch. We should have a freaking dog. Let's go to the shelter tomorrow in Grand Junction and pick out a dog for each of us."

"What's Mom going to say?"

"Who cares? If she doesn't like it, we move out."

"And go where, Callie? We don't have any money."

"I'm kidding, Rory. Geez. Mom loves dogs. I'm surprised we've gone so long without one. I guess she never got over Hedwig. Hedwig was a great mutt, but he died over two years ago."

"You know?" Rory nods. "I'd like a dog, Callie."

"Me too. It's settled then. Tomorrow we drive to the shelter in Grand Junction, and we get dogs."

"I kind of have students tomorrow. And last time I checked, you have a job as well."

"True . . . This weekend."

"It's a date. But until then, what do we do?"

"Leave that to Donny and me. We're going to do some research. Try to find out when Pat got back into town, and why he's here."

"Good enough. Damn, I wish I could sleep."

As if on cue, a giant grin splits my face.

"Not all of us have someone giving us orgasms to make us sleep well," Rory says, sarcasm lacing her tone.

"I promise you won't be alone for long."

"What makes you think I want another relationship? I'm sick and tired of people not being able to accept me for who I am. And that goes for men *and* women."

"I get it. I mean . . . I don't get what it means to be bisexual, but I'm sorry your last couple of relationships have failed because of it."

"Seems like each side just wants me to pick a team. It doesn't work that way."

"I know."

"Do you? Really?"

"I'm not bisexual. I can't pretend to understand what it feels like to *be* bisexual. But I would hope that if I loved a person, I would accept everything about him. Or her."

"Can you accept everything about Donny?"

"Yes. I don't have a choice. I love him. And everything he's into or is going through is part of him and part of what I love about him."

"You're lucky. I'm not sure I've ever felt that way about anyone."

"Not even Raine?"

"I'll admit Raine was the most serious relationship I've been in, but no."

"You'll get there, Rory."

"But my little sister got there first."

"It's not a freaking contest. Jesse is older than you are, and he's not there."

"Jesse is a guy. He doesn't have to worry about his biological clock."

"Ror, if you want a baby that badly, go to a sperm bank. A partner isn't necessary in this equation."

She smiles then. My sister actually smiles. It took the thought of her being a mother to get it out of her, but I did it. For Rory, apparently a baby trumps everything—even this Pat Lamone mess.

"I've thought about it, but until this whole thing is settled, I'm certainly not bringing an innocent person into the mix. Plus, the thought of doing it alone is pretty daunting."

"You wouldn't be alone. You have all of us. Your family."

My words are certainly true, but I wonder… Will our family be supportive if those nude pictures of Rory and me surface? I can see Jesse going off half-cocked, and probably my father as well. None of that will end up good.

Which means we have to nip this in the bud.

Now.

CHAPTER EIGHTEEN

Donny

At six thirty a.m., I stumble out of my room clad only in my lounge pants. Mom is in the kitchen, fixing coffee, and to my surprise, Dad is also up, sitting at the kitchen table, sipping a glass of orange juice.

"Good morning, sleepyhead," Mom says. "Coffee will be ready in a minute."

"Sleepyhead? This is when I get up. What in the world are you two doing up? Dad, you need your rest."

"What I need is a cup of your mother's coffee. They didn't let me have any caffeine in the hospital."

"But you're allowed to have it now?"

"Yes," Mom says. "Do you think I'd allow him to have it if the doctor hadn't given the okay?"

I can't help a smile. Mom and Dad are home, and they're back to normal.

"You're not planning to work today, are you?" I ask Dad.

"Not out in the orchards, no. But I thought I might go into the office."

"The office can come to you," Mom says adamantly. "You have a perfectly good setup here at home."

"You heard her, Dad. She *is* the boss."

Dad laughs and then winces.

"Are you okay?" I ask, my voice higher than usual.

"I'm fine. I still get a little bit of pain when I laugh or cough."

"Then stop doing those things."

"You want me to stop laughing?" Dad shakes his head. "Not in this lifetime. A man has got to be happy."

I can't fault his logic, so I say nothing.

Mom brings two steaming cups of coffee and sets one in front of Dad and the other in front of me. I inhale the roasted goodness of its steam. "Mom, do you know when you'll be coming back to the office?"

Mom pauses a moment, clears her throat. "Donny, your father and I have been talking about that."

"Of course, you should take all the time you need here home with Dad. I've got things under control."

"I know you do. And with Troy, Alyssa, and Callie to help you, I realize I'm not really needed."

"Not needed? You're the city attorney. Of course you're needed."

Mom returns to the counter, pours herself a mug of steaming coffee, and then joins us at the table, sitting between us. "I never thought I'd retire in this lifetime."

"I know that."

"But you've done me a favor, Donny. I took you away from a huge opportunity in Denver."

I hold my hand up. "Don't go there. You know I was glad to do it. Then, with what happened to Dad, I'm really glad I was here."

"I am too, and I know I have the right person in that job."

"Yeah, so take as much time as you need. We've got things under control."

Mom smiles. "You don't know how happy I am to know that. Not that I ever doubted it."

"Well, you don't have to."

"Good." She takes a sip of her coffee. Then she looks at my father.

What's going on?

"So," Mom says, "I've decided to retire. Effective immediately."

I have to stop my eyes from popping out of their sockets. I set my mug down with a shaking hand, nearly spilling coffee on the table. "Did I hear you right? You're fifty years old, Mom. Not anywhere close to retirement age."

"You heard me right. Dad and I had a lot to talk about while he was recuperating in the hospital. And we've decided... we don't want to miss one more minute of our lives together. We want to spend *more* time with each other, not less. He can't give up the orchard, not yet. Not until Brianna is a little older and more established. But I *can* give up the city attorney's office because I have the best attorney in Colorado ready to take my place."

I look at my mother, and then I look to my father. I don't know what I'm searching for... Maybe some indication that this is all a big joke, because I can't imagine that it can possibly be true.

"Mom, you love working."

"But I love your father more. I almost lost him, Donny. I'm not going to waste another moment of our time together."

"Working isn't a waste of time. You love being an attorney."

"I do. I was a damned good one for twenty-five years. I've made my mark, and now it's time for you to make yours. There are other things for me to do now. I want to be home. Taking care of your father when he needs me. I may just do some writing. Maybe start a business."

I open my mouth to speak, but no words emerge. I have no idea what to say. I'm shocked, to be sure, especially since my mother has always encouraged all four of her kids to reach for their dreams and make their own way in the world. She was a working mom all her life. None of us suffered for it. We were well cared for, and she and Dad spent a lot of time with us on the weekends.

"Are you sure this is what you want?" I can't help asking.

"I know it's a little off brand for me," she says, "but I'm sure."

"Trust me, son," Dad says. "She and I had a lot of words about it. I even tried to talk her out of it because I wasn't sure she could be happy as a housewife. But she won't be just a housewife. She's got lots of other things to do, and I have to also tell you, I'm looking forward to seeing her more often."

"If you're both sure."

"We are," Mom says. "I'm truly happy about the decision. I'm already thinking about ideas for a legal thriller."

"I'm sure you'll write a great one. Then you can be the second member of the family who's a published author, after Aunt Melanie."

"Maybe I will be. I also want to help Marjorie. She and I are thinking about an event-planning business."

"Serving grilled cheese and tomato sandwiches and chocolate cake?" I chuckle.

"Ha-ha, good one. She'll be the cook, of course. I'll work on the business side."

"Starting a business. Writing a novel. I had no idea you had such aspirations, Mom."

"To be honest, neither did I. I thought I would practice law until the day I met my maker. But Marjorie has been after me for a while to put together a business plan with her and Ava, and the idea for a novel has been percolating in me for years now. I never thought I'd find the time to do either, but now, with you here, I can do all that *and* be here with your father more often."

Darla bustles in then. "Sorry, Miss Jade. That was my mother. Unfortunately, she broke her hip, and I'm going to need to ask for a few days off."

"Of course, that's no problem. Will you be back for the party Saturday evening?"

"I'm not sure."

"No worries. I can manage," Mom says.

"Who will take care of all of you? Do the cooking?"

Mom smiles. "I will. I can handle it for a week. Take all the time you need."

"Who are you, and what have you done with my mother?" I can't help saying.

Dad, Mom, and Darla all erupt in laughter.

"Damn, that hurts," Dad says.

★ ★ ★

An hour and a half later, I'm in the office. Callie, Troy, and Alyssa are all at their stations, and I'm getting ready to go down to court by nine o'clock. I have another two speeding tickets to prosecute, and I peruse the files. I haven't told my staff that I'm now the actual city attorney. Not yet. I'm giving Mom a chance to change her mind.

"Donny?" Alyssa's voice comes through the intercom.

"Yeah?"

"I have a Pat Lamone on line one for you."

My eyebrows pop up on their own. What the hell does he want? "Sure. Put him through."

"You got it."

"This is Donny Steel."

"Hey, Donny. It's Pat Lamone."

"To what do I owe the pleasure?" My tone is slightly sardonic. Make that really sardonic.

"I want to file a complaint."

"Then you should be talking to the sheriff. Not to me."

"Oh?"

"Yes. If you have a criminal complaint, you go to the police. If they decide it should be prosecuted, then they come to me."

"Oh. I'm sorry to bother you, then. I'll talk to the sheriff about my complaint against Callie."

Ice pricks the back of my neck. "Callie?"

"Yes, Callie Pike. She assaulted me."

"You're full of it."

"I'm not. She threw hot coffee all over me the other day."

"And did this quote *assault* unquote lead to any damages?"

"Yes, my skin was burned slightly, and my clothes were ruined."

"And you want to file charges. Against Callie Pike. For spilling coffee on you. Am I correct?"

"Yes, you're correct."

"I'm going to try to give you the benefit of the doubt, Pat. I'm going to assume that you don't realize how completely ridiculous you sound. I'm going to assume you actually think you can file charges against someone for spilling coffee."

"Hey, I did my research. Some woman got a ton of money from McDonald's when she spilled hot coffee on herself."

"First of all, that was a civil lawsuit, not a criminal one. If you want to file those kind of charges, I suggest you find a private lawyer."

"No, this was an assault, plain and simple."

"Assault with deadly coffee. I see."

"If you're not going to take me seriously—"

"Oh, please, I *am* taking you seriously. I want you to go straight to the sheriff and tell him the same story you told me. That's where you start with this."

"Thank you. I will."

I slam the phone down.

What is this man after? No way will Hardy take this complaint. Spilling coffee, for God's sake. I rise, walk out of my office and to Callie's cubicle. "Take a walk with me."

"Sure." She stands, and together we leave the office, walk down the stairs, and outside.

"What's the matter?" she asks.

"Nothing. I just want to warn you. I just got a call from Pat Lamone."

She lifts her eyebrows. "And . . . ?"

"He wants me to prosecute you for assault. Get this. For spilling coffee on him the other day."

She drops her beautiful lips into an O.

"Yeah, that was my reaction too."

"What did you tell him?"

"I told him to go to Hardy. If he wants to file a complaint, that's where you start. With the police report."

"You don't think . . ."

"Of course not. Hardy is a good guy. He's not going to

take this shit seriously."

"Okay. Good."

"Honestly, Callie, I don't think he'll even go to Hardy. I'm pretty sure he just wanted to call me. Find out whether I even knew you had spilled your coffee on him."

"He thinks I might have kept that from you?"

"I don't know. Maybe. He's trying to mess with our relationship apparently."

"Yeah. Just like when he told you those lies about Rory and me. And when he said the same thing to Raine."

"I'm not sure what his angle is yet," I say, "but I *will* figure it out."

"I wonder... Maybe you should call him back. Tell him you'd like to hear more about this complaint about me."

"Oh?"

"You're a brilliant attorney, Donny. You can interrogate him. Find out why he's here."

A smile spreads over my face. "You're right. I had a shot at finding shit out, and I didn't take it."

"That's okay. If it had been me, I probably would have slammed the phone down on him."

"That's pretty much what I did."

She smiles. My God, she's beautiful.

"Can you call him back?"

"Better yet. I'll go see him in person."

"Do you know where he lives?"

"Easy enough to find out." I lean down and give her a searing kiss on her lips. "You're fucking brilliant."

"So are you. I think between the two of us, we can take him down."

"I know we can."

"I have to get to court, baby." I give her another quick kiss. "I'll visit Pat this afternoon."

She nods.

Pat Lamone is nothing. Him, I can handle.

It's the secrets of my own family that have my skin crawling.

CHAPTER NINETEEN

Callie

My nerves jump a little. Not that I think Pat Lamone can make charges against me stick. I did spill the coffee on him, but it was a total accident. He's just trying to get under my skin.

I can't let him.

I sit back down at my cubicle and then jerk at the sound of my name.

"Hey, Callie."

I look up. Brock Steel stands in front of me.

As tall as Donny but the opposite to him in looks. Dark where Donny is light but nearly as good-looking. Tall and muscular and an imposing presence.

"Brock, what are you doing here?"

"I need to talk to Donny. Is he in?"

"He's in court. Didn't they tell you downstairs?"

"There wasn't anyone at reception, and Alyssa isn't at her desk either."

I stand and take a quick look around the office. "That's strange. Anyway, I think he said he only has a couple of tickets to do this morning. He shouldn't be too long."

"Good, I'll wait. It'll give us a chance to talk."

"I'm kind of in the middle of working. Do you want to just wait in Donny's office?"

"When I have a lovely woman out here to talk to? I don't think so."

"Okay. But like I said, I'm—"

"Working. Yeah, I know. How's your sister doing?"

"Rory or Maddie?"

"Rory. How's she handling the breakup with Raine?"

"She's fine. I think she's made her peace with it."

Brock grins. "I'm glad to hear that."

I cock my head. Is Brock Steel interested in my sister? Can't be. He's younger than she is by about four years. Plus, he's a known womanizer.

Of course, so was Donny before he and I got together.

I can't help the smile. Wouldn't it be hilarious if Rory ended up with one of the Three Rake-a-teers? The term she herself coined? If two of the Pike sisters ended up with two of the Rake-a-teers?

But Brock is so not Rory's type.

Sure, she likes men as well as women, but she never goes for the obvious types. Someone like Brock… It just isn't going to happen.

"She's over at the studio. Teaching her lessons."

"You and Rory will be at our party this weekend celebrating Uncle Talon's homecoming, right?"

"You know we'd never miss a Steel party."

"Is Rory singing?"

"I have no idea. Neither Jesse nor Rory has mentioned playing at the party."

"She has the voice of an angel, that one."

I nod. "I can't disagree with you there."

Donny comes bustling through the hallway then. "Brock, what are you doing here?"

"Just chatting with your lovely lady, but I do need to talk to you."

"Sure, come on into my office." Then Donny looks over his shoulder. "Callie, you come too."

I rise and follow them into the office. I take a seat next to Brock, while Donny sits behind his desk.

"What do you need, Brock?"

Brock nods to me. "I need to talk to you about something in private."

"I've brought Callie up to speed. I want her involved."

"Well . . . okay, I guess."

"So what's up?"

"Dale and I are going over to the north property tonight. We wanted to know if you wanted to come along."

"I don't know. Dad just got back from the hospital."

"I know, but Dale and I don't want to wait on this."

"What about your dad?"

Brock clears his throat. "Dale and I have talked. We're going to keep this on the down low, away from Dad for the moment."

"Why?"

"You know why. Dale and I are hotheaded enough without bringing my father into it. We think it's best left among our generation for now."

Donny nods. "I can't fault your logic."

"So are you in?"

"How about you, Callie?" Donny says to me.

"I . . . think this is a family thing."

"Baby, you *are* family."

"I doubt Dale is bringing Ashley along tonight."

"I suppose you're probably right. That means I can't see

you tonight, though."

"It's okay. Rory and I have a lot of things to talk about. Plus, we were thinking about going into Grand Junction to adopt dogs at the shelter this weekend. Maybe we can do it tonight instead."

"Good enough." Donny nods. "Count me in, then. Text me where to meet you and Dale. Why the hell didn't he come to me with this?"

"He's in the city, meeting with vendors all day. He'll be home by seven." Brock stands. "Good to see you both." He leaves the office.

"This doesn't feel right," Donny says.

"What part of it?"

"The fact that Brock wants to leave his dad out of it. That can only mean one thing."

"What's that?"

"He's worried. He and Dale both. They're worried we're going to find something that will either implicate our fathers or send them on a rampage."

I bite my lip. "Donny, you need to deal with your own family stuff. This Pat Lamone crap is small potatoes compared to what is going on with you."

"There are no small potatoes, baby. We can get through all of this. Let's go for a quick lunch, and then I'll visit that fucking asshole Lamone."

I nod.

Donny has everything under control.

I wish I felt the same.

CHAPTER TWENTY

Donny

Five minutes. That's all the time it took to find out that Pat Lamone is renting a room on the east side of town. Instead of calling him, I decided to see him in person. The house is owned by a widow, Carmelita Mayer. Her husband, Jensen Mayer, passed away a few years ago, and she rents out the rooms in her small house to help pay the mortgage he left her with.

I rap on the door quickly. A dog begins barking, a high shrill bark. Probably a small dog.

Then the door opens, and Mrs. Mayer shoos the dog out of her way. "Mr. Steel. What can I do for you?"

"Hi, Mrs. Mayer. I'm sorry to bother you in the middle of the day, but I understand you have a new tenant in one of your rooms. Pat Lamone?"

"Yes, I don't think he's here right now."

"Do you know where I might find him?"

"I know he's working at the Snow Creek Inn."

"Is he working now?"

"I think he has the evening shift. I wish I could help you. Do you want me to have him give you a call?"

"No, don't mention I was here, actually."

"Okay, no problem. How's your father doing?"

"He's good. He came home yesterday, and of course he

can't wait to get back to work."

"And I suppose your mother will be coming back to the city attorney's office?"

"Actually, she won't be. She's going to retire."

"Jade is retiring? I never thought I'd see the day."

"Believe me, I didn't either. Sorry to take up your time this afternoon."

"Never a problem. Let me know if there's anything else I can do to help." She smiles.

"Thank you. If there is, I'll be in touch."

I walk down the cobbled pathway and then turn and regard the small one-story house.

Does Carmelita Mayer know that my family holds a lien on her home?

Does anyone in Snow Creek know?

Surely they must. All those things are required to be disclosed at closing.

This is all so surreal.

But I can't think about that now. Right now, Pat Lamone is my target. So he's not home. But at least I got confirmation that he does live here.

I walk away from the house, through the residential area a couple blocks, until I hit Main Street.

Why not check the hotel? Maybe he's covering someone's shift. The red-brick building is down the street a ways, and I head straight toward it.

I open the door, and—

Who is manning the desk but yes, Pat Lamone.

"Donny," he says, "you need a room?"

"No, I need some information."

He nods to a stack of newspapers on the side table.

"Today's journal just arrived. Have at it."

He thinks he's being funny. He thinks he can outsmart Callie and me.

Yeah, right.

"You know exactly why I'm here. Why have you come back to Snow Creek?"

"Uh . . . because it's my home."

"You and your family left midway through your junior year at Snow Creek High. No one has seen or heard from you since then. Until now."

"So?"

"So . . . Now here you are. And it seems like you've come to make trouble for Callie and Rory."

"Why would I do that?"

"I don't know, Pat. Why would you tell lies to me about Callie and Rory? Why would you say the same thing to Raine? Seems you're out to damage Callie and Rory's relationships."

"I haven't lied."

"Don't give me that song and dance. We both know you never slept with Rory or Callie Pike."

"I never said I slept with Callie. I said she was waiting in line."

"Yeah, and I'm just that gullible."

"You don't have to believe me."

"I know I don't have to, and I don't. But I do know one thing. I know you're the person responsible for my sister being hospitalized for alcohol poisoning ten years ago."

He shakes his head slowly. "So that's what Callie and Rory told you, huh? I shouldn't be surprised."

"No, you shouldn't, because unlike the shit that comes out of your mouth, this happens to be the truth."

"Prove it."

"Why? As you know, the statute of limitations for those crimes has long lapsed. It doesn't matter if I even have the proof."

"Still . . . if you had proof, you could make it public. You could hurt me that way."

"That's not the way we roll, Lamone. The Steels don't play dirty tricks like that."

"That's not what I hear."

Anger wells within me. He thinks he has something on the Steels? He can think again.

Unless . . .

A lot of shit is going down for us right now, but there's no way Pat Lamone could know about any of it. He's a nobody.

"We both know why you're back in town, Lamone," I say. "You heard that Callie Pike and I were dating, and you thought you could come out here and get some money out of me."

"You're full of it, Steel."

"Am I? Let me tell you this. If those photos that you have see even a *sliver* of the light of day, it will be the end of you."

"Photos? What photos?"

"Don't play idiot with me, although I admit you do it well. We both know what I'm talking about. You don't have anything else on the Pike women."

"Don't I?"

"No, you don't."

"What if I could prove something to you?"

"Like what?"

"What if I could prove to you that the fire that destroyed the Pikes' vineyards was actually started by one of the Pikes?"

My blood goes cold. "Nice try." I force myself to remain calm.

"Have it your way."

"If you really had any evidence like that, you wouldn't be running to me wanting to charge Callie Pike with assault with coffee. You'd be trying to have her arrested for arson."

"Who says it's Callie?"

I keep my face straight. I can't let the anger roiling through me show. I will not let Pat Lamone get the upper hand. "Who, then? Who do you think started that fire?"

"I could tell you," he says, "but what fun would that be? I think my information is worth a lot more than just getting on Donny Steel's good side."

"You'll never be on my good side."

"Fair enough. I might tell you what you want to know… for a couple hundred grand."

"This conversation is over. You want to take the Pikes down? Give it your best shot. My entire family will be standing in your way." I walk swiftly out of the hotel lobby.

I text Callie quickly that I'm not coming back to the office.

Then I text Dale and Brock.

I'm going to the first coordinate now.
See you there later.

CHAPTER TWENTY-ONE

Callie

"I love them all!" Rory gushes. "We live on a ranch. Can't we take them all home?"

I commiserate with my sister. Every dog in the shelter looks at us with pleading eyes, and they're all beautiful. They all deserve a good home.

"We can only take two, Ror. But I wish we could take them all."

"How are we supposed to choose? They're all wonderful."

I meet the gaze of what appears to be an Australian shepherd and golden retriever mix. She's a female, with one brown eye and one blue eye. Instantly, we bond.

"Hey, pretty girl, I think you're mine." I gesture to one of the employees. "How old is this one?"

"We think about two."

"Perfect. I want her."

"Great! She's really friendly. I'll get the paperwork started."

I stroke her head through the kennel. "We'll be going home soon, precious. What should your name be?" I regard her golden fur speckled with red and black. "Dusty, I think. You look like you're flecked with colorful dust."

"She's beautiful," Rory says. "But I still can't choose."

"I think you already have." Rory is absently petting a blond lab mix.

"He is gorgeous, isn't he?"

"What's his name?"

"Zach," she says without hesitation.

"There you have it. You've already named him."

"But all the others . . ."

"I know. I hate it too. But at least we can save these two."

★ ★ ★

Dusty and Zach are friends already. We've only been home for an hour, and they're chasing each other and playing in our backyard.

"Saturday we go see Doc Sheraton," I say. "Get these two checked out, updated on their shots. And then we casually ask what's going on with Brittany."

"Saturday night is the Steel party. Jess and I are playing."

"So? Doc Sheraton has Saturday morning hours. It's not going to conflict with your busy performance schedule."

"We don't have an appointment, and his Saturday hours probably book up quickly. I'll call him tomorrow morning to see if he can squeeze us in."

"That gives him the chance to say no, Rory."

Already I'm feeling better, though. A dog will do that. Dusty and Zach stop frolicking and come to the deck for a drink of water. Already they seem to know which one of us they belong to, as Dusty comes to me for pets on her soft head and Zach ambles to Rory.

"You're such a good boy," she says. "You're Mama's good boy."

Already, Rory is mothering her new dog.

"And you're a good girl," I find myself saying.

And I find myself thinking about being a mother.

Will it ever happen? Eventually, most likely. But we have so much crap to deal with before we can think about that. Both Donny and me.

Besides . . . he hasn't mentioned marriage or family.

It's still very early in our relationship. Only a day ago he was telling me to let him go.

The dogs bound back out into the yard, and Mom comes out on the deck.

"Rory," she says, "Lonnie Jefferson had to cancel Janae's lesson tomorrow. She's come down with a virus."

"Okay. Thanks, Mom."

"I've missed having dogs around here." Mom's eyes mist over a bit. "Maybe I should have gone to the shelter with you."

"Mom, you totally should go," Rory says. "There are so many other dogs there that need good homes."

"You've convinced me. I'll go tomorrow."

Rory and I smile at each other. We just saved another dog.

Life has been caving in on both of us lately, and it helps to see the light in those panting furry faces.

Mom goes back inside, and though I'm still smiling as the dogs frolic, Rory's countenance goes dark.

"Callie," she says, "I'm going back to the tree."

I widen my eyes. "Why?"

"We must have missed something. Some kind of evidence that Lamone was there."

"For all we know, he could have followed us ten years ago and taken it then."

She shakes her head. "You're right. He may have. But I'm

going back. And I'm going now."

"It's nearly dark."

"So I'll take a flashlight."

I sigh. "All right. I'm not letting you go alone."

CHAPTER TWENTY-TWO

Donny

It's the quiet that affects me the most.

I don't expect Brock and Dale for another couple of hours. I'm still on Steel land according to the property divisions and titles. Dale has been here before, and he told me what to expect. A few old buildings, not much else. He admitted he had only taken a cursory look. We're going to take a more thorough one this evening.

I'm dressed in older jeans, my working cowboy boots, and a tattered T-shirt. I'm even wearing a Stetson. An old one. It's been so long since I've done any work on the ranch, and I haven't bought a new one in a while.

Once I moved to Denver to attend college and then law school, I never really considered myself a cowboy anymore.

I don't have a full-length mirror here, obviously, but I'd bet I look the part now. I even drove my old truck. It's been sitting in one of Mom and Dad's garages for years, but it started right up. I threw shovels, plastic garbage bags, work gloves, a wheelbarrow, and . . .

My Glock 38.

Then I thought better of it, strapped on a holster, and my Glock 38 now sits at my hip.

Dad taught Dale and me how to handle guns when we

were teenagers. In fact, I haven't handled one since then. I'm probably a little bit rusty, but Dad was a good teacher. Apparently Uncle Joe taught him and Uncle Ryan when they were kids because their father—the man who was clearly keeping secrets—didn't want to teach them.

Why wouldn't you want to teach your sons to defend themselves?

There's a story there. One I'll probably never know.

There are a lot of stories I may never know, but I can at least find some answers. And I can start here, on this tract of land identified by a stranger who left me a clue in a safe-deposit box.

Where to begin?

I walk toward one abandoned building, which looks like it may have been a barn decades ago. The wood is splintered and rotting. The door is hanging on its hinges, and I swing it open easily and step inside.

I inhale and immediately regret it. The scent is thick with rot and waste. I expect to see animal carcasses, but when I flick on the flashlight and check things out, all I see are a few clumps of dirt here and there. The ground is slightly moist under my feet, but nothing is growing in here, since no sunlight can get in.

I walk around the perimeter of the inside, shining my light on the rotting walls and then up to the ceiling—an actual ceiling, instead of rafters like in most barns. I'm not sure what I'm looking for, but then I jerk my head at some markings on the wall. About knee high.

I squat down to get a better look. From an animal most likely. Or a human with long fingernails. Long hard fingernails.

A woman. Probably a woman who wears acrylic nails.

"Stop it, Donny," I say out loud.

My imagination is already running away from me. No women have been missing in the area. We would have heard if that were the case.

I look around further. I don't see any more scratch marks like the first, but I do see some discoloration. It could be normal. This wood is old and rotting. But it's almost like splatters of something. A darker brown on the wood.

It could be blood, but it could just as easily be stain or something else. There's no way to know. It's obviously been here for a long time. It's old. It could be animal blood. Most likely is, since this is a barn.

I continue walking along the inside of the building, when—

"Oh, crap!" Literally. Something mushy around my foot. Those clumps of dirt? Dog shit. Obviously a dog has been in here recently, because it's fresh. The indent of my foot brings up the odor, and I hold back a gag.

Great, just great. I was so busy holding the flashlight up to the walls, looking for more scratch marks and discoloration that I wasn't watching where I was going. Serves me right, I suppose.

A dog has been here, and recently. Which means . . . there's food somewhere. A dog could have taken shelter in here. I flash my light around. Several more piles of shit, older than the one I just stepped in, lie on the ground.

Which means the dog comes back here for shelter. And food.

Except there's no food here.

There could be food close by, and the dog simply comes here for shelter. But this is the middle of nowhere. I certainly didn't see any food here. Perhaps there are wild rabbits running around. That could make sense.

I sigh and walk toward the door. Outside the building, I find a patch of grass to wipe my boot on. After I get as much crap off as I can, I look around.

This time, I watch where I walk. Good thing, because I find more dog shit.

And then I wonder . . .

If a dog comes here for shelter, why would he relieve himself *inside* the building? Dogs don't normally do that. You don't shit where you live.

Interesting.

So perhaps *someone* was here. Someone with a dog—a dog who doesn't live here. Because if a dog thinks of this place as his shelter, he wouldn't be shitting inside. He'd be shitting out here.

I continue to search around the outside perimeter of the building, when something red catches my eye. I kneel to take a closer look. It's a fingernail. A woman's fake fingernail—the kind you glue over your own nails. It's painted fire-engine red.

How old could this be? It's probably made of plastic, and plastic is forever. Is this a fingernail that made the scratch marks on the inside of the building?

I doubt it. If it came off the nail it was on, it wouldn't have been strong enough to make those scratches.

Then again, what the hell do I know about women's fingernails? Not a lot.

I slide the fingernail into the pocket of my jeans and continue my search.

More dog shit. No more fingernails. But I can't help but wonder, why was there even *one* fingernail? Who was here? I'll assume it was a woman, but is that even a fair assumption?

Someone could have just dropped a fake nail here to throw someone off.

Someone.

Someone who knows I'm coming here. Whoever put that information in the safe-deposit box with my name on it knew I would come here.

So I'm here for a reason. I just don't know if that reason is good or bad.

We're going to have to raze this building. Dig all the way around it, tunnel underneath it. Something is here. Something that someone wants me to find.

Or someone wants to throw me off the scent of something else.

"Fuck," I say aloud.

"Fuck what?"

I turn toward my brother's voice.

"I didn't expect you guys until later," I say.

"Didn't you get my text?" Dale says.

"No." I pull my phone out of my pocket. "I don't have a text."

"I sent one." Dale shoves his phone at me. "See? It says delivered."

"The service sucks around here. It'll probably show up once we're back in a better area."

"Where's Brock?"

"Back at the truck, gathering our equipment together. When I saw your old truck, I figured I'd better come find what you're up to."

"Not much. All I've found is a fake fingernail and a lot of dog shit."

"Great. I guess we dig, then."

"We should start on the inside. I found some strange scratch marks."

"Probably from the dog," Dale says.

"Yeah, maybe. But the dog can obviously get in and out on his own, so why would he scratch?"

Dale cocks his head. "Maybe that wasn't always the case."

"Maybe. But I'm thinking the dog doesn't actually live here. If he did, he wouldn't shit where he sleeps. Obviously he can get in and out."

"Good point." This from Brock.

I turn and regard my cousin. "When did you get here?"

"A minute ago. So you found dog shit, huh?"

"Yeah. Let me show you guys the scratch marks. I guess that's where we start."

The three of us enter the building.

"Oh, man." Brock pinches his nose. "That's nasty."

"I suppose I should have warned you."

"That's not just dog shit, man," Brock says.

"No," Dale says. "It's decay. Damn... Do you smell it, Don?"

"Decay? Yeah."

"No, I mean..."

"What?"

"Don't you remember?"

"Remember what?"

"We've smelled this before."

I inhale.

Decay, yes. Waste, yes. And... something else.

And I remember...

It was the day...

The day I first laid eyes on Talon Steel.

CHAPTER TWENTY-THREE

Callie

The tree is exactly the same as it was when we dug up the box several days ago. Rory and I each have a shovel, work gloves, and a flashlight. Rory also grabbed a camping lantern from the garage, and we set it up. It gives us pretty good light over the area.

"I don't know what we're looking for, Rory."

"I don't either. But I bet we find it." She pushes her shovel into the dirt.

"Find what?"

"For God's sake, Callie, if you're not going to be supportive, just go. But I'm not leaving here until I find something. Anything."

"All right. I'm with you, sis."

We both have work in the morning, but what the heck?

I've moved several shovels full of dirt when I say, "Maybe we shouldn't be looking underground. If Pat were here recently, we should probably be looking on *top* of the ground. Maybe he dropped something.

"Yeah, I thought of that. But we were only looking for the box when we were digging here earlier, so if there *is* anything underground, we wouldn't have noticed it. Not unless it was really obvious."

"I doubt he left any red herrings for us to find," I say. "He's not that bright."

"Normally, I would agree with you. But I think we need to stop thinking that he's not our intellectual equal. He *has* managed to get the best of us."

"Has he?"

"Callie, for God's sake, you're not the one who's going to be hurt by this. He won't dare expose your photos. But I was over eighteen."

"Think about it though, Ror. The worst thing that can happen is the town sees you naked. You were gorgeous then and you're gorgeous now, with a body to die for. What's the harm?"

I hate the words as soon as I utter them.

"Believe me, I've thought about that," she replies. "I'm not ashamed of my body. I wasn't then and I'm not now."

"You shouldn't be."

"But still, I don't want it plastered across social media."

"I understand that. Really, I do. I'm sorry if what I said sounded harsh. I wasn't thinking. I wouldn't want my body exposed for the town either. Of course, mine isn't as good as yours."

Rory rolls her eyes at me. "You're a beautiful woman, Callie. You're the only one who doesn't know it."

I don't reply. She's right. It's time to stop being so self-deprecating. "I'm in this for you and with you Rory," I say. "Whatever you want to do. Because you're the one who will ultimately be more harmed by this if those photos get out."

"I suppose we don't even know if he has the photos," she says. "Except we do know."

"Yeah." I sigh. "I mean, we kept *our* evidence even though

we agreed to destroy it."

"And that son of a bitch got his hands on it."

"Tell you what," I say. "Why don't you have a look around? Walk around the perimeter of the area, but stay in the light so I know you're okay. I'll do the digging. We can kill two birds with one stone here."

"Good plan." Rory leans her shovel against the tree, takes her flashlight, and shines it around the area.

I continue digging. It's kind of a form of self-flagellation. I shouldn't have said what I did to Rory about the photos. I've always wanted to look like my sister. The perfect face, the perfect body—thick dark hair and dark eyes that could mesmerize a person. But I vow, here and now, to stop holding her up as some vision I want to attain.

I'm Callie. I will never be Rory, no matter what I look like. And that's okay. In my way, I'm as beautiful as she is. And Donny doesn't seem to mind that my boobs are smaller.

I can't help letting out a soft chuckle.

Rory turns. "What's so funny?"

"Nothing. I'm just… I'm sorry, Rory. I'm really, really sorry."

"For what? The photo comment?"

"Yeah, that… and so much more. I've been so envious of you over all the years."

Rory's mouth drops open, and she walks back to me. "Envious? Of me?"

"Well… yeah. You're a beauty queen like Mom was. And me? I'm kind of the black sheep of the Pike family."

Rory bursts into laughter.

"What the hell? I don't see what's funny from where I'm standing."

She pulls me into a hug. She's still laughing.

I push her away. "Seriously. What the fuck?"

"Callie, it *is* funny. It's funny because I've always been jealous of you."

This time my mouth drops. "Uh . . . why, exactly?"

"For many reasons, but one big one is that you have normal-sized boobs. You can wear button-up blouses without the fabric puckering. You have a gorgeous ass and gorgeous legs. And those eyes. So bright and fiery. Mine are dull brown. But none of those are the main reason."

My jaw is still dropped, so I say nothing.

"The biggest reason is your intellectual ability. You think I could ever get through law school?"

"I haven't actually been to law school yet."

"I know, but you killed it on the LSAT, and I know you'll kill it in law school. And then there's the whole bisexual thing."

My jaw drops again.

"I mean, I'm happy with who I am. I'm not ashamed. But it makes life a little harder, you know? To not be the norm."

This time I carefully pick up my jaw. "Oh my God, I had no idea. All this time, I look at you, and you're so beautiful, and so talented, and everyone loves you, men and women alike. And you love them. You're like the ultimate person in my eyes."

Rory smiles. "That's not at all how I see myself. And you don't see yourself the way I see you. Isn't that just crazy?"

"Everyone sees you the way I see you, Rory."

"And everyone sees you the way I see you," she says. "I hear it all the time. Callie is so smart. Callie is so beautiful."

"Who the hell says that?"

"Well, the smart stuff I've been hearing since day one from Mom and Dad. Jesse and I have commiserated about it over the years. I'm not sure our parents were exactly thrilled when the two of us decided to go into the performing arts."

"They're very proud of both of you."

"I know that, and I know they love all of us. But you're the one who's going to make a name for herself. You're the one who's going to do something amazing."

"By practicing law? You and Jesse have your faces out there, your voices out there."

"Yeah, I was supposed to be a huge operatic mezzo soprano, but I sing part time with my brother's rock band. And Jess? He's an incredible talent, but he's still here in Snow Creek. He's not in LA making waves."

"You're an amazing voice and piano teacher."

"I am. I get that. But someday I'm going to have a student who surpasses me. Who makes it when I didn't."

"Maybe. But you'll help that happen. You'll always be that guiding force in that student's life."

"I love my job. I love teaching. But my first love is and always will be performance."

I regard my sister—everything about her—her beauty, her gentleness, her nurturing nature, and of course her incredible talent. How in the world could she covet *my* life?

"But you, Callie," she continues. "Your brain is so brilliant. The way you can solve problems, come up with solutions that are so logical. You don't let your emotions enter into it, and that gives you such strength."

"That's not exactly true. My emotions control me all the time. I just don't let them make decisions for me."

"That's my point, Cal."

This time I join in her laughter. "Who would have thought, after all these years, that we each envy the other?"

"I never knew you envied me," she says. "I just figured you considered my life kind of—I don't know—*fluffy*."

I laugh at her word. "No. You're not fluffy. You're kind and gentle, and you're going to make an amazing mother."

"Oh." She swallows. "Let's not go down that path. I'll end up in tears, and we've already got enough to cry about."

I nod. "Right. Let's deal with the here and now. I know you weren't looking for long, but did you see anything that seemed out of place to you?"

"Not yet." She flicks her flashlight back on. "I'll continue now."

"I'll keep digging."

I shove back into the dirt. It's softer than it was the other night because we just recently disturbed it.

Damn, this is a waste of time. But it's important to Rory, so I'll continue.

I dig, and I dig, and I dig, until I'm a farther down than where we buried the file box in the first place. There's no reason why anything would be down there farther, so I decide to widen the area. I push my shovel into the ground and—

I gasp as I hit something hard with a *clank*.

CHAPTER TWENTY-FOUR

Donny

Dale and I huddle in the corner of the concrete room. Our large T-shirts are gray with grime, and today our wrists and ankles are bound with white rope. Dale is quiet. Distant.

Dale is always quiet and distant, but it's worse today.

Something happened to him. I wasn't blind to blood that soaked the bottom of his T-shirt in the back. We often bleed, but this is worse. Much worse. It's mostly brown and dried now.

But yesterday . . .

Yesterday was bad.

They took Dale away, to another room. They came for me, but Dale protected me as he always does. So they took him instead. I don't know how long he was gone, but when they brought him back, he was limp. For a minute, I thought he might be dead.

But he wasn't dead. They threw him onto the concrete, his shirt soaked in fresh blood, and then they took me.

Dale didn't protect me that time. He could barely open his eyes.

When they brought me back later, they tied us up.

They came this morning to untie us so we could eat and use the bucket.

Then they tied us up again.

Dale doesn't talk to me, even when I try. At least he holds on to me.

We still have each other.

I open my mouth to try to talk again, when—

A shrieking siren pierces through the room. I scream, my voice hoarse.

Dale jerks but doesn't utter a sound.

"Dale!" I try to nudge at him as well as I can with my hands and feet tied. "Dale! What is that? Is it the police? Are they coming to rescue us?"

Dale shakes his head slowly, tears pooling in his eyes. "No one's coming, Donny. Not ever."

I don't talk again. Just listen to the siren until it becomes the new normal. Then—

The door to the room bursts open, and three men stand there, all tall, all dressed in black, all wearing those masks.

"Hold it together, Tal," a man yells. "Please! We'll get them out of here!"

Another man runs to me and grabs me. My heart is racing.

"No!" I yell. "No! Please! No more!"

"We won't hurt you!" the first man yells.

The siren stops, but I pound against the man with my bound fists, shrieking. "No! No! No! Please don't hurt us anymore!"

"Hey, hey," the man holding me says. "You need to be quiet if you don't want the bad people to come. We're not going to hurt you. I promise." Then he sets me down for a moment and works the knot binding my hands and then my feet.

I look to Dale, silently asking him what to do. He's crying. Which is weird. Dale doesn't cry. Sure, he gulps back a sob every now and then, but he's crying now. Not screaming crying but quiet crying.

"Can he walk?" the second man asks.

The man helping me rubs my wrists lightly. "Of course he can't walk. Look at him. Look at both of them. They'll stumble. They're starved and malnourished. They'll need our help."

"Tal," the second man says. "Get a grip. We need them to be strong if we're going to help them. You walked out, remember?"

"I had help."

"You had Larry, who let you out, but you didn't have anyone to help you walk. They do. They have us. They'll be okay."

Who is Larry? Who are these men? My little heart is racing, and my brother... My strong brother is... I don't know what he is. Dale, *I plead silently.* Tell me what to do. What do we do?

"Listen, mon," the third guy says. "We can't take them right now. We don't know what we're walking into. The siren has stopped. Things will settle down and get back to normal. We need to find who's in charge here and get him taken care of. They'll slow us down."

"We are not leaving them here," the first man says through gritted teeth. "I'm paying your bills, goddamnit, and you're going to help me get these boys out of here."

"Talon's right," the second man says. "We're not leaving them here."

I scream. I scream like there's no tomorrow. I don't know these men. They look just like the ones who hurt us, with their black masks. Like ski masks.

The second man clamps his hand over my mouth. "Hey, I know you're scared. But we're going to help you. We need you to be quiet. If you scream, someone will find us and we won't be able to help you. Do you understand?"

My tummy is doing weird things. I think I might puke, and the hand on my mouth makes me feel like I can't breathe. But I nod. I nod because I want his hand gone. When he moves it, I scream.

I scream and scream and scream until it hurts my throat.

"He doesn't trust you, Ryan," the man who untied me says. "He doesn't trust any of us. He can't. He's been through hell."

The second man looks to the third man. "Raj, you still have the tape?"

"We will not tape his mouth!" the first man yells. "Damn it, Ryan. We can't put them through more shit."

"Tal, I understand, but they have to be quiet."

"I'll get them to be quiet," the first man says. "I know what they need right now." He sets me down on the floor next to Dale and then sits beside us.

He takes off his black mask.

I shriek again. He has dark hair, dark eyes. He looks like a normal guy, but he could easily hurt us again.

I don't know him. I don't know anyone here except Dale.

The third man covers his ears. "Damn it, mon! We've got to leave them."

"We are not leaving them," the second man says.

The first man holds me so I can see him. "Shh. You see? I took off the mask. I'm just a normal person, like you. Only the men who wear masks hurt you."

I don't believe him. I don't believe anyone anymore except Dale, and he told me no one was coming. This man is not a nice man. He's mean, like the others. I don't scream again. I just cry.

"You two," the first man says to the other two. "Take off your masks. Show him he doesn't need to be scared."

"Mon…"

"Do it! Just fucking do it!"

The third man sighs and pulls off his mask. He has dark

skin and dark eyes. The second man has brown hair and brown eyes, light skin, and looks kind of like the first man.

"See?" the man holding me says. "We're not going to hurt you. I promise. As long as you're with us, you're safe."

Dale is still cowering in the corner. He's crying. He's not helping me. Why isn't he helping me?

The man holding me nods to Dale. "Ryan, get that one."

The second man walks forward, and Dale cringes.

"Please," the man says. "It's okay. We're friends. I promise." He pulls Dale into his arms.

"We know you've been around some bad people who hurt you. We won't hurt you," the first says. "I know how you're feeling right now. You're scared, and you're hurting, and you don't know who to trust. You're also a little embarrassed. You never imagined the things that have happened to you, that such horrible things could even exist. But there is good in the world still, and you'll be okay. You'll be okay again. I promise."

I cling to the man. Then he kisses the top of my head. Like my mommy used to.

And I feel a little bit safer.

"I don't want to scare you guys," he says, "but we have to put the masks back on. We won't be able to get you out of here if we don't, because the bad men will recognize us and know we're not supposed to be here. Will you be okay if we put the masks back on?"

I let go. It feels good to let go. I decide to trust this man. "Yes," I choke out.

I don't hear Dale answer, but I think he nods.

"All right," the first man says in a soft voice. "I'm going to put the mask on now. And the others will too. Then we'll go."

Somehow he gets the mask on while still holding me.

"Are you both ready?" he asks.

I look over at Dale in the second man's arms. This time I see him nod.

"Uh-huh," I gulp out.

"I still think you're crazy," the third man says, donning his mask.

The man carries me out of the room, and now we're in a hallway.

I breathe in and gasp. What's that smell?

"Be quiet," the man holding me says. "If you see another masked person, just be quiet. Act scared."

Act scared? I am *scared. Especially because of that smell… I swallow hard so I don't puke on the guy. That will just make him mad, and if he gets mad…*

We go down the hallway, and the smell gets worse.

"No!" the man holding Dale yells.

"What is it, Ry?" my man says.

"Nothing. I'm fine."

"This is ridiculous," the third man says. He has a weird accent. "We don't even know where we're going."

"We'll take them back to the yacht. One of us will have to stay with them," my man says.

"Then it'll be one of you," the third man says. "I'm not paid to babysit."

"You're paid—and very well—to do what we say, damn it."

"Tal," the second man says. "We can't get them back to the yacht. They're in no condition to swim, if they even know how."

"All right. All right. We'll find somewhere safe to hide them. But damn it, we're getting them out of here."

I close my eyes, hoping it will ease the smell of—what is it? Rotten garbage?—that's making me gag.

We're getting them out of here.

Maybe these men really are helping us. I start to feel hope. Is Dale feeling hope?

I remember… If we get the chance… I remember the promise we made to each other.

Finally we go through a door, and—

Light! The sun! My eyes close against it, and Dale and I both scream. It hurts. Hurts my eyes so bad!

"Shh," my man says. "You have to be quiet so the bad men don't hear you."

I stop yelling and squeeze my eyes shut against the light.

At least the nasty smell is gone.

CHAPTER TWENTY-FIVE

Callie

"Rory!"

My sister rustles back, shuffling through the falling leaves and pine needles. "What?"

"Help me. I've hit something."

"What is it?"

"I don't know yet," I say, "but it's hard."

"It could just be a big rock."

"I suppose, but it clinked."

"What do you mean it clinked?"

I bang my shovel against the object. "Hear that? It sounds kind of hollow, doesn't it?"

"Yeah, I suppose." She digs her shovel into the dirt. "Let's figure out what it is."

We both dig furiously, and my arms are already exhausted. Heck, we haven't quite recovered from our first digging escapade.

"I can't really tell what it might be," Rory says. "We're down deep enough that the lantern isn't really helping."

I flick my flashlight over the object. "It looks like . . . I'll be damned."

"What?"

"It's another file box. But this one isn't ours."

"Why would anyone bury another file box under ours?"

"Well, we already know that he was here and that he got our key out of the first file box. Maybe . . ."

"What?"

"Maybe you're right, Rory. Maybe we've underestimated his intelligence all this time. Because where is the one place he might be able to hide something where we wouldn't look?"

A smile spreads over Rory's face. "Underneath where *we* hid something."

"Help me pull this thing out of here."

Within a few minutes, we've pulled up what is, without a doubt, another file box. This one is graphite metal. And, of course, it's locked.

"Do you have a bobby pin?" Rory asks me.

"Do I look like someone who would wear a bobby pin?" My hair is back in its signature low ponytail.

"Ha-ha. What about a paper clip?" she asks.

"Didn't bring my office supplies with me," I say. "Let's just take it home. We can easily pick this lock there."

"Or cut it open with a damned ax."

"I get it, sis. You're pissed off. But we can't take the chance of ruining whatever may be in here."

"True. It may not belong to Pat Lamone anyway."

"In the meantime," I say, "we should throw all this dirt back in and make it look like it did when we left the first time. We don't want him to know we've been here."

Rory nods and begins shoveling dirt back into the hole. I help her, and within about fifteen minutes, my arms feel like they're going to fall off, but everything is back in order.

"While we're out here," I say, "do you want to look around a little bit more?"

"Oh, hell no," she says. "I want to get this damned thing home and find out what's inside."

★ ★ ★

It's nearly eleven by the time Rory and I get home. Surely everyone's asleep. The house is dark, so we park the car, take the box—which is pretty light—and head into the garage.

Only to find—

"Jess!" Rory says.

Our brother is zipping his guitar case shut.

"You weren't practicing, were you?" Rory says.

"This late at night?" Jesse shakes his head. "Nope. I just got back from Dragon's, and I'm putting Roxy to rest."

Roxy, of course, is Jesse's Fender Stratocaster.

"What are you two doing here?" He eyes the box. "What's that?"

"Nothing."

"It looks like you just unburied it."

Rory and I send a look to each other. Time to think of an excuse and quick. Luckily, this time I come through, unlike the time with Mom and the rabbit story.

"Yeah," I say. "We were in town, and Rory was pulling some more things out of her old apartment, including this box. It had been left out in the yard, and she forgot about it."

"Yeah, and I'm glad we found it. It has some of my old music in it."

Jesse cocks his head but then seems to accept our explanation. "Okay. Where's the other stuff? I'll help you move it in."

I feign a big yawn. "No, we're going to wait until morning, but thanks."

"Have it your way." Our brother exits through the garage and into the house.

"That was close," I say. "I don't really want to tell our big brother that there are naked pictures of us somewhere on the loose."

"No shit. Though I've been thinking about that bonfire."

"Yeah?"

"Jesse and Donny Steel were there that night. I'm the one who insisted they show up."

"Yeah, that has crossed my mind as well."

"We should go let the dogs out before we do anything," she says.

"You're right."

Dusty and Zach are in kennels. They're full-grown dogs, but we need to make sure they're house-trained before we let them run loose.

Rory and I go in the house and into our respective rooms, where our dogs are eagerly wagging their tails.

"I'm freaked out," I say, "but I have to tell you, these dogs help."

"They do," Rory agrees.

They bound out of their kennels, through the house, to the sliding-glass doors leading out into the backyard. Rory and I sit on the deck as they play after they do their business.

My heart races. As much as I love these dogs and would like to stay in their presence all night long, we need to get back to the garage and figure out what's in that box.

"You good?" I say to Rory.

She nods. "Come on, Zach!"

We gather Dusty and Zach, bring them back inside where they lap up some water, and then we take them with us to the garage. They can run around while we open the box.

Except . . .

Rory gasps.

The file box, and whatever it contains, is gone.

CHAPTER TWENTY-SIX

Donny

"I do remember," I say. "It's nasty. But what the hell is it?"

"It's remains," Dale says. "Human remains."

Brock clamps his hand over his mouth.

I'm tempted to, but as much as I want to puke right now, I hold it back.

I can't let my emotions get to me here. If I allow that, I'll lose it. I can't think about that time. About being caged.

"How? How do you know?" I demand.

"Because we've smelled it before, Donny. You remember as well as I do."

"But how do you know it's . . . *human*?"

"I asked Dad a long time ago, after we'd been here for a few weeks. He was straight with me. I couldn't tell you. You were so young. Besides, we grew up on a ranch, Don. You and I both know what animal remains smell like. It's not pretty, but it's not *this*."

He's right. I know the smell of rotting flesh, and this is definitely it, but it has an odd sickeningly sweet smell as well.

"This is our land," I say.

"I know, Don."

"You're telling me that we have rotting corpses on our land."

Brock gives in then. He turns and retches.

I'm about to follow suit, but I'm determined to hold it together. Not just for Brock but for myself.

Dale pulls a red bandana out of his back pocket and hands it to our cousin.

Brock wipes his mouth. "Sorry."

"No need to apologize," Dale says. "I nearly upchucked myself."

"Yeah, but you didn't," Brock says.

"Don't go by Donny and me. We've seen more than we should."

Brock nods. "I'm still not over that. I can't fucking believe what you two have been through."

"That's way in the past," I say. "Right now, we need to figure out who the fuck put dead bodies on our land."

"Not only dead bodies, but recent dead bodies. Anything that had been here for long wouldn't smell anymore, would it?"

"It's hard to say," Dale says. "I don't think any of us are scholars on how long it takes a body to decompose. How long the smell lasts."

Here comes the puke again. I swallow fiendishly to hold back hurling.

Brock places the hanky over his mouth, his Adam's apple working as fiendishly as mine is.

"What do we do?" I ask. "Start digging?"

"Man," Brock says. "I don't want to find what we're going to find."

"Neither do I," Dale says.

"Maybe we do bring Uncle Joe in on this," I say.

Brock speaks then. "Guys? I'm kind of afraid to bring Dad in on this."

"You don't think your father—"

"God, no. He didn't kill anyone. And he certainly didn't bring anyone here. But he'll go ballistic if he finds out what's going on."

"Maybe we need him to go ballistic," I say.

Dale speaks then. "Don, I'm pretty ballistic myself right now. Once I can breathe without wanting to gag, I'm going to figure out what to do here."

"That may take a while," I say dryly.

Brock gulps. "No shit."

We swiftly leave the barn, and I hold back more dry heaves.

"This is fucked up," Brock says. "What if we start digging? What if we find shit we don't want to find? And what if we get blamed for it?"

"We can't get blamed for it," Dale says. "We didn't do anything."

"Right, but it's on our property. Whatever evidence is here, we're disturbing it."

I lift my eyebrows. "That's a good point. One I should have thought of as an attorney. Of course, I'm not exactly thinking clearly right now through the stench of dead bodies."

"What if we say we didn't know the evidence was here?" Dale asks.

"You and I both know what we're smelling," I say.

"Whatever it is, it's buried. Or we'd see it, right?"

I lift my eyebrows again. He raises a good point. If it were buried—buried so deep that there's no evidence of it on the ground—would we still be smelling this shit? I mean, graveyards don't smell like this, right? Of course, those bodies are embalmed and buried inside airtight caskets.

Something doesn't sit right with me. "Why are we smelling this so strongly?"

Dale shakes his head. "I don't know, man."

"We need to bring in an expert," Brock says.

"I'm afraid I don't know any experts on how we're smelling decayed human flesh." This time Dale speaks dryly.

"I'm not sure we have a choice," I say. "I think we bring in your dad, Brock."

"Guys . . ."

"What?"

"I'm honestly . . . afraid to. No, I don't think he has anything to do with this, but it's like I said before. He'll go off all half-cocked, and before we know it . . ."

My heart is racing. I've never had a panic attack before, but I think I may be having one now. I breathe in deeply. Let it out slowly. Again. Again.

"You all right, Don?" Dale says.

"Yeah. Just trying to calm down, you know?"

Dale nods. "Trust me, I know."

"Brock," I say, "have you had a chance to look through the crawl space yet?"

"No, I haven't. Damn. We should have done that before your dad and mom got home."

I nod. "Yeah, we should have. But now we don't have a choice. We need to go through that stuff, and we need to do it now."

"Now?" Dale says. "While we know there are bodies rotting somewhere on this property?"

"Yeah, now. Let's find out what there is on paper before we start literally digging up our past."

In reality, I just want to get out of here. So does Brock. I can see it on his face. He's yellowish green.

Dale, though, is made of sterner stuff. "We're here now, guys. I think we should look around a little more." He walks to the truck, pulls a shovel out of the back.

"You want to go digging?" I say.

"Yeah. I want to go digging. I want to dig right around the place where you found that fingernail."

"Good. At least it's not inside the damned barn."

"Good enough," Brock says. He grabs a shovel. "I'll help."

I head back to the truck behind my cousin, grab a shovel and work gloves, and walk slowly to the spot.

"That fingernail hasn't been here for very long," I say. "It doesn't look old."

"It's plastic, man."

"I know that, but still . . . It would have been washed away by rain or wind or something."

"Maybe not. Not when it's so close to the shelter of the barn. It protected it."

I'm not sure I believe my brother, but I'm okay with doing a little bit of digging. As long as we're out here in the fresh air. Although, now that I know what it is? I smell that fucking rotting flesh. It's like it has lodged inside my nostrils.

I push my shovel into the dirt. The four of us dig for a while until we're down about four feet.

"Nothing that I can see," I say.

"Let's go just a little bit farther," Dale says.

His forehead is tense and wrinkled. I've seen this look of determination on him before.

All those years ago, when he stood defiantly, demanding that our captors take him instead of me.

He was determined then, and he's as determined now.

So I keep digging. I keep digging because he's my brother, and I owe him everything. I owe him my life.

I dig and I dig and I dig, until my phone vibrates in my back pocket. I grab it. It looks like it's trying to send a text through, but because the service in this area is so sketchy, I'm not getting anything.

I don't like the idea that I'm missing something. What if something has happened to Dad? Callie? Anyone?

"You okay?" Brock asks.

"Yeah, my phone vibrated, but I got nothing."

"Shitty service."

"I've got a bad feeling. I feel like someone's trying to get in touch with me. I have to leave. Now."

CHAPTER TWENTY-SEVEN

Callie

I got no response from Donny.

That in itself is odd, but I can't worry about it. I have more pressing things to worry about. What the hell happened to that file box?

"Let's look around," Rory says frantically. "Someone was here, and they must have left evidence. Someone would have driven up, right?"

"Yeah. I didn't hear anything, did you?"

"Of course not, but we were out back with the dogs. Mom and Dad are in bed. Where's Jesse?"

"He probably went to bed as well."

"Let's have a look around."

We leave the garage, brandishing our flashlights still, and look closely. Our driveway is asphalt, so there's not really any way to tell if a car has been here. Footprints?

The same. Not really any way to tell without knowing what we're looking for.

"Damn," I say.

"Looking for this?"

Our brother stands in the doorway from the kitchen to the garage. In his hands is the file box, and it's opened.

"Damn it, Jesse!" Rory says. "That isn't yours."

"No, it isn't, but I'm going to need you to explain the contents."

"We don't have to explain a damn thing—"

"What contents?" Rory interrupts me, her voice dropping to a low timbre.

"Let's just say it's something a brother never should have to look at."

My heart falls to my stomach. "Oh, shit."

"It's a thumb drive, along with hard copies. I only looked at one. That's all I could take."

"Which one of us was it?" I ask.

"It was you, Rory. But does that mean there's photos of both of you? Christ." He pulls out his man bun and lets his hair float around his shoulders. "Christ," he says again.

I'm oddly thankful that my brother didn't see the picture of me first.

"I think, girls, we need to have a little talk."

"It's a long boring story, Jesse," I say. "And . . . thanks for not looking any further."

"Are you kidding me? I feel like I need to have my eyes burned out just from seeing one. What were you thinking, Rory?"

"Ease up," I say. "She didn't do anything. Does she look conscious to you in that picture?"

"I don't know. I tossed it aside once I realized who it was. I didn't commit it to memory, thank you very much. If you didn't do anything wrong, where the hell did these come from?"

"I guess we have to tell him," I say to Rory.

"Yeah, I guess so." She sighs. "Let's go inside. Better yet, out on the deck. We can let the dogs run around. I don't want there to be any chance that Mom and Dad can overhear us."

"After you." Jesse gestures to the door.

We herd Dusty and Zach through the house and out again into the backyard.

The sky is clear, and I can make out both the Big Dipper and Little Dipper. I stare at the stars for a moment, thinking about the beauty and the vastness of the night sky. How I wish I could just float upward, become a part of it, and not have to deal with real life for just a few minutes. Only a few.

Alas, that's not going to happen.

"I'll tell him, Callie. I was the adult in the room back then."

"Being a few days older than eighteen doesn't make you an adult," I say.

"Except that it does. Legally." She bites her lip.

"I don't really care who tells me. Just start talking. How did this happen? And who do I have to fucking kill?"

"You're not going to kill anyone, Jesse," I say. "If Pat Lamone—"

"Pat Lamone? Who the hell is Pat Lamone?"

"Yeah, you wouldn't know. You were long gone from high school by the time all this went down." I suck in a breath. "What I was saying is, Pat Lamone probably has other copies of all this shit."

"Great, just great." Jesse shakes his head. "I'll fucking kill him. Tell me where he is. I'll go now."

"Normally I'd be all over that," I say, "but I don't really want you getting arrested. And trust me, Lamone *will* have you arrested. He tried to have me arrested for spilling coffee on him."

Jesse goes red in the face, his hands curling into fists.

"Simmer down, Jess," Rory says. "Let me tell you the whole story."

Jesse listens intently, growing more tense as Rory pours out the story of what happened all those years ago.

By the end, our brother is growling. Seriously growling. Like a freaking wolf.

"He's probably at the inn right now," Jesse says. "See you girls later."

I stand then, and so does Rory. We block him from the door.

"Nice try, but I can move you both with one hand tied behind my back."

"We know you can," Rory says. "We're asking you not to. Callie and I are trying to figure out how to deal with this. And Donny—"

"Steel knows about this?" Jesse shakes his head. "You don't trust your own brother to help you, but you go to Donny Steel?"

"Donny is my boyfriend, and it's about time the two of you put this stupid-ass high school rivalry behind you."

"Fucker got MVP instead of me because the Steels own this damned town."

I open my mouth to refute him but then close it abruptly. My latest research shows the Steels *do* own this damned town, so what do I have to stand on? Nothing.

"Callie and Donny are together," Rory says. "You need to deal with it. He's a good man."

"Yeah, yeah, yeah. He's all right. Still..."

"Still, that was fourteen years ago, Jesse," Rory says. "Give it a rest. We all know you were more talented than Donny."

I open my mouth to disagree but then shut it quickly again. I can't take sides between my brother and my boyfriend. So not happening. Not tonight anyway.

"We've got bigger problems now," Rory continues.

"What's your plan?" Jesse asks.

"We don't really have one yet. We can get him if he in any way publishes the photos of Callie, because she was a minor at the time. We'll bring him up on child porn charges. But... my photos are another story."

"Easy enough," Jesse says. "If those photos ever see their way anywhere, I'll kill the son of a bitch."

"For God's sake," I say. "We have to figure out how to be smart about this. For example, did he bury these underneath the place where we buried the safe-deposit box key on purpose, knowing we would find them? Or did he think he was being so smart, putting them in a place where we wouldn't look, so we would *never* find them? If the latter is the case, these may be his only copies. In which case we can end this now."

"But if it's the other," Rory says, "we've fallen right into his trap."

"What a fucking dick," Jesse says. "I'm still open to killing him."

"We have a preliminary plan. We think Brittany Sheraton, Doc Sheraton's daughter, is the person who impersonated Rory to get into our safe-deposit box, which means she has a fake ID. Saturday we'll take the dogs over there and find out how to get in touch with Brittany."

"And if that's a dead end?" Jesse says.

"Then we put our thinking caps back on," Rory says. "We haven't had a lot of time to deal with this."

"Why don't you just have your boyfriend pay him off?"

Rory raises her eyebrows. She's thinking the same thing. She's been thinking it since the beginning, and I can't blame her.

"No," I say.

"You think he wouldn't?" Jesse scoffs.

"I think he would," I say. "In a minute. But where does that get us? Lamone will never give us all the evidence. He'll always keep a copy. Then, when he runs out of the first payment, he'll come back for more. No. First of all, I don't want to ask Donny to do that, and second of all, it doesn't get us anywhere. It's a temporary solution at best."

Jesse nods, to my surprise. "You're probably right."

"Exactly. So what's the next step, then? If the Doc Sheraton thing doesn't pan out?" I ask.

"That, I suppose, is what we need to figure out." Rory twists her lips into her thinking pose.

"Let's figure it out," Jesse says. "The two of you aren't in this alone anymore. I'll do everything I can to help you."

"Thank you," Rory says. "Thank you so much, Jess. And I'm really sorry you had to see that."

"So am I. But that's nothing compared to what he has put the two of you through. We'll get him. We'll figure it out, and we'll get him."

I nod, as my phone starts ringing. It's Donny. "Sorry," I say. "I need to take this."

"Donny?" I say frantically into the phone.

"Callie, is everything okay?"

"Yeah, I tried to text you, but I didn't hear back from you."

"I just got into a place where I could get service and got your text. You said it's urgent."

"Yeah, at the time I thought it was." I quickly fill him in about finding the file box and then having it disappear. "Turns out Jesse had it, and he opened it. So Rory and I had to let him in on what's going on."

"Okay, okay. This is good. Maybe this is the only copy of his evidence."

"That's what we're hoping, but we can't depend on that."

"True."

"Are you okay?" I ask. "Where were you?"

"Near the Wyoming border. I'm still about an hour out. I was... checking out one of the GPS coordinates. Dale and Brock are still up there."

"Why did you leave?"

"Because my phone vibrated, and then nothing happened. I didn't know if it was you or Dad or anybody. But I was freaked out enough that I needed to know."

"I'm sorry. I didn't mean to make you worry."

"It's okay, baby. Trust me, I was glad to have an excuse to leave."

"Why?"

"Oh, Cal, I'd tell you, but I just can't talk about it right now. Can't lay it on you. Don't worry about me, though. I'm fine. Dale and Brock are fine. It's just... Damn. So much going on."

"All right. I understand." Though I'm a little upset that he doesn't want to confide in me. "I guess I'll see you tomorrow at work."

"Actually... I'll be taking the rest of the week off."

"What?"

"Yeah. I've got shit to take care of in the city. I'm sorry, but I had Alyssa clear my schedule for the next three days. I'll be back Friday evening."

My heart aches, and tears threaten. *Why? Why didn't he tell me he was planning to leave town for a few days?*

"Okay," I finally say.

"I'll miss you, baby."

"Yeah. I'll miss you too. Right. Then I'll see you at the big party, I guess."

"Right. Steel party. Rah, rah, rah."

"Donny, you're freaking me out a little here."

"I'm sorry, baby. I'm just exhausted. I think I need a good night's sleep, though it's doubtful I'll get one."

"Try some melatonin. Or a stiff shot of your dad's Peach Street."

"Maybe both," he says with a soft chuckle. "I love you, Callie. I'll see you Friday."

"I love you too."

I move back to my brother and sister.

"Everything okay?" Rory asks.

"No, actually. He's leaving town for a few days. Something's bothering him, but he doesn't want to talk about it. Which is fine, because I don't want to talk about what's bothering me, either. Though I did tell him what happened here tonight because he was worried. Apparently my text started to go through but then didn't. He was in a place where there wasn't good service, so . . ." I plunk my ass into an Adirondack chair on the deck. "You know how it goes."

"All right," Jesse says. "What's your next step?"

"I just don't know," Rory says, her lips still twisted into a grimace. "I just don't fucking know."

I say nothing.

"Maybe we just sleep on it," Jesse says.

Except who could sleep? I know I won't. And looking at Rory, I'm pretty sure she won't either.

And Jesse?

He looks like he needs to run ten or twenty miles before

he'll be able to relax.

"Damn," Jesse says, "I could use a drink."

Rory smiles. It's not a big smile, but it'll work. "You know? That's the best idea I've heard all night."

Jesse rises. "I'll get us all a beer."

"Diet Coke for—" I rethink my statement. "Never mind. Get me a beer. In fact, get me two beers."

CHAPTER TWENTY-EIGHT

Donny

The lady called Marabel is kind. She gives us water to drink. Everyone keeps trying to get us to talk.

Dale doesn't talk, and I don't do anything that Dale doesn't do.

Until Marabel touches my chin. Her brown eyes are kind. "What's your name? Please, honey. We want to help you."

I open my mouth despite Dale giving me his big brother eye. "My name's Donny. His name is Dale."

Another lady comes out. She's pretty, with dark hair and blue eyes. I notice eyes now, since they're all we could see of the men who hurt us.

It's funny to be able to see people's faces. For so long, we saw only those black masks.

"Miss Ruby!" Marabel says. "I have wonderful news. The little boy finally revealed his name. It's Donny, and his brother's name is Dale."

The pretty lady smiles and sits down next to Dale. He has scratches up and down his arms.

So do I.

But the hardest part is sitting. It hurts down there.

Dale is petting one of the yellow puppies. His name is Bo, I think. The pretty lady sits down next to him.

"Dale," the lady named Miss Ruby says. "That's a nice name. Can you tell me how old you are?"

I know Dale won't answer, so I do. These people are nice. I want to believe that they're nice. "He's ten, and I'm seven."

Dale keeps petting the puppy.

Another lady joins us. She's wearing a black T-shirt and gray pants, and she has pretty blond hair. "I know they hurt you, Dale. They hurt me too. But we're going to be okay now. It will just take time."

Dale nods slightly.

"Would you stay with him for a little while?" Miss Ruby asks.

The other lady nods, stroking Bo's soft head. "We should take the puppy down into the yard so he can play. Would you like that?"

No slight nod this time, but Dale stands, releasing the pup. He follows the blond lady out onto the green grass.

I'm sitting next to Marabel with the other two puppies. They squirm away from me and follow Dale and the other puppy onto the grass.

"Are you hungry, Donny?" Miss Ruby asks.

"Yeah. A little."

Marabel gave us water. She said we shouldn't eat quite yet because our tummies have been empty for so long that eating might make us sick.

No way will eating make me sick. I don't think there's enough food in the whole world to make me full again.

"Do you think we could give him something to eat?" Miss Ruby asks Marabel.

"Just a little. I'll get him something." Marabel walks back into the big house.

"Do you remember your last name?" Miss Ruby asks me. "Or your mommy's or daddy's names?"

"We don't have a daddy. Just Mommy. Our daddy died when I was a baby."

"I grew up without a daddy too." Miss Ruby smiles. "Do you remember your mommy's name?"

"Her name is Cheri. She has blond hair too. Our last name is Robertson. We live in Colorado."

"Really? That's where I live too."

"I like the mountains. We could see them outside our back window. They look purple." I squirm in my chair. "My bum hurts."

Miss Ruby looks sad then. Sad and mad at the same time. Her eyes even get a little glassy, as if she's going to cry. Did someone hurt her too?

"I know you took a shower, but have you had a bath?" she asks me. "That might help a little."

I close my eyes against the pictures in my mind. Against the hurt. I can still feel it. Everything they did. I don't even understand it all, but I know it hurt more than anything. "No, not yet. The bad men did things to us."

"I know. But you're safe now. And you will heal. I promise." She touches my hair.

I don't flinch at the touch. Already I trust her.

And if I can have a bath…

"Dale protected me a lot," I say. "They hurt him worse. He stopped crying after a while."

She tries to smile. "He's a good big brother, isn't he?"

"He's the best. He's my hero."

Marabel brings out some apples. They're cut into slices and spread with peanut butter, and they're the best thing I've ever tasted. Even better than Mommy's macaroni and cheese. She brings me a little bit of milk too, but then she says I have to go back to water.

I don't mind. I love water. I've been so thirsty for so long.

"Come with me." Miss Ruby stands and holds out her hand.

I look into the grass where Dale sits with all the dogs. Should I take the lady's hand? I want to ask Dale, but I also don't want to.

I want to take her hand. I want a grown-up to be nice to me. I like people being nice to me, even though I'm going to do what Dale told me to do.

So I put my little hand in hers, and she leads me through the house to a bedroom that has its own bathroom. And a big tub. She runs the water into the tub and puts something in the water that smells nice.

"Mommy used to give me bubble baths," I say.

"Your mommy is going to be so happy to know you're okay. You and Dale both." She turns off the water. "You're a big boy. You probably don't need my help to take a bath."

"Right. I can do it myself."

"I'll just stay in here, in case you need me."

She can't stay in here. She won't let me do what I have to do. Or maybe she will. Maybe the niceness is fake. How do you tell?

"No," I tell her. "You don't have to."

"Donny, have you ever taken a bath by yourself before?"

I decide to lie. Mommy always watches me still when I take a bath, but I need Miss Ruby to go away. "Yeah. Dale doesn't get in with me anymore. He says he's too old for that. So I have to do it alone."

"You mean your mommy doesn't stay in the bathroom with you?"

I feel bad about lying. But I still do it anyway. "Sometimes. But sometimes not. I'm getting too big for that too. I mean, I'm a boy and all."

"You sure you'll be okay?"

"Yup. I'll be fine."

"I'm not leaving you."

"Please..." I start to whine. "I'm... embarrassed."

It's not a lie. Those bad men did things to me. Bad things that hurt. They made me scream and cry, and they laughed. Laughed at what they did to me.

I don't want this lady to see me. I don't want anyone to see me. That's why I'm going to do what I have to do.

Miss Ruby smiles. "You don't have to be embarrassed. I'm a police officer, and I'd never hurt you. I just want to make sure you're okay."

"But... they did things... Please."

She sighs. "Okay. Just sit in the water for a while. It will help. There's a washcloth and towel on the rack. Some shampoo on the shelf if you want to wash your hair. I'll be right in the next room. Just holler if you need anything."

"Okay."

She closes the door, and I step into the tub. The warm water sloshes, and it feels good when I sit down. I like the heat. So I give myself a minute. I sit. And I let it feel good.

But it's time.

Time to do what I promised Dale I'd do if I ever got the chance.

I slide into the water all the way, head and all.

I hold my breath as long as I can. Then even longer.

I sit up and gasp in a breath.

No. I have to be strong! Strong like Dale is. Strong because

I promised him.

I go underneath the water again, hold my breath, until finally I can't.

I breathe in water. I breathe in . . .

I breathe in . . .

I choke. I breathe in . . .

And . . . nothing.

★ ★ ★

I jerk wildly, nearly running my truck off the road.

My heart is racing. I don't know what time it is. Well after midnight. I'm about a half hour away from home, I think.

But my mind doesn't stop. The images . . . The feelings . . . Being in a fishbowl, breathing in water . . .

Choking.

I pull to the side of the road and close my eyes.

These things I never think about. That I never *let* myself think about. Why now? Why?

I *thunk* my head on the steering wheel, and I let the pictures play.

★ ★ ★

I'm coughing. Throwing up warm water. I gasp.

Gasp.

Gasp.

Air. I'm breathing air. What happened?

Miss Ruby sits above me. I'm lying on carpet somewhere. She's crying. Why is she crying?

A man holds her. One of the men who rescued us.

"It's okay, baby. He's okay. He's breathing."

The man named Talon touches my forehead. "Can you sit up?"

I cough. This isn't supposed to happen. "No. I was supposed to die!"

"You're alive," Talon says. "And we're all glad you're alive. Your brother will be glad."

I cough again. It's hard to talk. Hard to breathe. "No, he won't. We made a pact. If either of us had the chance to end our own life, we'd do it."

Talon shakes his head. "Why?"

"So the bad men wouldn't hurt us anymore."

He grabs me and pulls me to his chest. I gasp in some air.

"The bad men won't hurt you anymore. I promise. They won't. You're going to have a long life. I promise that too."

But Dale… I promised Dale…

He'll be mad. He'll be mad because I wasn't strong. Like him.

"It's my fault." Miss Ruby's voice.

"How is this your fault? Ruby, you saved him. He's alive because of you."

"No. I put him in the tub. He said… He said his bum hurt. I thought sitting in a tub would help. He said he could do it himself. But I kept watch. The door was cracked. It was only a few inches of water. I didn't leave him!"

Voices keep talking, but I'm not sure who they belong to anymore. I pant against the man's chest.

"Of course you didn't. You didn't do anything wrong."

"But then I heard something from the office."

"I'm so sorry. That was—"

"It doesn't matter what it was. I shouldn't have stopped watching for a second."

"He's old enough to take a bath by himself."

"He's only seven. What was I thinking?"

"Ruby, how old were you when you started taking a bath by yourself?"

"I don't know. Five, I think."

"So was I. You didn't do anything wrong."

"He was doing so well. He was talking. He was eating. Playing with the puppies. I never imagined . . ."

"You couldn't have known what he'd try. Please. You didn't do anything wrong, baby."

The man named Talon talks to me. "You're safe now. There's no need for your pact anymore."

I pull away just a little. "But Dale said—"

"Shh. When was the last time you talked about the pact?"

"In the room. Before you came."

"Well, things are different now, aren't they? You're here, and no one here will hurt you."

"But Dale won't talk. Not even to me."

"Dale is just . . . Dale's going through some stuff. But it's over now. He'll come around. I'll make sure he's okay."

I sink my head against his chest again. Is he right? Is it okay not to be strong right now? Is it okay to like this man? The others? To believe them?

"Donny!" Dale's voice. "Are you all right?"

I lift my head from the big man's chest. "I'm sorry, Dale. I tried."

"No!" Dale grabs me and hugs me. "No, God. I'm so sorry. I never meant . . . I'm so glad you're okay. That you're alive."

"But we made a pact."

"It was a stupid pact. We were starving and hurting. But now we're not. I want to live, Donny, and I want you to live too."

CHAPTER TWENTY-NINE

Callie

The hoppy flavor of the Fat Tire Jesse brought me hits the spot like even Diet Coke couldn't tonight. Already it's the early hours of the morning. Rory and I both have work tomorrow, but man, it feels nice to relax.

I'm not thrilled that Jesse knows about our Pat Lamone issue—most specifically the compromising photos of his little sisters—but in all honesty, it feels good to have his strength on our side.

He and Rory are talking about that night, and I'm listening.

"It was ten years ago," he says. "Donny and I weren't there very long and didn't drink any of that shit."

"Be glad you didn't," Rory says. "Callie made me promise not to have any more of it after she saw Carmen acting weird, but honestly? I'd have drunk another whole cup. It was that good."

"What was so remarkable about it?" Jesse asks. "Looked like basic trash can punch to me."

"Is that what you guys call it? We called it hairy buffalo."

"Whatever. You didn't answer my question."

Rory takes a sip of her beer. "It was sweet and refreshing. Better than any other hairy buffalo I had."

"Do you think the drugs made it sweeter?" he asks.

"I have no idea. I doubt it."

"Maybe you were just high on life that night, Ror," I say. "You know, after being crowned the most beautiful and popular girl at school."

Rory rolls her eyes. "You call me beautiful and popular. You admit you were envious of me. Neither of you knew, back then, how I was struggling."

"Struggling?" Jesse asks. "You mean with your bisexuality?"

"Yeah, that was a big part of it. But another part was that I just didn't think I had what it took to be a star, even then."

I drop my mouth open. "Are you kidding me?"

"Geez, Cal, have you noticed lately? I didn't make it. I'm not an operatic mezzo. I'm a music teacher in a one-horse town."

"And I'm not a rocker in Hollywood," Jesse says. "That's fucking life, Ror."

"For God's sake." Rory downs another draw on her beer. "I'm not feeling sorry for myself. Forget about now. I'm talking about *then*. Everyone expected the best from me. I was homecoming queen. Voted most likely to sing at the Met. Plus I was dealing with my attraction to women as well as men. I knew I wasn't as smart as you, Callie—"

"You're every bit—"

"Oh my God, would you let me finish?"

"Sorry." I look down at my lap.

"I knew I wasn't as smart as you. Mom made that clear every day. So there I was, the most popular, and I could sing and act, but I was Snow Creek good. Maybe Denver good, but far from New York or Hollywood good. I was bisexual, though I wasn't sure how to put it into words at that time, and I wasn't brilliant. Not even close. But everyone expected great things from me. Rory Pike, what a beauty. But beauty's only skin deep. Deep down, I knew I didn't have it. Think about that for a hot minute. Put it all together and what do you get?"

Jesse lifts his eyebrows.

"The freaking hairy buffalo was sweeter than syrup because I was struggling, and it gave me a high. A high I needed that night of all nights. The night I became the homecoming queen, because deep down I knew that was the best I'd ever be."

"I'm sorry." Jesse takes another pull of beer. "I should have seen what you were going through."

"Me too," I add.

"You were a kid, Callie. And Jess, you were four years older. Gone. Maybe Mom and Dad should have seen it, but you two bear no guilt."

"You're so much more than a pretty face and an amazing voice," Jesse says. "You know that now, I hope."

"I do. But I'm ten years wiser. I'm talking about that night. About why I drank that shit and wanted more. Why it tasted so good to me."

"I get it," I say. "But I'm glad you didn't drink any more of it."

"I don't break promises to my sister." Rory smiles weakly.

"Still," Jesse says, "I wish you had come to me about the photos. About everything."

"Maybe we should have," I say, "but how exactly do you tell your big brother that some derelict drugged you and snapped naked photos of you? It's not dinner conversation, Jess."

"The girl's right," Rory agrees.

"I can't fault you there, I guess." Jesse gives Zach a pet on the head. “How much of it do you think Diana Steel drank?”

I shrug. “Who knows? She was fourteen or fifteen. Tall like all the Steels. We didn’t know her well. Did you see how much she drank, Rory?”

Rory shakes her head. “I wasn’t paying any attention to anyone but myself that night.”

“Here’s the thing,” Jesse says. “No one else got alcohol poisoning, and I’m willing to bet others drank as much or more than Diana.”

“Maybe,” I say. “But stuff affects people differently.”

“True.” He nods. “But what if Diana was *specifically* poisoned?”

I widen my eyes. “Why would anyone want to poison Diana?”

“Envy, pure and simple,” Jesse says. “And I know that emotion better than anyone.”

“Because of Donny.” I stare at my empty beer bottle. Good thing Jesse brought me two.

“That’s right. Envy is a powerful emotion. I’m still not over the rivalry between Donny and me. Sure, I’m a grown-up. It doesn’t rule my life. But even now, when I see him, I still feel it. It’s not pretty.”

“Jess,” I say, “Donny and I are serious. We’re in love.”

“I know, sis, and I’m happy for you. I’ll deal.”

“But you’re saying someone may have singled Diana out.” Rory rubs Dusty behind her ears.

“I’m saying it’s a possibility. If she didn’t drink any more than anyone else did, it’s certainly a possibility, especially considering she’s a Steel. The Steels are the envy of everyone in this town.”

My brother’s not wrong. How many times have we heard

something similar? The Steels are golden. The Steels have everything.

The Steels own this town.

The Steels . . .

"So when I overheard Pat talking to Jimmy outside the algebra room"—I'm thinking out loud—"he didn't say specifically that he spiked all the punch with angel dust. He asked Pat why he let her, meaning Diana, drink the stuff. Pat said he thought it was just alcohol, but Jimmy called him out and Pat admitted that some dude told him it was angel dust. But they didn't say anything about spiking *all* the punch with angel dust. Maybe they just spiked *Diana's* drink."

"Oh my God," Rory says. "Then, when I got him to confess, all he said was that he spiked the punch. He didn't say he spiked it with angel dust."

"Maybe he spiked the punch with Everclear," I continue. "I mean, someone always did, but this was some seriously strong hairy buffalo, according to you and to Carmen. But did you feel drugged? High?"

"I'm not sure. I've never used drugs, but I just felt drunk and giddy. It was a release for me. A release from everything piling up on me."

"Any hallucinations?" Jesse asks.

"God, no!"

"Does angel dust cause hallucinations?" I ask.

"Yeah, visual and auditory."

"And you know this . . . how?"

"Dragon got some for us a few years ago. Trust me, I'll never touch that shit again."

I swat my brother on his arm. "That's for doing drugs. But damn, Jesse, I think we just solved an integral part of this mystery."

CHAPTER THIRTY

Donny

I considered booking a suite at the Carlton for the next few days but ultimately decided against it. With Darla gone, Mom and Dad may need me as Dad continues to recuperate. Mom, of course, wouldn't be thrilled with me taking a few days off work, especially since I'm now the official city attorney… which is why I didn't tell her.

I made sure my calendar was cleared for the rest of the week, and Troy, Alyssa, and Callie have things under control.

I really hate being away from Callie, and I also hate lying to my mother.

But I have an appointment this morning that needs to be kept.

Now, I stand outside a small jewelry store in the city. It's low-key and far from ostentatious, but inside is one of the best resources for precious stones in the nation, Drew Campbell. He's about my dad's age, and Uncle Bryce found him years ago when he needed to have some rare yellow diamonds appraised. Since then, he's been the jeweler to the Steels.

Drew, gray-haired with a beer belly but wearing a designer suit, meets my gaze from behind the glass as he moves his sign from closed to open. Then he opens the door.

"You're early."

"Only a few minutes."

"Sorry to keep you waiting. Come on in."

"I suppose it's too much to ask you to close the shop for the next half hour. I'll make it worth your while."

Drew rubs at his goatee. "Nah. Almost no one comes in until noon. I use this time to work on repairs and do research. We'll be fine."

I nod. This is why I like Drew. He just turned down money to close up shop for a half hour when he probably won't sell anything until after noon anyway. He's a man of character and a man of class.

He'll give it to me straight.

"What can I do for you, Don?" he asks, stepping behind his counter.

I pull the ring—the one from the safe-deposit box—out of my pocket. "I need you to take a look at this. Let me know, first of all, what it is and how much it's worth, and second, if you can figure out who it belongs to."

"Possession is nine-tenths of the law," Drew says. "You're a lawyer. You ought to know that."

"It was left in a safe-deposit box."

"Your safe-deposit box?"

"Yes." I don't need to tell him I have no clue who left it or who even opened the safe-deposit box in the first place. "I need this to be on the down low."

"Not a problem." He takes the ring from me and examines it. "This is quite a piece. Extraordinary color."

"A little lighter than my girlfriend's eyes." I'm not sure why I said that. It kind of popped out.

"Lucky man." He pulls out a jeweler's loupe. "Let's take a look."

He picks up the ring and first examines it with the naked eye and then with the loupe. He looks at all angles—of the stone itself, the surrounding white stones, and even more white gold. This man literally leaves no stone unturned.

I drop my gaze to the glass counter and the pieces on display. Drew deals mainly in antique jewelry. I don't know if my ring is an antique, but Drew knows more about stones and metals than anyone I know. He will at least be able to tell me what this ring is made of.

He also traces his pieces back to last known ownership.

That's where I'm really hoping he can help me.

Drew clears his throat. "Don, I need to take this in the back for a few minutes, run a few tests. Help yourself to some coffee." He nods to the pot sitting in a corner.

"Thanks."

I won't take any coffee, of course. Everyone else's coffee sucks compared to my mother's.

I do, however, continue looking at the few pieces he has on display. One is an old Rolex. It's just the watch itself with no band. A gorgeous piece, but I can't do it. I may have all the money in the world, but spending fifty grand on a watch? Nope.

He also has a diamond tiara.

Sure, I can afford it, but Callie in a tiara?

I chuckle out loud. The look on her face would be worth all the money to buy it. She would truly get a laugh out of it, but then what would she do with it? Does anyone actually wear such a thing?

But the rings . . .

There are nine altogether. One is all diamonds. One is a large sapphire that looks a lot like the ring that once belonged to Princess Diana.

Two are emeralds—or green stones—not that I would know. One is a beautiful ruby. I'll have to mention it to Uncle Ryan, as his and Aunt Ruby's wedding anniversary is coming up next month.

They're all beautiful, and all unique.

But not one of them is as beautiful or unique as the ring Drew is appraising now.

I need to know what kind of stone it is. What kind of metal.

But more than that . . . I want to know its history. Why did it end up in my hands? Whose is it? Because if I have to return it, I'll do so.

But if I don't have to return it . . . it's going on Callie's finger.

A pair of earrings catches my gaze. They're screw-on, which you hardly ever see anymore, but their beauty astounds me. The metal is silver, clearly, and the cabochon looks like some kind of black enamel. A silver figure is etched onto it—perhaps a harlequin or a dancer of some sort.

I can't take my eyes from them.

"That's Siamese silver," Drew says.

I look up. "I didn't realize you'd come back in."

"Yeah . . . I have some interesting information."

The Siamese silver ejects from my mind.

"What did you find out?"

"This ring is worth a hell of a lot of money, Don."

Although I'm not surprised, my jaw drops anyway. "What kind of stone is it?"

"It's a diamond."

"An orange diamond?"

"Yeah. Sometimes they're called pumpkin diamonds. They are the second-rarest type of diamond."

This time my jaw does drop. "What's the rarest type?"

"Red."

"Oh my God."

"Let me put this in perspective for you. I've been in the precious stone business and jewelry business for thirty-five years, and my father before me fifty years. I've never seen a pumpkin diamond before."

"Have you ever seen a red one?"

"No, I haven't. I have nothing to compare this to to appraise it."

"Okay. I'm slightly disappointed, but I'm not selling it, so the price doesn't actually matter. What else can you tell me?"

"The white stones are diamonds, as you probably guessed, and it's set in fourteen-karat gold."

"Can you find out who it belongs to? Or who last owned it?"

"I did a bit of research while I was in the back, and I was able to trace this particular stone back a couple of generations." He holds up the ring. "I'm going to give you the loupe. See if you can read what's inscribed on the inside of the band. It's small and very hard to make out."

I hold the jeweler's loupe to my eye and then hold the ring in front of me. I see nothing but a blur.

"You have to bring the ring pretty close to the loupe. But not too close or it'll blur up again."

I use trial and error a few times, and finally I'm able to see clearly. I'm not sure I see anything, though, except a couple of scratches.

"See it?" Drew asks.

"Just a couple of scratches."

"Look more closely. You're not a seasoned jeweler,

obviously, so you don't know exactly what you're looking for, but stare at the scratches, and you will eventually see that they're initials."

I squint my eyes, willing myself to see something.

And then, as if by magic, they appear.

"It's an *L*. And a *W*."

"Right. I'm making some calls. Anyone who's come across this stone will definitely remember it. Do you know anyone with the initials LW?"

"Not off the top of my head. I sure don't."

"Someone clearly wants you to have it. There must be papers on this stone somewhere. I just have to find them. Do you mind if I take some photographs of the ring?"

"Not at all."

He takes the ring from me again and heads back. A few minutes later, he returns and hands me the ring. "I took the liberty of putting it in my ultrasonic cleaner. Look how sparkly it is."

Sparks seem to shoot from it, and then, at a certain angle, it's embers from a dying fire.

"I didn't want to leave it in there too long," Drew continues. "It shouldn't mess with the engraving, but just in case. That engraving needs to be intact if we're going to find out where this ring came from."

"Absolutely."

"Like I said, I've put in some calls. I'll let you know as soon as anything comes up."

"How long do you think it will be?"

"My sources usually get back to me within forty-eight hours."

"Your sources?"

"Yeah. I have certain sources in the markets . . . and in the black markets."

"Shit. You don't think this is stolen, do you?"

"We can't rule that out, Don. This is a priceless item. It's nearly four carats, and it's almost the rarest of all diamonds."

"Still, it's not the Hope Diamond."

Drew chuckles. "No, it's not the Hope Diamond. But it's worth a lot. Like I said, I can't appraise it because I have nothing to compare it to. I'm going to do more research on its value, and I'll come up with a valid appraisal for you so you can get it insured."

"If it's even mine."

"You know what? Do yourself a favor and get that puppy insured now. Insure it for half a million at least."

"What if it's not mine? And will any company insure it without an appraisal?"

Drew takes a card from behind the counter and hands it to me. "Call this guy. He's with Lloyd's. He'll insure anything. If it turns out the ring's not yours and you have to give it back, you'll only be out a few bucks, and he's good about refunding unused premiums."

I pocket the card. "Thanks, Drew."

"I'll call you as soon as I have anything," he says.

I shove the ring back in my pocket.

Drew shakes his head and hands me a velvet box. "Put it in here, and don't shove it in your pocket like that. It's literally worth the moon."

I nod, deposit the ring in the box, and then gently put it in the pocket of my coat.

"If I were you, I'd put that thing back in the safe-deposit box."

"No worries. I have a safe at the house."

"Perfect. Get it in there. Don't keep it on you. You can't risk losing that, Don."

"I get it." It belongs to Callie and only Callie, if I have anything to say about it. But just in case . . .

"Can you replicate this ring, Drew?"

"Not another pumpkin diamond like that, but I can create a reasonable facsimile."

"With what?"

"An orange sapphire is the best bet. It's a much less expensive stone and pretty easy to come by. Then of course the white gold and diamonds are no problem."

"How soon could you do that?"

"I could probably have it for you by Friday, but it'll cost you. I'll have to do a lot of rush ordering."

"Price is no object. This ring was made for my girlfriend. It doesn't yet belong to me, but someday I will put it on her finger. In the meantime, I'd like to give her the next best thing."

"Not a problem. I took a lot of photographs of the piece, so I should be able to easily replicate it."

"Your work is always stellar," I say. "I probably won't even be able to tell the difference."

"Oh, you won't. I will, but I have the eye of a pro." He laughs.

"Thanks. Give me a call when it's ready, and I'll be right in to get it. In the meantime, when you get any information on its ownership, call me right away."

★ ★ ★

Later, as I'm getting ready to drive back to Snow Creek, I find myself in front of a dive bar on the outskirts of town.

It's a place I recognize. Dad brought me here on my twenty-first birthday.

★ ★ ★

"Talon Steel!" an old barkeep says. "What's it been . . . three years?"

"Almost exactly," Dad says. "This is my son Donny. Today's his twenty-first birthday."

The barkeep nods to me. "You look a lot like your brother."

"You brought Dale here?" I ask.

"Three years ago, when he turned twenty-one," Dad says. "Didn't he tell you?" Dad sits down on a barstool and nods to me to sit next to him.

"Nice to meet you," the bartender says. "I'm Luke."

"The usual," Dad says. "Two."

"You got it." Luke slides two drinks in front of us.

Dad raises his glass. "To my second born."

I grab mine and clink it to his. When will he get the idea that I'm not a fan of whiskey? But this is my dad, the man who saved my life. He means well. The least I can do is taste the stuff. I take a sip.

And I unceremoniously choke. "Damn, Dad. What is this stuff?"

"You were expecting Peach Street?"

"Of course not, but my God." Yeah, not a fan of Peach Street either, but there's no telling Dad that.

"You get used to it," Dad says. "In fact, you learn to like it on occasion."

"I'm not sure about that." I absently push the glass away from me.

Dad takes another sip and then exhales. "It takes a bit, but there's a strange beauty in the causticity of it."

"That beauty is eluding me, I'm afraid."

"Sometimes you find beauty where you least expect it," he says. "I learned a lot about myself in this place. Met a man named Mike, who in some ways I think might have been my guardian angel."

Guardian angel? Surely I didn't just hear those words from Talon Steel.

"I was older than you. Thirty-five," Dad continues. "I remember because I'd just met your mother."

I raise my eyebrows. It's no secret that my mother means the world to me. She and I are close in a way she isn't with Dale, Diana, or Brianna.

"Tell me more," I say.

"Nothing more to tell," he says, "except to remember that sometimes the most beautiful things in life aren't obvious. Not at all." He takes another sip, finishing his rotgut bourbon.

I pull the drink back toward me, pick it up, take another sip, this time holding back the grimace. For my father. For the man who rescued me all those years ago.

Talon Steel never does anything without a reason, so I vow to understand his motive in bringing me here.

I vow to always see the beauty in everything.

★ ★ ★

How quickly one forgets.

I've let all the shit that's been raining down on me the past several weeks fuck with me. I put my ethics on the back burner. I almost let Callie—the best thing that ever happened to me—go.

And now I'm lying to my mother, telling her I'm in the office doing the job she trusts me with when I'm in the city dealing with more secrets I'm keeping from her.

Stick a fork in me. I'm done.

I speed up the car. No need to go in and drink rotgut to find answers.

I already have them.

They lie at home. At the ranch. With Callie. With Mom and Dad. With Dale and Ashley.

They lie within *me*.

I pick up my phone and make a call.

CHAPTER THIRTY-ONE

Callie

"Donny?" I say into the phone.

"Change of plans," he says. "I'm on my way back to town, and I won't be in the city the rest of the week."

"What happened?"

"Nothing. I just got a big dose of what's important. That's all. So . . . how about a dinner date?"

"Sure, but—"

"No buts. I'll swing by the office and pick you up."

"My car . . ."

"Got it. I'll swing by your place and pick you up, then. In fact, I should be there right about the time you get home, so that works out great."

"Okay, Donny. Are you sure you're all right?"

"More sure than I've been in a while, baby. I can't wait to see you."

I smile into the phone. "I can't wait either."

"Love you, baby."

"Love you too."

★ ★ ★

We end up at Donny's, where he and I prepare dinner for Talon and Jade.

Yes, I'm totally serious.

Callie Pike, whose kitchen repertoire consists of Hot Pockets and Trader Joe's Moo Goo Gai Pan, is cooking dinner for her boyfriend's parents.

God help me.

"So this is your idea of a dinner date, huh?" I say to Donny.

He looks up from the lettuce he's shredding. "Darla's out of town for a while. Her mom got hurt. I didn't want to leave—"

"I'm kidding, Donny. I don't mind. It's just . . . I suck at cooking."

"You're doing great."

"I've sliced a tomato. What else you got?"

"I'm no gourmet chef either, but I'm actually having fun, Callie." He kisses my lips. "I kind of like playing house with you."

Hamburgers. Donny and I surely can handle that. Still, I'll let him man the grill. If I do it, the glorious Steel beef burgers are likely to end up as hockey pucks.

Talon and Jade are sitting on the deck, the dogs bounding around them.

"Your dad looks great," I say.

"Yeah. Nothing keeps him down for long." Donny starts squishing ground beef in his hands and shaping it into patties.

"What else can I do?" I ask.

"Slice up an onion? There's a bunch of them in the pantry." He gestures toward the door.

I've been in the pantry once before, when Mom, Rory, and I came over after Talon was shot. It's huge and well stocked with everything from onions to imported spices. I grab an onion and bring it to the cutting board I used for the tomato. I breathe through my nose to keep the fumes from getting to me.

It doesn't work. Soon my eyes feel like I've been exposed to tear gas. I sniffle.

"You okay?" Donny asks.

"Just onions."

"Breathe through your nose."

"Doesn't work." I sniffle again.

He chuckles. "You're right. It doesn't. Just an old wives' tale. I guess my mom's an old wife."

I laugh. "Don't let her hear you say that."

He tilts his head back in a roar of laughter. "No shit. She'd kick my ass." He finishes the burgers. "I'm going to get these on the grill."

I nod and pile the sliced onions on a platter with the tomatoes, lettuce, and pickle slices. Another platter holds fresh-baked buns from Ava's bakery.

★ ★ ★

Later, Donny drives me home. "You were in a good mood tonight," I say.

"Yeah. I guess I was. I am. Even though I can't sleep with you in my arms."

I lean against him, let my head rest on his shoulder. "I'm just happy to see you happy, Donny."

"How about you?" He kisses the top of my head. "You seemed happy for the most part, but I know you, Cal. You're still worried."

"Of course I am. Aren't you?"

He inhales. "Yeah, I am. Big time. Still, there's beauty in the world. My mom and dad need me whole. You need me whole."

"I need you to be you. You don't have to pretend for me."

He kisses the top of my head again. "Your hair always smells so good."

"Nice pivot."

He sighs. "I know. Of course I'm worried, but I had a kick in the pants today as I was leaving Grand Junction."

"Oh?"

"Yeah. I just remembered what's important. You. Mom and Dad. My brother and sisters. And . . ."

"And what?"

"And me, Callie. I need to stay whole for myself as much as for others."

"You're whole, Donny. You're the strongest man I know."

He doesn't reply. Does he not believe that? I pull back, meet his gaze.

His gorgeous hazel eyes are troubled. "You're an angel, Callie Pike, but there are many guys stronger than I am."

"I'll never believe it."

"God, I love you." He pulls me back toward him, and our mouths slide together in a searing kiss.

It's so hard and passionate that I wonder if we're going to fuck in Donny's car, but—to my disappointment—he pulls back.

"I love you," he says.

"I love you more." I smile.

"Not possible." He brushes his lips over mine once more and then opens his car door.

In a flash, he's at the passenger side, opening the door for me.

Such a gentleman. I grab his hand and exit the car.

"Thank you," he says.

"For what?"

"For helping me. For helping me see the beauty in everything. I meant it when I said you're an angel."

"I'm hardly an angel."

"And I'm hardly the strongest man in the world, but Callie, you make me feel like I could be."

His eyes are so green in the moonlight, and I stand on my toes and kiss his lips gently. "We're better together, aren't we?"

"We are." He walks me to the door, kisses me again, and then leaves.

From the window, I watch him drive away.

So much I need to tell him. But not tonight. I won't spoil what's left of his good mood.

What will he do, though, when I tell him the new theory Rory, Jesse, and I came up with? That Diana was targeted and drugged on purpose?

We could very well be wrong.

Or we could very well be right.

CHAPTER THIRTY-TWO

Donny

"Dad, I have to talk to you."

Dad is in his office typing something into his computer. He turns. "Sure, son. Are you okay?"

I take a seat across from his desk.

Hours ago, I vowed to continue to see the beauty in everything. My mood reflected that.

Now? All I can see is my father—my big, strong father who could be dead if not for some random ranch hand out for a jog.

I'm not ready to lose him.

"No, I'm not okay. My father was shot. And then poisoned. I'm far from okay."

"I'm going to recover fully, Donny. I'm going to be fine."

"I know, and I'm grateful, but Dale and I are going to find out who did this. I swear."

"You leave that to the pros."

"We have resources the pros don't."

"Don..."

"It wasn't the pros who found Dale and me. Got Dale and me out of that wretched place. Saved our lives. It was you. You, Dad."

He nods. What else can he do? I'm right on target.

"Dale's got a wife to think about now, and you've got Callie."

I nod. "I love her, Dad."

"That was pretty clear tonight. Your mother and I are thrilled for you."

"Are you? You don't think it's too fast?"

Dad smiles—that smile I saw so often as a kid. The smile that said *I've got your back*. "I had this same talk with your brother only weeks ago. I fell hard and fast for your mother, and look how things worked out for us. When you know, you know."

I nod. "Speaking of Callie . . ." I pull the velvet box out of my coat pocket.

I texted Dale earlier that I was going to ask Dad about the ring. He agreed that we could trust our father.

Dad raises his eyebrows. "Ideas already?"

I clear my throat. "I *am* going to marry Callie, but this isn't what you think it is. I mean, it is, if possible, but—I know I'm not making any sense."

"Just start at the beginning."

I open the box and hand it to Dad. "This was left for me in a safe-deposit box in my name. The key to which was left in my bathroom. In this house, Dad. Someone got in this house."

"*What?*" Dad stands, one hand over the wound near his liver.

"Sit, Dad, please. I've got Monarch looking into it."

"Fuck," Dad says. "Fuck. Is history repeating itself?"

I jerk backward in my chair. "What's that supposed to mean?"

He shakes his head. "I can't. I can't think about that now."

"Dad, you can't dump that on me and—"

"Enough, Don."

"All right, all right. But sit down, for God's sake. I can tell you're hurting."

"I'm fine," he says harshly. "Fucking Monarch, for what I pay them..."

Dad's cheeks turn ruddy. He's pissed, and rightfully so. I'm pissed too.

"I'll call first thing in the morning and check in with Monarch. In the meantime, take a look at this ring. Please."

The box is still clutched in his hand. He pulls the ring out and examines it closely. "It's beautiful, but I don't know anything about gemstones."

"Neither do I, but Drew does. It's a pumpkin diamond, the second-rarest type of diamond in the world. It's worth a mint. He told me to have it insured for half a million."

Dad's eyebrows rise.

"The initials inside are LW," I say. "Do you know any LW?"

Dad wrinkles his forehead, still staring at the ring. "I don't see anything."

"They're hard to see. Do you have a loupe?"

"A what?"

"A jeweler's loupe. You know."

"Do I look like I keep a jeweler's loupe in my office? I'm a rancher."

Good point. "A magnifying glass, then. You know what? Never mind. It doesn't matter. The initials are there. LW. I saw them. Do they ring a bell to you?"

"Not offhand... Actually... Yeah. But that doesn't make any sense. They didn't have that kind of money."

"Uh... Dad, you're going to have to say all the words. I don't know what the hell you're talking about."

"Right. Sorry. My grandmother. My mother's mother. Her name was Lucy Warren. No. Lucy Wade. My father changed my mother's birth certificate."

"You're talking in weird circles, Dad."

Dad rubs his forehead. "I'm sorry. I'm tired, and these meds..."

"Let's get you to bed." I rise.

"No, no. I'm fine. God, there's so much you don't know."

"I know that, Dad. Maybe it's time you let me in the loop."

"It's a long story, Donny. I'm not up for it tonight."

No, he's definitely not. "Just tell me who Lucy Wade or Warren or whoever is."

"She was your great-grandmother. And her married name was Wade. It's a long story why my father changed my mother's maiden name. But either way, LW are the initials of my maternal grandmother. But this can't be her ring. My mother didn't grow up with money. Not the kind of money that could afford a ring like this, anyway."

"So *all* the money comes from your dad's side?"

"Yeah. All of it. My mother's parents lived in a suburb of Denver called Westminster. She was on a scholarship to college, where she met my father."

"How come you never talk about your parents?"

Dad inhales and rubs his chin. "I don't remember much about my mother, Donny. She... Man, this is a long story. Suffice it to say she checked out when I was around ten years old."

I gulp. "Right around the time..."

"Yes. When I was taken. She never got over that. The stress forced her into preterm labor with your aunt Marj, who wasn't expected to survive, but miracle of all miracles, she did. My mother was never the same after I came home, and she... Well, she left a year or so later."

"What do you mean she left?"

Dad inhales. "I guess we're talking about this now."

"It's okay, Dad. We don't have to."

"No, I can tell you at least this much. We thought she died. That's what my father told us. In reality, she declined mentally, and Dad put her in an institution."

For a moment, my head spins. I can't form a thought.

"You all right?" Dad asks.

"Would *you* be?"

"Don, I've told your brother this, and now I'll tell you. Your mother, uncles, aunts, and I made a conscious decision after you and Dale came here and before Dee was born. We decided to mask the horrid parts of the past. None of it would affect you anyway, so why should you have to carry it?"

"Except it *is* affecting us, Dad. For God's sake, someone tried to kill you."

"We don't know if that was related to our history. Besides, they weren't successful."

"But what if they are the next time? Or what if it's Uncle Joe? Or Ryan? Or Marjorie?" I gulp. "Or Mom?"

Dad's eyes go dark and fierce. "Nothing will happen to your mother on my watch."

"On mine, either. Which is why Dale and I *will* figure this out."

"Donny..."

"Dad, we're all-in now. Someone went to the trouble to get this ring to me. To..." I shake my head. "I don't get it. Why leave a safe-deposit box key? Why not just leave the ring? They obviously got in the house."

"Would you leave this ring sitting around?" Dad asks.

"Good point." I sigh.

Dad clears his throat. "Someone wanted you to have that ring. If it was truly my grandmother's, it should have gone to my mother and then to Marjorie."

"There are a lot of LWs in the world," I say. "It could just as easily belong to someone else."

"Then why would someone leave it with you?"

"Hell if I know." I rise. "I'd like you to put it in the safe. For now, we don't even know if it belongs to us."

Dad nods. "Good enough."

"And Dad?"

"Yeah?"

"If it turns out that it belongs to the family, I'd like to purchase it and give it to Callie. She's meant to have it. I felt it as soon as I saw it."

He stands, takes the box from me, and moves toward the wall to the right of his desk. "Well, someone wanted you to have it. I don't see why anyone would object."

"Thanks, Dad."

On the wall hangs an oil painting of a pure-black horse. Dad's horse. His name was Phoenix. Dad says he never had another horse that understood him so well.

I remember Phoenix. Dad taught me to ride on a much tamer animal, but once I could handle the best horses on the ranch, he let me ride Phoenix.

"He was gorgeous," I say.

"Your aunt Marj wanted me to name him Barney." Dad chuckles.

"No way." A smile tugs at the corners of my lips.

"She did. I almost let her get away with it. She had me wrapped around her little finger." He sighs, staring at the painting, as if he's talking to it instead of me. "I think it was

Marj who truly saved me when I returned. She was such a strong and beautiful baby. She helped me remember there was still beauty in the world."

Still beauty in the world.

His words speak to me more than he knows. I've vowed to remember the same since driving by his old dive bar this afternoon.

"Let me get that for you, Dad." I walk to him and remove the painting from the wall.

Behind the painting is the wall safe. I know the combination. We all do. Dad entrusted it to each of us when we turned eighteen.

The numbers are committed to my memory, but I've never once opened it.

Never.

But…

Surely there's nothing in there that could shed light on any of this. Otherwise, Dad wouldn't have given us the combination.

He opens the safe carefully and sets the box inside. Then he closes it, locks it, and replaces the painting of Phoenix.

Phoenix.

The bird that rises from the ashes.

The way Dad rose from his past. The way Dale and I did as well.

Except now, I have a feeling of foreboding.

A feeling that we're burning into ashes once more, and then we'll have to rise once again.

CHAPTER THIRTY-THREE

Callie

After the rest of the week passes in a blur, luck appears to be on our side Saturday morning. After a fitful night of sleeping, Rory and I woke early, ate a quick breakfast, and made it into town with Dusty and Zach in tow.

And who is manning the reception desk at Doc Sheraton's? None other than Brittany Sheraton herself.

How did we not know this?

We have animals on our small ranch, some of which required treatment after the fire. We should have known Brittany was back in town.

"We need to see Doc Sheraton," Rory says to Brittany. "We just rescued these two dogs, and they need an exam and their distemper shots. They're up to date on rabies."

Brittany flounces her bleached-blond curls. "Do you have an appointment?"

"No, but we didn't want to wait until Monday."

"My dad's really busy this morning, and we close at noon on Saturdays."

"Which is why we're here first thing this morning," I say, trying not to sound too snide.

I doubt I'm doing a good job. In front of me stands the woman who most likely impersonated Rory and got into our safe-deposit box.

Already I want to go off on her.

Rory's a lot nicer than I am—or at least she's a much better actress.

"Would you mind checking with him?" she asks sweetly. "We came all the way from our ranch."

"I'm afraid—"

Doc Sheraton bustles into the reception area then. "If it isn't the Pike sisters. I thought I heard voices." He kneels down and pets the dogs. "And who do we have here?"

"Dusty," I say, gesturing, "and Zach."

"Well, aren't they a couple of happy pups! About two years old, I'd say?"

"That's what the shelter told us." Rory dazzles him with a smile.

"Let's bring them on back and have a look."

"Thank you, Doc," Rory gushes. "We appreciate you seeing us without an appointment."

"Not a problem. There's not much on the book this morning."

I dart an angry gaze toward Brittany. She's looking down at her lap.

"Can you go back with the dogs?" I ask Rory. "I need to make a quick . . . phone call."

Rory meets my gaze with understanding. "Of course. Just join us when you can." She takes Zach's leash, and Doc Sheraton takes Dusty's.

I stalk toward Brittany's desk.

Stay calm. Don't put her on the defensive.

"Booked, huh?" I begin with.

"Sorry." Her cheeks are red. "I was looking at Monday

morning." She taps on her computer. "Just had the wrong day on the screen."

"Wasn't it lucky that your dad came out, then? So we got in today?"

"Yeah. Lucky." She smiles. Sort of.

I take a seat and scooch it up next to her desk. "So tell me, Brittany. What have you been up to lately?"

She clears her throat. "Nothing."

"Oh? I don't recall you working here the last time I came by." I have no idea when that was, but I'm thinking she won't know that.

"I've only been here a few weeks. I just moved back to Snow Creek, and Dad gave me the job."

"Isn't that convenient that you got a job right away?"

"Well, I know the boss pretty well." She laughs. A nervous laugh.

"Someone else just came back to town recently," I say.

"Oh?"

"Yeah. Pat Lamone. Remember him?"

The redness extends down to her neck at the mention of Lamone. "From high school, right? He left after his junior year?"

I nod. "I believe you're right."

"I didn't know he was back in town."

Right. Because I was born yesterday. "He's working at the hotel."

She nods and then pretends to be thoroughly engrossed in the copy of *Dogster* magazine sitting on her desk.

"You and he used to be pretty tight," I say.

"Pat and me? Not really."

"Hmm. I'm thinking Daddy might be interested to know

how you stole his tranquilizer gun and drugged Rory and me ten years ago."

She gulps audibly. "You can't prove any of that."

"You sure about that?"

"No. No." She looks frantically toward the closed door heading to the exam rooms in the back. "You can't. If you could, you'd have done it a long time ago."

"What have you been doing since you've been back, Brittany? Make any trips to Denver lately? To a bank?"

She picks up her phone. "I'm calling the cops."

"Please do."

She bangs her phone down on the desk. "What the hell do you want?"

"You know exactly what I want. Show me. Show me the fake ID that got you into Rory's safe-deposit box."

"I . . . I don't know what you're talking about."

"Sure you do. Or you'd be a lot madder than you are now. What the hell has Lamone ever done for you? Why are you helping him?"

"I don't know what you're talking about. Daddy!"

"Good, good. Bring Daddy out here. I think he'll be interested to know what you've been up to."

"Damn it, Callie. What do you want?"

"Give me the ID, Brittany."

"I don't have any fake ID."

"Then how? Tell me how you two got into that safe-deposit box and stole property belonging to Rory and me."

She opens her mouth, and—

Doc Sheraton booms through the door again. "Come on back, Callie. Dusty's a little nervous, and I need both you and Rory to hold her while I give her the shot."

Lousy timing, Doc.

I give Brittany a look that I hope says *this isn't over*, and I follow Doc back.

"Hey, Cal," Rory says. "Dusty's really nervous. She's already peed everywhere."

"Sorry about that."

"No worries," Doc says. "It happens a lot. Especially with rescues. If you can hold her and Rory can talk to her, that will help. Rory's voice seems to soothe her."

Not surprising.

I love this gorgeous dog, and I'll do what I can to make her more at ease and keep her healthy.

But I also know something else.

When we get back out to reception, Brittany will be gone.

CHAPTER THIRTY-FOUR

Donny

I lift my eyebrows when I find Dad at the breakfast table Saturday morning. Mom is nowhere to be found. I've slept a little later than usual. Eight o'clock a.m. After tossing and turning for several hours, I finally fell off near four o'clock, so I'm still pretty darned tired.

Still no word from Monarch Security or Drew, despite both their assurances that they'd have information within forty-eight hours, though I did see Drew yesterday when I picked up the new ring. It's nearly as gorgeous as the one nestled inside Dad's safe.

"Shouldn't you be resting?" I ask Dad.

"I rested enough for a lifetime in that damned hospital bed," he says. "You're usually a little more of an early riser than this."

"I had trouble sleeping."

"Insomnia? Is this new?"

"Happens from time to time. Where's Mom?"

"Over at Marjorie's. Big party tonight."

Shit. That's right. Dad's big welcome home party. Which means I'd better get some shut-eye between now and then or I'll be falling asleep. Fat chance of that happening, though, with everything else that's going on.

"I hope you're planning on doing a lot of resting today, then," I say to Dad. "They're going to expect to see a lot of you at this big shindig."

Dad smiles. "I suppose you're right. Your mother and her parties . . ."

"Yeah. Seems a bit much sometimes."

"Really? You used to love them."

He's not wrong. I had a devil-may-care attitude for most of my life. I chose not to dwell on my past, but instead, I embraced the present. And my present was pretty darned good. As a Steel, I had the best of everything, and I never wanted for anything. Always the present. Never the past.

Until now.

The present is a big fucking mess.

I wish I could confide more in the man sitting across from me. But damn, he just got out of the hospital. Someone fucking shot my father. My father could be dead right now but for circumstances that day.

Not only that—someone tried to do him in while he was in the hospital getting treatment. Atropine poisoning.

More research to do.

And who do I trust? Besides Dale, Brock, and Callie . . . I just don't know.

My father . . . My father who fucking rescued us that day.

And I'm not sure I can trust him.

Was the bullet really meant for Uncle Joe? Makes me wonder, because whoever did it obviously came back and tried to finish the job on Dad in the hospital.

And here's the part that scares me the most. Perhaps the bullet *was* meant for Uncle Joe, but there was another one coming for Dad. And there might be one more coming for

Uncle Ryan, Uncle Bryce. Aunt Marj.

My mother.

Oh, God.

What the hell is happening to my family?

"What's bothering you, Don?" Dad's voice is low, serious.

If only I could tell him the whole story—more than just the safe-deposit box and the ring. If only I could confide in this amazing man who saved my life.

But I can't.

"I'm good. Just exhausted."

"That may work on anyone else in the family, son, but it won't work on me."

I drop my mouth open to speak but then close it.

"Don't forget that I know what you've been through. Don't forget that I've been through it too. You're different from your brother, and I don't pretend to understand everything about you. But you are my son, and I know when something isn't right."

"It's nothing, Dad. Really. I just haven't heard from Monarch or Drew yet, and it's got me on edge."

He nods. "I'm sorry I haven't asked before now. Those meds keep me kind of groggy."

"You concentrate on healing," I say. "That's your only job right now. Please don't worry about me. I'm fine."

"I know it wasn't easy for you to leave Denver and come back here to work with your mother."

"Turns out I'm not going to work with her at all. She's leaving."

"That surprised me as much as it did you, believe me," Dad says. "But I support her decision. When you look your mortality in the eye, you realize what's important."

"Dad, you looked your mortality in the eye a long time ago."

"I did. But I was a boy then, like you were."

"No, you weren't. What about the military?"

Dad's eyes go narrow. "Okay. You got me. I didn't give a shit about my mortality until I met your mother."

"I know. I'm sorry."

"But you have always given a shit about *your* mortality, Donny. Your brother, not so much. But you? You live in the present, not the past. Which is why I know something's bothering you. Something's bothering you right in the here and now."

You've always given a shit about your mortality.

Not that one time. I erase the images from my mind. Why, when the present sucks, do I dredge up the past, which also sucked?

I shake my head. "I'm fine."

Megan, Darla's temporary replacement, whisks into the kitchen then. "Good morning." She nods to me. "What would you like for breakfast?"

"Just some toast, Megan. Thanks."

Dad eyes me solemnly. Dead giveaway. Good job. I usually eat a lot for breakfast, and Dad knows that.

He won't badger me, though. Not while Megan's here.

"Could I have some more coffee?" he asks.

"Sure thing, Mr. Steel." Megan pours Dad another cup.

"I'd get it myself but . . ." Dad smiles.

"You stay off your feet as much as possible," Megan says. "Mrs. Steel's orders."

"Yes, Jade's orders, when she's throwing a huge party for me tonight where I will be expected to talk to everyone.

Interesting how I'm going to have to stay off my feet." Dad laughs.

Even I, in my current state, can't help a slight chuckle. "That's Mom, but she'll probably set up a throne for you on the deck so you can hold court."

Dad rolls his eyes. "That's what I'm afraid of."

My phone buzzes then, and I grab it.

It's a text. From Dale.

Come to the guesthouse. Now if you can.

CHAPTER THIRTY-FIVE

Callie

"Shocking," I say quietly to Rory after we're done in the exam room and we come back out to the reception area to make the next appointment for our dogs.

Brittany, as I suspected, is nowhere to be found.

"I guess I'll make the appointments myself." Doc Sheraton walks behind Brittany's desk and taps on the computer. "I'll need to see them both back here in a couple of weeks just to make sure there aren't any issues. How does two weeks from today sound?"

"Sure," Rory says. "Saturdays are good for us."

"Great." He scribbles an appointment on a card and hands it to Rory.

"Thanks."

"Where's Brittany?" I ask.

"Got me. Usually she lets me know if she's taking a break. I'm sure she'll be back in a few minutes."

"Yes, I'm sure."

Rory darts me a stink-eye at my snide tone.

"Doc Sheraton," Rory says. "When did Brittany come back to town?"

"A couple of weeks ago. She and her boyfriend moved back here."

"Boyfriend?" I ask.

"Yeah, a guy who used to live here a while ago. His name is Pat."

"Pat Lamone?" I say, trying to sound normal.

"Yeah. That sounds right. Nice guy."

Right. I knew she was lying to me. "How long have they been together?"

"Several months, I think. They were both up in Laramie, working, and they got together."

That sounds like a manufactured story to me, but I keep my mouth shut.

"We're very happy for her," Rory says with a smile.

Doc Sheraton returns her smile, looking a little besotted. Rory has that effect on men. And women. And anything in between.

"Where are they staying?" I ask.

"Brittany's staying with me, and Pat has rented a room somewhere in town."

I nod. I already knew where Pat was.

"What's Pat up to?"

"I believe Brittany said he's working over at the Snow Creek Inn. Evening hours, I believe."

Still no new information.

Rory gazes at her wrist and then turns on her dazzling smile once more. "You know, Doc, I think I may have left something in the exam room. Would you mind if I go back in for a second?"

"Not at all. Go right ahead. I'll just stay here and chat with Callie."

"Thank you so much. You're a gem." She dazzles him with a smile once more and then slides back through the door.

I'm not exactly sure what she's up to, but I know it's my job to keep Doc Sheraton engaged.

"So . . . do you get a lot of rescues from the Lifeline Shelter in Grand Junction?"

"Here and there," he says. "It's a long way to go to rescue a dog."

"But so many of those amazing animals need homes."

"I know. I wish more people were like you and your sister. And I wish more people here in Snow Creek got their animals spayed and neutered. I can't tell you how many barn litters we have, and then we have to find homes for the puppies or kittens."

I nod. And I've effectively run out of things to talk to a veterinarian about.

"So how are your parents doing, Callie?" Doc Sheraton gives me the obligatory *I feel sorry for you* head tilt.

Here comes the pity party. But I have to use it to my advantage.

"It's tough," I say. "We lost a lot in that fire."

"If you need any help, with your animals or anything, don't hesitate to reach out."

"That's very kind of you." I force a smile and hope it looks genuine. "I'll let my mom and dad know that you're here for them."

"Please do. Everyone in town is. We all feel terrible about what happened."

I have to hold back the peristalsis in my esophagus. Otherwise, I'm going to puke from all the sympathy I'm getting. Doc Sheraton doesn't mean any harm. He's always been a nice guy, as far as I know. But I do have to wonder . . . How can a nice guy have a daughter who runs around impersonating other people and breaking into safe-deposit boxes? Not to mention stealing tranquilizer guns and shooting high school girls with them, and then watching as her boyfriend disrobes them and photographs them in compromising positions.

Nature versus nurture. It's a timeless debate.

Rory bustles out then. Thank God, because I will truly hurl if I have to play the pitiable young lady for one more second.

"I found my bracelet!" She holds it up.

I'm pretty sure Rory wasn't wearing a bracelet when we went in there, but of course I don't say anything. Apparently, she had one in her purse.

"I'm so glad." Doc Sheraton smiles. "I guess I'll see you two young ladies in a couple of weeks for the dogs' next appointment."

"Yes, we'll be here." Rory dazzles with a smile once more.

We get Zach and Dusty out of the vet's office and walk the block to where our car is parked.

"Tell you what," Rory says. "Let's take a walk around the park. Let these two do their business and stuff. Plus . . ."

"What? I know that's the bracelet Raine gave you, and I also know you weren't wearing it this morning."

"Nope. It was still in my purse from when I took it off a week ago. But I wanted to go back in there, Callie. I had a feeling."

"What feeling?"

"I actually went through the exam room and into Doc Sheraton's office. I knew I didn't have a lot of time, but I was just looking for something, anything, that might give us a clue to what's going on with Brittany and Pat Lamone."

"And did you find anything?"

"I found an address in Laramie. I wrote it down."

"What good is an address in Laramie going to do us?"

"Probably nothing, but it's a start. Pat and Brittany were both in Laramie when they got together, and now they're here."

"True enough."

"And then tonight… I guess we're all going to be at the Steels' big party. I'd skip it, but I already told Jesse I'd sing."

"I can't skip it, of course, because of Donny. Why would you want to skip it anyway, Rory?"

"Are you kidding? I sure as heck don't feel like partying. And now that I'm no longer in a relationship, everyone and his brother and sister are going to be hitting on me."

I scoff. "Since when is that a bad thing?"

"It's a bad thing when I've got all this other shit on my mind. I mean, who knows when those photographs are going to turn up somewhere to haunt us?"

"First of all, we may have his copies. Remember? And second, if it's money he's after, he won't get anything by putting the photos out before he makes a demand."

"I know you're right, but…"

"I know." There's really nothing more to say. I get it. She doesn't want to be exposed to the whole town, and neither do I.

"Does he know when my birthday is? Because if I were even one second younger than eighteen when those were taken…"

"A birth date is easy to find, and he obviously has yours, because someone got a fake ID."

"It doesn't have to have my actual birth date on it. I doubt the bank would check that closely." She sighs. "I guess these guys have had enough of a walk. Let's get home. They have way more area to run around there. Besides, I have to rehearse with

Jesse and the band this afternoon."

"And I . . ."

"What?"

I shake my head. "I have nothing to do. Donny will probably be helping set up for the party. What the hell do I do this afternoon?"

"Actually, why don't you do some research? On this address? Can you get into the office?"

"I can. I have a key. And a card, and the code. But why would I be going in on a Saturday?"

"Maybe Donny gave you some work."

"I don't know . . ."

"Just text him. See if he cares."

"All right." I send Donny a quick text. This time I make sure I hit send, and I make sure it shows that it went through.

But he doesn't get back to me right away.

Which is odd. Especially on a Saturday when I know he's home.

"He's probably just busy," Rory says, as if reading my mind.

"Probably."

Except that something feels off.

And not in a good way.

CHAPTER THIRTY-SIX

Donny

Change of plans. Meet
Brock and me at the winery.

I read the text from Dale that comes in as I start the engine of my truck. The winery. Will anyone be there on a Saturday? Surely there will be employees there, as wine is fermenting. What about tastings? And Uncle Ryan? We don't really want to bring him in on this.

Dale wouldn't have told me to meet him at the winery if there were any problems.

Twenty minutes later, I'm at the winery, and Dale and Brock are standing outside the door.

"What's up?" I say, slamming the truck door.

"We needed to get out of the guesthouse," Dale says. "Willow was having a hard time, having a crying spree about Dennis, and Ashley needed to be with her. I didn't think it would be a good idea for all of us to be there talking about… well, shit that someone in mourning really doesn't want to hear about."

Ice pricks the back of my neck. "What are you talking about?"

"Brock and I went back up to the border last night."

My stomach churns. "And . . . what did you find?"

"We're not exactly sure," Brock says, "but . . ."

"For God's sake, just tell me."

"Bones," Dale says. "And from Brock's and my limited biological expertise, we think they're probably human."

Puke gurgles in the back of my throat. "I suppose it's not surprising, given the stench."

"Except that these bones have been there for a long time. They didn't have any smell, and they were just bones. No flesh."

"None at all?"

"No. Which makes us think they may have been planted." Brock rubs his chin.

"But what about the smell?"

"I suppose it could have been planted too," Dale says.

"What the hell else smells like that?"

"Hell if I know," Dale says. "But there was no evidence of decaying human flesh anywhere in that barn."

"No evidence that we saw, anyway," I say.

"Don, you know as well as I do that if the bodies had been buried deep enough, we wouldn't smell them. And there was absolutely no evidence of any decaying body anywhere we could see."

"Right . . . Anywhere that we could see."

"Dude," Brock says, "are you suggesting like they were on another plane or something?"

"Where the heck did you get that?" I shake my head. "No . . . but I'm wondering. Now that I think about it. The ceiling of the barn . . . There was a ceiling."

"I'm not sure I ever looked up," Dale says.

"I did, though. And it was something that I thought was

weird for a minute before you guys got there. Instead of rafters, there was an actual ceiling."

"Are you suggesting that there are decaying bodies up there?" Brock covers his mouth.

"I'm suggesting maybe we take a look."

"You're not getting me up there," Brock says.

"I don't really want any of us to go up there," I say, "but who else do we trust?"

"If they're up there," Dale says, "wouldn't there still be evidence? Like . . . you know . . . drippings or something?"

This time my hand goes to my mouth. This is all too disgusting.

"Maybe I'll do some research," I say, once the gag reflex is under control. "Find out if there are any missing persons in that area."

"Yeah," Brock says, "because if what you say about the smell is true, the bodies can't really be that old, can they?"

"I wouldn't think so," Dale says.

"Let's just get through this damned party tonight," I say. "Then I guess tomorrow we go back."

"Not how I was expecting to spend my Sunday," Brock says.

"Why? You got a hot date?"

"I may."

"Are you seeing somebody new that we don't know about?" Dale asks.

"Not yet. But after tonight, I figure I may be."

"No. Please say you're not thinking about Rory."

"Why not? She's the hottest thing walking."

"She just got out of a relationship, Brock."

"Yeah . . . and I love being the rebound guy."

Leave it to Brock to be able to go from possibly finding decaying bodies to picking up his latest conquest without so much as a transition. I used to be the same way. As the founding member of the Three Rake-a-teers, I can't really fault Brock.

He's also so young. Twenty-four as opposed to my thirty-two. And Dale's thirty-five.

And . . . he's not in love. Both Dale and I are, and it's funny how once you find that person who you fall for—who you can't imagine your life without—things change. You want to make the world a better place. You want to make your family better.

And whatever's going on in our present right now is *not* making our family better.

"Honestly, cuz," Dale says, "I don't know how you can talk about picking up a woman when we're dealing with this shit."

"I'd say I have a one-track mind," Brock says, "but you already know that. But seriously, I'm as freaked out as you guys are about this whole thing. Your father took a shot that may have been meant for my father. Or maybe they want all the Steel brothers dead. And who the hell is hiding dead bodies on our property? You think this doesn't get to me?" His cheeks go red. "I'm just not ready to abandon everything else about life while we deal with this."

Again, I understand Brock's attitude. It was my own a mere month ago.

"Ease up, Dale," I say. "We can't let ourselves live like this."

"I know that." Dale shakes his head. "And I won't. For Ashley's sake. For all our sakes. I can't let myself get inside my own head too much. You all know how good I am at that."

"Yeah." What I don't tell my brother is that I understand him more than ever now. For some reason, the mess of our present has dredged up our past in ways that I never allowed myself to think about before. My brother continually lived in the past, and he only broke free of it recently. Me? I didn't forget the past. I just didn't let myself think of it. So why in the hell is it at the forefront of my mind now?

Then there's Brock. Uncle Joe in miniature. Except not miniature. He's every bit as big and tall as Uncle Joe. Brock, who lived the charmed Steel life from birth. Just like Diana and Brianna did. Just like all our cousins did, except for Henry, but he's too young to remember his former life.

There's still a part of Brock that isn't quite accepting what we've stumbled onto. He can't, because he's never had anything horrible happen in his life. So of course he's thinking about getting some ass tonight. Hell, a month ago, I'd have been thinking the same thing.

"Just go easy on Rory," I say. "Breakups aren't easy."

"Like you'd know," he says.

He's not wrong. I've never been serious about a woman in my life until now. I can't imagine a breakup with Callie, even though I was determined to let her go mere days ago. In the end, I couldn't, of course. Giving up the love of your life? It's not really ever an option, no matter what the circumstances are.

It wasn't an option for Dale, and it's not an option for me.

But Brock isn't looking for the love of his life. He's looking for some action, and he's looking for it with Callie's sister.

I don't want to see Rory hurt.

"Every eligible young lady in town will be at that party tonight," I say. "Maybe you could look around. Rory will probably be singing with Jesse anyway."

"I suppose I could look around," Brock says. "But there's

not a woman alive who's hotter than Rory Pike."

"Except her sister," I say.

"Love is clouding your eyes, cuz," Brock says. "Callie is gorgeous, but Rory . . . That girl is model material."

"Just go easy on her," I say again.

"I've never in my life done anything without a woman's consent," Brock says. "And fuck you for thinking that I would."

"That's not what I meant, and you know it. I'm just saying that I care about Callie, so by extension I care about Rory. I don't want to see her hurt. She's probably vulnerable right now after the breakup with Raine. She may not be looking for anything like a one-nighter."

"And if she's not, I'll move on."

"Good enough," Dale says. "You can't protect Rory, Don. Not if she doesn't want to be protected."

I nod. My brother is right.

But I have a bad feeling about this party tonight.

And I wonder . . .

If most people from town will be here . . . does that mean Pat Lamone is coming?

And if he does . . . What will happen?

With everyone here at our place, the time would be right to do some searching around town. Is that what Lamone will be up to? And if so, I want someone on his tail. I pick up my phone, thinking.

And spy a text I missed from Callie earlier.

I'm going into the office to do some research. Hope that's okay.

CHAPTER THIRTY-SEVEN

Callie

It's weird being in the office on a Saturday.

I feel like I need to keep looking over my shoulder, though that's silly. No one else is here. No one even knows I'm here other than Donny. And it's strange that he never returned my text.

My phone buzzes.

"Speak of the devil," I say out loud.

Yeah, that's fine. But I don't like
the idea of you being alone.

Strange. Why would he be concerned about me at the courthouse and city administration building? He knows it's Saturday. No one's here.

I text him back quickly.

No worries. I'm fine.
Just getting started.

But then something pricks the back of my neck.

Why *do* I feel like I need to be looking over my shoulder? And why would Donny think it's not good that I'm alone here?

What secrets does this building hold?

I already know one. It's owned by Henry Simpson. Well, not technically Henry Simpson, but a trust for his benefit. Mental note: check into Henry and the building later. First... The address Rory found in Doc Sheraton's office.

Easy enough. Google Maps will show me a picture of it.

I fire up my computer, make sure the VPN is up and running, as well as my firewall and all other security systems, and then I type in the address.

Huh. That's strange. It's vacant land.

Google is pretty good at keeping their records up to date, so why would Doc Sheraton be keeping an address of vacant land in his office?

Whatever it is, it's obviously not the place where Pat Lamone and Brittany were staying, unless they were camping out. I so cannot see Brittany Sheraton living the rugged life.

I shrug. No harm done. Although Rory wasted her dazzling smile for nothing.

Or maybe not. I have access to all Colorado state databases. This piece of property is in Wyoming.

Will Doc Sheraton be at the party tonight? Was he at the last Steel party?

Honestly, I don't remember. I had eyes only for Donny that night, even though I spent a lot of time being pissed at him for leaving me in the closet.

There were a lot of people there—almost everyone from town—so it's probable that Doc Sheraton was there.

Doesn't really matter.

Okay, then. Since I'm already here, time to research the trust for the benefit of Henry Simpson.

I start tapping keys on the computer.

And I get…

Nothing.

Apparently trusts are not public information.

Just to be sure, I check out the legal research websites. Trusts are not recorded anywhere, so they are not available to the public. As a would-be law student, I probably should have known that. Donny could have told me. So much for finding out more about Henry and this building.

No big deal. Back to Doc Sheraton. I flash back to the initial research I did for Donny regarding liens. Doc Sheraton's veterinary office is located on business property that has a lien by the Steel Trust, like almost all business properties in the city with the exception of Ava's bakery.

Doc Sheraton may have answers for me. If only Rory were here. She could get him to talk.

I'm not going to ask him about any liens on his business property, though. I can't. Donny hasn't asked me to talk to any of the townspeople about my research, and I won't go behind his back. However… I *can* pump Doc Sheraton about information on Brittany and Pat. After all, this morning Brittany claimed she didn't know Pat.

Doc Sheraton closes the office at noon, so he's probably home. I do a quick search to double-check his address, and then I gather my purse and my sweater, wrap it around my shoulders, and head out, making sure to lock up carefully.

Saturday afternoon in Snow Creek is pretty dead. Some of the small businesses close both days of the weekend, and others are only open until noon. Ava's bakery is open, but there's a sign in the window saying she's closing early for a family event.

Of course. The notorious Steel party tonight.

Rita's is open, and though I could use a cup of coffee, since I haven't been sleeping well, I bypass the café and head straight to the residential area and to Doc Sheraton's house. My heart beats faster than normal. Why? There's nothing strange about what I'm doing. No reason to be scared of Doc Sheraton. Rory and I just saw him this morning. But for some reason, I'm freaked.

I knock on the door.

It opens and—

I gasp. Standing before me is none other than Pat Lamone, a ball cap hiding most of his dark hair.

Now I know why my heart was beating fast, why I was fearful. On some level, I must have known he was here.

"Callie," he says. "What the hell are you doing here?"

I gulp back the fright that is trying to overwhelm me. I won't give him the satisfaction. "I'll ask you the same question. What the hell are *you* doing here?"

"Not that it's any of your business, but Brittany and I are . . . seeing each other."

I feign surprise. "Really? That's odd, since I saw Brittany this morning and she claimed to hardly remember you. She didn't even know you were back in town."

His cheeks redden. Ha! I got him.

"She was just . . . I'm sure she was just nervous."

"About what? About the fact that she was talking to one of the women she shot with her father's tranquilizer gun ten years ago?"

He doesn't reply right away.

"Cat got your tongue, Lamone?"

"You can't prove any of that."

"I can prove you're an asshole. Did you really think Donny

Steel was going to bring charges against me for spilling coffee on you?"

"I've got some burns."

I shake my head. "You're something else. I know exactly why you called Donny. For the same reason that you lied about Rory and me and our ties to you. The same reason you told the same lies to Raine. You're trying to mess with Rory's and my relationships."

"You think so? If that's true, I guess I was successful with Rory."

"She and Raine were over before you came back to town. I won't let you take credit for that breakup."

He scoffs. "You won't *let* me?"

This is going nowhere fast. "Just get Doc for me. Or get the hell out of my way and I'll find him myself."

"I think he's out back."

Pat shuts the door in my face.

The door opens again a few seconds later, and Doc Sheraton stands before me. "Callie, is everything okay with the new dogs?"

"Yeah, I was just wondering if you had a minute."

"Sure. Do you want to come in?"

Pat is inside, which means Brittany is probably also inside. "Could we talk out here?"

"I suppose so. Let me grab a jacket." He returns a minute later wearing a denim jacket, which looks really odd on him. "What can I do for you?"

"I was wondering if you could answer a question for me."

"I'll try."

"How long have you practiced here in Snow Creek?"

"Since Brittany was a little girl. You know that. Wasn't she in your class?"

"Actually, she was the year between Rory and me."

"And Rory is . . ."

"Two years older than I am," I say.

"Is Rory seeing anyone?" Doc Sheraton asks.

Seriously? He's not thinking . . .

"She just had a bad breakup."

He lifts his eyebrows slightly. "I'm sorry to hear that."

"Yeah, she just needs some time alone, I think."

"I see. So why are you asking me about my practice?"

Time to put that Callie quick-thinking gene to good use. "I'm doing some research on the town and its business owners for an article I'm writing. You've been here since Brittany was little. I'm trying to remember. I was in elementary school when we moved here, and Brittany was already here, so you've been here longer than we've been here."

"I bought the practice when we moved here. Brittany's mother had just passed away, and we needed a change."

"Where were you working before?"

"In Wyoming. Around Laramie."

"Oh. That makes sense. Why Brittany would go back there to live."

"Yeah, she loves it there. She always talked about home. Even when she was a little girl. She never quite fit in around here. At least she never thought she did."

Nice segue, Doc. I can dig more about Brittany. Thanks. "Oh? I'm sorry she felt that way."

"I remember back in high school, she always spoke so highly of you and Rory. How pretty you both were. How popular."

Pretty? Popular? Those words described Rory's high school experience but certainly not mine.

"That's kind of her."

"The poor girl wanted to fit in so badly. I think she would have done just about anything to be popular."

Oh, you have no idea.

But I'm not about to tell Daddy Dearest that his little Brittany most likely stole one of his tranquilizer guns and sank darts into Rory's and my flesh and then let Pat Lamone take compromising pictures of us.

"High school can be difficult," is all I say.

"It certainly was for her. She seems to have things together now. She seems happy with Pat."

I force a smile. "I'm so glad." Then I clear my throat to dislodge the phlegm from the ridiculous lie that just came out of my mouth. "Will I see you at the Steel party tonight?"

"Of course. I'd never miss one of their parties. Will Rory be there too?"

"I'm not sure," I lie.

"Oh. I'll see you there, then."

"Wonderful. And thanks again for fitting Rory and me in this morning without an appointment. We really appreciate it."

"Anything for the gorgeous Pike sisters." He smiles. "Good luck with your article."

My article. Right. I nod.

I've known Doc Sheraton since I was a kid. Of course, I never dealt with him. My parents did. With the animals we had on the farm.

He always seemed like a nice enough guy.

Now he seems kind of sleazy.

He's a nice-looking older man with a head of thick silver hair and a goatee. Not as tall as the men I'm used to—my father, my brother, and all the Steels. But a good lean build.

Old enough to be my father, of course, so the thought of him drooling over my sister kind of makes me want to retch.

"Give Brittany my best," I say. "It was so good to see her today." Yuck. Another big-ass lie.

"She said the same thing."

"By the way, what happened to her? Remember? She wasn't there when we came out from the exam room."

"Right. She said she wasn't feeling well."

"Then I suppose she won't be at the party tonight. Too bad."

"No, she and Pat aren't planning to attend."

"What a shame. We'll certainly miss them."

Except that that makes me a little more uneasy.

The whole town will be at the Steel ranch tonight.

Which gives Pat and Brittany a chance to do whatever the hell they want. And I wonder… Will they go to the old ponderosa pine, dig up the photos they think are buried there?

Or were they meant for Rory and me to find after all?

I'll be at the party, so I won't know.

But I wish I could clone myself and meet them by the ponderosa pine tree.

CHAPTER THIRTY-EIGHT

Donny

Callie alone in the city building is freaking me out. I'm not quite sure why, but it's enough that I leave Dale and Brock at the winery and drive into town.

Callie's car is parked right by the building. Parking is easy on the weekends.

I breathe a sigh of relief, park behind her, walk to the entrance, and slide my card through. Then I nearly run up the stairs to the city attorney's office.

"Hey, baby, what are—"

She's not at her computer. Fine. Maybe she decided to use my office. Except that I keep it locked. I unlock it quickly just in case she somehow managed to get hold of a key.

Nope. No Callie.

I grab my phone and frantically send her a text.

Where are you? I'm at the office.

She texts me back quickly.

On my way. Just made a detour.

What detour?

No response, but a minute later she's walking into the office.

"I was so worried."

"Why?"

"You weren't here. And… I know it sounds stupid, but with everything else that's going on, I just feel like a vacant office on a weekend is a recipe for disaster."

"That's funny," she says. "When I first got here, I felt like I had to constantly look over my shoulder. All this crap with your family and Pat Lamone… It's getting to me."

"I suppose it's better that we're being overly cautious," I say. "Where were you?"

"Actually, I went to see Doc Sheraton."

"Why?"

"I wanted to see if I could get any information about Brittany and Pat Lamone. Plus, Rory and I did a little investigating this morning when we took our new dogs to see him. Rory found an address in Laramie, which is where Pat Lamone and Brittany were living before they came back to town. I wanted to check it out on the office computer. But it turns out that it was a dead end. It's just vacant land."

"Doc Sheraton has vacant land in Wyoming?"

"Well, he had an address in his office of vacant land in Wyoming. I didn't bother looking for the title because it's not in Colorado. I only have access to Colorado records."

"Actually, you have access to all national property records."

"I do?"

"Yeah. I guess I thought you knew that."

She's already tapping at her computer. "My God. Here it is. I'm not sure why I didn't at least try earlier."

"Because you have a lot on your mind," I say. "It's probably nothing important."

She continues typing. "Give me a minute. The databases are slow."

I watch her screen.

Then, "Hmm. This tract of land is owned by the Fleming Corporation. Why does that sound familiar to me?"

"I don't know."

"Just a minute." Callie pulls up a spreadsheet. "Here it is. The high school. Snow Creek High School, the building, was once owned by the Fleming Corporation. I didn't think much of it at the time, as I was looking for Steel names, but let me just pull this up."

She taps furiously.

Then she frowns, and I look over her shoulder.

"It's a Colorado corporation with a PO Box. The only thing listed is its registered agent. An attorney in Denver. Lucas Wade."

"Lucas Wade." Wade. Seems I've heard that name recently. I scratch my chin. Damn, I haven't shaved in a while.

"I don't know anyone named Wade," she says, "but I think…" She taps again, furiously. "Yeah. Here it is. I knew I'd seen the name before when I was doing research. The city attorney before your mom took over twenty-five years ago was a guy named Larry Wade."

"Larry Wade. LW."

Damn. My great-grandmother Lucy Wade. LW. But Larry Wade is also LW. So is Lucas Wade. But why would a man have a ring that's clearly a woman's?

"Check him out," I say. "Do a search."

Minutes pass. Minutes that seem like hours, as I watch

Callie pull up screen after screen. "Finally," she says. "It's a death certificate for Laurence Wade. He died in New Mexico nearly twenty-five years ago. Parents were Jonathan Wade and Lisa Wade."

Not Lucy Wade. But another LW. Damn. "Anything else?"

"He was married," she says. "Divorced, actually. A woman named Greta. And they had two kids. I suppose one of them could be Lucas Wade."

"Maybe a grandkid," I say.

"Yeah, maybe. But Wade isn't like Hornswaggle. It's a pretty common name."

"True enough." I scratch at my chin again.

"You know," Callie says, "I have the strangest feeling that this Laramie property means something. Rory was just looking for anything that could give us any information about Pat Lamone and Brittany. All she found was this Laramie address, which may or may not be related to Pat and Brittany even though they used to live there. But now . . . with Fleming Corporation and all . . ."

"You think you may have inadvertently stumbled upon something important with regard to my family."

"I don't know. But the Fleming Corporation did transfer the high school building to the Steel Trust all those years ago. I wonder . . ."

"Yeah?"

"I didn't see the Fleming Corporation on the list of other business properties or government properties in the city," she says. "But I haven't looked at the residential properties yet."

"I could ask my dad," I say, "but I don't want to bother him with any more of this. Not until he's fully recovered."

"What we have here, Donny, is a lot of little pieces but no

context holding them together yet."

"You're thinking like a lawyer, Cal." I smile. "And you're right."

Should I tell her about the horrid smells and the bones on our property to the north? It's not property we use. But clearly, someone has been using it.

Her lips are parted in that sexy way, her gaze glued to her computer screen as she continues to type.

She's invested in this. Invested not only in her own issues but in mine.

As if they're one and the same…and it's looking increasingly like they could be.

I place my hand over hers, stopping her typing. "Callie, let's let this lie for the time being."

She turns to me, her eyes wide.

"I want to leave it alone for a minute. For the evening. I need to be at that party for my father. Not just my presence, but I need to be there wholly. I need to truly be there for him."

She nods. "I understand."

"Let's go."

She rises. She's beautiful, as always, but this morning she's wearing old jeans and cowboy boots. A T-shirt with a heart on it. Man, she looks good. Such a delectable ass. An ass that I've spanked, licked… and God… I want to…

Here we are… In an empty city building.

Owned by my cousin.

What a fucking mess.

But I don't want to think about it. I want to wipe it from my mind, concentrate on the beautiful woman before me. I need her. I need this. I need to wipe my mind clean so that I can be present for my father tonight.

Already my dick is tightening in my pants. I want her.

I want her right here out in the open. Where anyone could walk in.

After all, Callie and I aren't the only ones with keys to this building. The judge, the mayor, the few other employees… They could all get in if they wanted to.

I grab her, pull her toward me, and crush my mouth to hers.

CHAPTER THIRTY-NINE

Callie

It's easy to see where this is going, and I have no plan to stop it. Seconds later, my jeans are around my knees, and Donny's inside me, thrusting me against my desk. It's a quick fuck. We're good at quick fucks.

But it's also necessary.

Donny needs to be whole for his father this evening, and he won't be if all these other things are on his mind. In the same way, I need to be whole for Donny. He needs me, and I want to be there for him.

He thrusts into me hard, and my hip bones dig into the side of my desk. The pain is fleeting, though, and I don't care anyway. I'll do anything—everything—for Donny.

All our time together—the quick fucks, the spankings, that amazing night in Denver—every one of them is special. This one is no less so.

Too soon it's over, but he stays inside me, panting against my back.

"I needed that," he says gruffly.

"Me too, sweetie."

"Sweetie?" he whispers against my ear. "You've never called me that before."

"It sort of just popped out. Don't you like it?"

"Baby, you can call me whatever you want. I love you, you know."

"I know. I love you too."

"I swear to God, Callie, when all this is over, you and I are going to have a fucking huge sexfest. It's going to be days long. Weeks, even. We'll never leave the bedroom."

"I think we might starve to death if we never leave."

"We'll have food delivered."

"One of us will have to leave the bedroom to get it at the front door."

He chuckles and gives my ass a quick slap. "You're so fucking literal. God, I love you."

I warm all over. "I love you too."

He withdraws then all the way and turns me around to face him. His jeans are around his thighs, mine still around my knees.

He looks at me. So intent, his eyes so full of love. "I need you in my life, Callie Pike."

"I don't plan to go anywhere."

"I thank God for that. I gave you the chance to walk away, and I'm so glad you didn't take it."

"You're not getting rid of me that easily."

"Damn. This isn't how I meant to do this . . ."

"Do what?"

"Marry me, Caroline Pike. Be my wife."

My jaw drops.

"I mean it. I should drop to one knee, but my jeans are preventing that. I should give you the biggest fucking rock in the universe. I will. I'll do all that. I already have one picked out. But right now, I just need you to say yes." He cups both my cheeks, kisses me lightly on the lips.

I swallow, my heart racing.

"Well?" he asks.

I pick up my jaw from the floor. "Donny, are you sure? We haven't known each other for that long."

"We've known each other for years."

"You know what I mean."

He brushes his lips over mine again. "I know exactly what you mean. I also know that this is right. Everything about it screams right. Apparently, we Steels are known for very short courtships. We fall fast and we fall hard. I watched it happen to Dale. And I've heard about my mom and dad's whirlwind romance. I believe in us, Callie. I believe in what I feel for you, and I want it to last forever."

"Oh, Donny," I say. "I love you so much."

"Ditto, baby. I have to tell you, I wasn't sure this would ever happen for me. You know, being one of the Three Rake-a-teers."

"I'm glad it happened. And if you're sure, yes, I will marry you, Donovan Steel."

His lips plunder mine then. A kiss of possession. Of passion, of enduring love.

Funny thing is, I don't need him down on one knee. I don't need a rock the size of my fist. I never needed any of that.

All I need is this man. This man and his love.

That's all I need to be complete.

CHAPTER FORTY

Donny

Back at the house, my phone buzzes. "Drew? What do you have for me? Did you finally trace ownership of the ring?"

"You're not going to believe this, Don."

"Yeah? Try me. I've recently come across a lot of things I wouldn't have believed a mere month ago."

"This one'll throw you for a loop for sure. The last known owner of this ring was Daphne Steel."

The phone slips from my grip, but I catch it and return it to my ear. "Daphne Steel? My grandmother?"

"She's the one."

"Then what about the LW?"

"I don't know. The papers don't show any prior ownership, unless they've been tampered with, but that's unlikely."

Not as unlikely as you might think. Apparently my family likes tampering with official documents.

"All right. At least it belongs in my family. How the hell did it get to me? If it was my grandmother's, it should still be with the family."

"I can't tell you any more than I have. I came across an old insurance policy covering a ring identical to what you brought in, right down to the initials carved inside."

"I was only seven when my grandparents died. They died

within forty-eight hours of each other. I never met either of them."

"Who has all your grandmother's belongings?"

"I have no idea."

"Well, it looks like you have one of them."

"It most likely belongs to her children. Not me."

"As I said, possession is nine-tenths of the law."

"Yeah . . ."

The funny thing is, especially now that I *know* it's a family heirloom, I want this ring.

I want it because it belongs on Callie's finger. It reminds me so much of her. Her fiery nature. Her beautiful eyes. The blaze we ignite when we're together.

This ring belongs to Callie.

"I guess I should talk to my dad and my uncles and aunts about it. Aunt Marjorie may want it, since it belonged to her mother."

"If you can, find your grandmother's will. This may be specifically bequeathed to someone."

"Good idea."

Perhaps I'll look through Dad's safe after all. I hate to do it, but . . .

"At least you know now that it *does* belong in your family. It's worth a ton. Did you get it insured yet?"

"Shit. I haven't. I've had a lot on my mind."

"Get it insured yesterday. Call the dude on the card. He keeps weekend hours."

"I will. I'll call him as soon as we hang up." I shake my head. "It must have been a gift from my grandfather. My grandmother's parents didn't have this kind of money."

"Someone had money to afford this bauble. This

particular stone came from the Argyle mine in Australia. Not too surprising, as that's where most orange diamonds come from. Some are found in South Africa, but the papers on this—"

"Papers? What do you mean, papers?"

"I guess I should have explained. Jewels like this are supposed to come with papers certifying where they came from, and their value. I found a copy of the papers with the insurance policy showing Daphne Steel last owned the ring. The original certification should be somewhere."

"None of this explains how it ended up in a safe-deposit box with my name on it."

"No, it doesn't."

"Fuck. Anything else?"

"That's all I've come up with so far. I'm sorry for the delay."

"No problem. This is good info. I think."

"I'll call if I find anything else."

"Sounds good. Send me the bill."

No sooner do I hang up on Drew when I get another call—this one from Monarch Security.

Finally.

And I don't like what I hear. I don't like it at all.

"What do you mean the surveillance video is *missing*?"

"I don't understand myself, Mr. Steel."

"For God's sake, for the amount we pay you…" Anger stampedes through me. "Someone got into my house, put a safe-deposit box key in my bathroom. I want to know who the fuck it was."

"I've questioned everyone. The material just seems to have disappeared."

"I don't buy that. You find out, or we're taking our business elsewhere."

"Absolutely, Mr. Steel, and I don't blame you. I'm pretty damned pissed myself."

"You're not half as pissed as I am. You find that surveillance tape, or you'll wish you had."

I throw my phone across the room to end the call.

Every cell in my body is jumping. Fucking jumping. Anger and tension and pure madness rage through my body. It's a good thing Callie's not here, or I'd be fucking her senseless, using her body to ease this tension.

I don't want to do that to her. Not ever.

When Dale feels like this, he goes to his basement and kicks and punches that martial arts dummy of his. I understand my brother so much better now.

I was always jovial Donny. Nothing ever got to me. Sure, two months of my life were pure torture, but that's in the past. Why let it bother me in the present?

Now my present sucks, and I don't know where to turn.

I could go over to Dale's house, go down to his basement gym—except he's probably moved all of it to the new place by now.

The guesthouse should be mine by now. It's taking him and Ashley too damned long to get the hell out. I need a place. I need a place so I can scream at the top of my lungs if I feel like it. Fuck my girlfriend whenever I feel like it.

Uncle Joe and Brock would be doing front crawl laps right now. Maybe that's what I should do. I'm already in my room, so I shed my clothes in seconds, slide on a pair of swim trunks, and head out to the backyard, luckily avoiding Dad and the temporary maid.

Mom is busy with Aunt Marj in the kitchen, and I manage to sneak by them as well.

Fred and Ginger pant around my feet, and I give them each a quick pet on the head, but that's it.

I'm on a one-track mission.

I want to get in that damned pool, and I want to start swimming.

It helped that night at Uncle Joe's, and it will help now.

It has to.

Because tonight I have to turn on the fucking charm and be jovial Donny Steel again.

CHAPTER FORTY-ONE

Callie

Maddie hitched a ride to the ranch from college with Brianna Steel, so I'm hanging out with her at the party when we first arrive. Rory came over early to help Jesse and the band set up, and Donny is hanging close to his father. So is Dale.

I feel a little like a fish out of water, though I shouldn't, as I'm secretly engaged to a Steel.

Donny and I decided not to make the announcement tonight. Tonight is about Talon. About how lucky we are that we still have him.

Maddie ends up dragging me toward the makeshift stage where Jesse and his bandmates are. She locks eyes with Dragon Locke. Dragon's a loner. Really sexy in a dark rocker kind of way. I don't particularly like the way he's looking at my little sister, but last I heard, he was dating someone in Grand Junction.

Bree is hanging with us as well. She also can't seem to keep her eyes off Dragon Locke. Or my brother.

She's not quite twenty-two years old—way too young for either of them.

But there is something about a rocker. Of course, one is my brother and one is my cousin, and the other two can't hold a candle to Donny Steel, who is mine and all mine.

The selfish part of me wants to tell the world. Shout from the rooftops that I'm engaged to Donovan Steel. That we're going to be married. I'm going to be the mother of Steel children.

I look around at the crowds of people making the rounds, and I spy my parents.

And it dawns on me for the first time. I'm going to be a Steel. *I can help my parents.*

Wow.

It was never my intention to get involved with Donny for any mercenary reasons—despite Lamone's assertion that Rory and I are gold diggers—but it *is* a nice fringe benefit.

Of course, my proud parents probably won't take any money from Donny. That's all in the future anyway. We didn't talk about when we'd get married. It could be a year or two from now for all I know.

But…

Donny is now the city attorney for Snow Creek. What about my law school? The only two law schools in Colorado are in the Denver area.

My heart sinks. No biggie, right? Donny and I can just wait to get married. But being away from him for three years… I can't stomach the thought of it.

Online courses are an option, but I wanted the in-person classroom experience.

We'll work it out one way or the other. I'll talk to Donny about it. But not tonight. Tonight is for his father.

Tomorrow, maybe… Still, law school will take fifth or sixth place on the list of what's important now. First we have to find out who shot Donny's father. Then why the Steels seem to own the town of Snow Creek, and what the heck the Fleming

Corporation is. Then… Pat Lamone and Brittany Sheraton and those damned photos.

Yeah… law school is way down the list of what's important right now.

Tonight, I'm going to try to have a good time. Donny won't leave me alone for much longer. He said he wanted to spend the first part of the party hanging with his dad, playing the dutiful son. It's certainly not role-playing. Donny *is* a dutiful son. He's slightly closer to his mother than to his father, but he adores them both.

I can see it in his eyes whenever he talks to or about his father. That man has Donny's utmost respect.

Of course he does. Talon Steel adopted them, took them away from…

I feel like I'm back in a damned cage.

Those words still haunt me when I allow them to float to the top of my mind. I try not to. I don't want to think about what Donny may have been through in his young life. Whatever happened, he's grown up to be an amazing man. A man with such strong ethics—when he was faced with breaching them, he couldn't.

There are so many things to love about Donny Steel. His strength is merely one of them. His brilliance, his sense of humor, and of course the fact that he's the most gorgeous man on the planet.

Rory scurries up to me then. "Hey, Cal, could you come up and help us for a minute?"

Brianna and Maddie say in unison, "I'll do it."

"Actually, I need Callie for this."

The two of them give us pouting looks as Rory drags me behind the makeshift stage.

"What is it?" I ask.

"It's Jesse. He just told me that he and the guys are going to go see Pat Lamone later tonight. They're going to get those pictures."

My heart drops to my stomach. "No. They can't."

"You're telling me."

"Shit. Does this mean he told Cage and the others?"

She shakes her head. "He promised me he didn't. He made up some stupid story about Lamone hitting on you and me."

"Why would the guys care about that?"

"Hell if I know. I've been trying to talk him out of it."

Brock Steel shows up then, his addictive smile splitting his handsome face. "Why are the two most beautiful ladies at the party hiding back here?"

"I don't know. Why don't you ask them?" I smirk.

"I think I just did, Callie."

I roll my eyes. "We're not buying your lines, Brock."

"Maybe you aren't. I know you've got it bad for Donny." He turns to Rory. "You, on the other hand . . ."

"Just got out of a major relationship," I say. "Leave Rory alone."

Rory drops her jaw open. Though I expect her to agree with me, she says, "I can speak for myself, Cal."

What? Perhaps Rory doesn't realize her comment just invited Brock Steel to inundate her with come-ons. Has she totally forgotten how men are? Especially the Rake-a-teers?

"In fact," Brock says, "Donny is looking for you, Callie. I told him I'd try to find you."

"You found me. I'll just text him and tell him where we are."

"He's up on the deck with Uncle Talon."

"I know that. He's hanging with his dad, and I totally understand."

"All I know is he was wondering where you are."

"Like I said, I'll text him."

Rory meets my gaze. "It's okay. Go ahead. I'm fine here."

Fine? With a Rake-a-teer? Who's clearly interested?

"Ror . . ."

"I'm good. Go ahead."

"Okay. If you say so." I walk back out into the crowd and toward the deck where Donny's still sitting with Talon.

And I hope my sister knows what she's doing.

CHAPTER FORTY-TWO

Donny

My phone buzzes. Hmm. I don't recognize the number, so I ignore it and shove it back into my pocket.

Callie approaches us then. "Hey. Brock says you were looking for me."

"I am." I smile.

"How are you feeling?" she asks Dad.

"Good, good," he says. "Happy to see everyone."

I clear my throat. "Could you excuse us, Dad? I need to talk to Callie inside for a minute."

"Of course. You and your brother don't have to hang around me as if I'm made of glass. I think it's clear by now that I'm made of steel."

I chuckle at his pun as Dale returns from the bathroom. "We'll be back in a few."

I lead Callie inside through the kitchen and then to my bedroom.

"What's this about, Donny?"

"I want to give you something." I open my top dresser drawer and withdraw the ring Drew crafted for me. I hold it toward her.

She gasps, bringing her hands to her mouth.

"This isn't the ring from the safe-deposit box, baby. That

one's not mine to give to you. Not yet, anyway. But my jeweler made this one especially for you."

"My God..."

"One day you'll have the real one. I swear. I found out today it once belonged to my grandmother."

"Donny, that means it's a family heirloom."

"It is. But someone—I don't know who yet—gave it to me. It's mine, now, and I knew when I saw it that it was meant for you. This one will have to suffice for now."

"It's stunning. What kind of stone is it?"

"It's an orange sapphire—not as rare as the orange diamond in the original. But it reminds me of you, Callie. First, it's so similar to your eyes, with that gorgeous amber sparkle. But even more so because you're as rare as any priceless gemstone, Caroline Pike. You're one in a million, and I can't believe I'm the lucky guy who gets to marry you."

I drop to my knees this time and hold the ring out to her.

"Will you marry me, Caroline Pike?"

"Yes. Yes, yes, yes." She holds out her hand, shaking slightly.

I, also shaking, place it on her ring finger.

"It fits." She falls to her knees then and kisses me. "I love you."

"I love you too, baby."

"So what about... tonight?"

"I know we decided not to say anything tonight, but Dad wants us to make the announcement. He says it's more of a reason to celebrate than his homecoming."

"It's a huge reason to celebrate," she says, "but it's no more important than your dad."

"And this is one of the many reasons why I love you, Callie.

So what do you want to do? We can make the announcement tonight, or we can wait."

"I guess it's up to your dad," she says. "It's his party, after all."

I smile. "Then I guess we announce tonight. We'll do it after dinner. After the toast to my dad's homecoming. Is that okay with you?"

"That's perfect." She looks down at her left hand. "I can't believe the sparkle of this stone. It's amazing."

I take her left hand, place a kiss on it, and then meet her gaze. "Wait until you see the diamond. But the real sparkle is in your eyes. They're a fiery blaze of sparkle."

She melts against me, our lips sliding together. Already I'm hardening. I could so easily take her here, in my bed, with no one the wiser.

But the whole blessed town is outside on our property.

"You just wait until tonight," I say against her ear. "You just wait."

★ ★ ★

Mom and Aunt Marjorie are helping the caterers serve dinner when Callie and I return. Dad, as the man of the hour, is up first, which is strange. Usually we let our guests eat first.

"You hungry?" I ask Callie.

"A little." She casts her gaze around the crowd.

"Looking for something?"

"Yeah, Rory. Brock's going after her big time."

"Damn," I say. "I told him not to do that."

Callie punches my arm. "You knew about this?"

"Brock has the hots for your sister. Then again, every

single unattached guy here probably has the hots for your sister."

"They do know she's bisexual, right?"

"I think it's pretty well known. It doesn't seem to bother Brock. In his words, 'it's hot.'"

Callie shakes her head. "I know Rory used to be the town siren, but those days are long gone. And Brock..."

"Is a known womanizer. I know. Of course, so was I before I fell for you. We *can* be reformed."

"Brock is a lot younger than you are, Donny. I can't see him settling down anytime soon."

"Truth be told, neither can I. But Rory's a big girl. I'm sure she can handle herself."

"She can," Callie says, "but I have a bad feeling about this."

"Why?"

"The thing with Raine hit her pretty hard. And she has... other things on her mind these days."

"The Lamone thing. I know."

"I'm actually not talking about Lamone. Donny, Rory really wants to have a baby."

I let out a gale of laughter. "Then there's nothing to worry about. Brock is so not ready for that. All Rory needs to do is mention that little fact, and he'll go running."

Callie laughs then too. "I never thought about it that way. If Rory wants a one-nighter with Brock, I guess she can have a one-nighter with Brock."

"Who even knows if it's going to get that far?" I say. "Rory may just be doing a little flirting. Brock's a good guy at heart. If Rory isn't interested, he won't push it."

"I know that. Still, I wonder where they are."

"The food is out, which means Brock will sniff that out

eventually. That man can put away more food than my brother and me combined."

"Really?"

"Oh yeah. Frankly I don't know how he stays in such great shape. It must be all the swimming he does."

"Right. I remember. Maddie always talked about what a big champ he was. I think he was a senior when she was a freshman or something."

Speaking of Maddie, she comes running toward us. "Callie, guess what?"

"What?" Callie says.

"The band invited Bree and me to go to Murphy's after the party."

As much as I don't want my little sister hanging out with the band, maybe this means they decided not to go after Lamone. "The band? You mean the band consisting of our brother and our cousin?"

"And Dragon Locke."

I scoff. "I swear to God, why are all the women infatuated with Dragon Locke?"

"Because he's a dream," Maddie says.

I roll my eyes, despite the fact that Dragon is pretty hot in that dark way of his. "If you say so."

"Mads," Callie says. "Dragon is way too old for you. But since Jess will be there, I don't have to worry. He won't let his bandmate near you."

"Yeah? Well, you and Jess are both party poopers. I'm going to get something to eat." Maddie flounces away with a pout and gets in line behind Angie and Sage.

"Come with me," I say to Callie.

I drag her over toward the makeshift stage, where her

brother, cousin, and Dragon are talking. Looks like the stage is set.

"Pike," I say.

"Steel."

Still our standard greeting. I wonder if it'll change once I'm married to his sister.

"Where's your dad?" I ask.

"I don't know. I haven't seen him."

"He and Mom are here somewhere," Callie says.

Jesse, standing on the stage, shades his eyes and looks around. "There they are, over by the pool."

"Great." I grab Callie's hand.

"He didn't notice my ring," Callie says.

"Just as well. We need to talk to your mom and dad."

"What about?"

"I'm going to ask for permission to marry you."

CHAPTER FORTY-THREE

Callie

"You can't be serious."

Donny turns and faces me. "I'm totally serious."

"We don't live in Victorian England."

"Nope. We live in twenty-first century western Colorado."

"Uh . . . yeah."

"Look, Callie. We're both up to our necks in crap right now. I want to do something right. I love you, and I want to ask permission to marry you."

"What if he says no?"

"Then we'll wait."

I drop my jaw, until I see the twinkle in his hazel eyes. He's kidding.

"He's not going to say no, is he?"

"I doubt it," I say. "But why give him the chance?"

"Because I'm a gentleman. I'm not sure anyone knows that, given my history, but I am. I want him to know how much I love you. That I'm going to take excellent care of you."

"Don't forget that I'm going to take excellent care of *you* too."

"Absolutely. I'll be back in a few minutes."

I grab his hand. "Oh, no. I'm coming along."

"How am I supposed to ask him for his daughter's hand if

you're hanging on to me?"

"Because this is a two-way decision, Donny. He needs to know that I want it. For God's sake, you just admitted we're living in the twenty-first century."

He grins. My God, he's handsome. "Okay, boss."

"I'm not your boss. Just like you are not mine. Neither one of us is a boss, Donny, we—"

"Easy, Cal. I'm kidding. You're a little on edge tonight."

"Can you blame me? All this other stuff that's going on, and now we have to go talk to my father? This is something we could easily avoid."

"Callie, I feel strongly about this. I feel like I've fucked so much up lately, and I want to do this right. Exactly right."

His hand is warm in mine. Just this light touch of our bodies has me feeling a little less tense. For that, I'm so thankful. I'm so thankful that Donny Steel came into my life. If he wants to do this, I have to support him.

We approach my father, who's talking with my mom and Uncle Scott and Aunt Lena, Cage and Jordan's parents.

"Mr. Pike," Donny says.

"Mr. Pike?" My dad erupts in laughter. "I don't think you've ever called me Mr. Pike, Don."

"Okay, Frank. I need to speak with you privately."

"With *both* of you." I gesture to my mother.

"You are determined to make this a feminist issue, aren't you?" Donny beams at me.

"My mother is just as much a part of this as my father."

"Okay, okay," my father says. "Scott, Lena, excuse us for a minute."

Donny leads my father, my mother, and me toward a gazebo that, oddly, is empty.

"Frank, Maureen," Donny says, "I would like your permission to marry Callie."

My father's eyebrows nearly pop off his forehead. "Already?"

"I realize we haven't been dating that long."

"Only a couple of weeks," my mom adds.

"Mom," I begin, "I—"

Donny squeezes my hand, and I close my mouth. I'll let him do this. Sure, it's completely patriarchal, but it's also kind of sweet.

"We realize it's soon," Donny says, "but when it's right, it's right. I watched my brother fall in love quickly. I've heard the stories about how my mother and father fell in love quickly all those years ago. I love Callie, and… Well, you're probably aware of my reputation. I'm hardly inexperienced. So when I know something is right, it's right."

I try not to wince at the mention of Donny's reputation. It's something I don't like to think about, and his bringing it up while he's asking for my father's blessing… Yeah, not sure it's the wisest idea.

My father's countenance is stern as he clears his throat. "Donny, I can't think of a better man to be my daughter's husband." He holds out his hand and smiles.

That's when I realize I'm holding my breath. I exhale sharply.

"Thank you, sir." Donny shakes my father's hand.

"Stop this *sir* nonsense. I'm Frank, just like I've always been. Especially now that we're going to be related."

"If you're sure, Callie." Mom smiles at me.

"Mom, I don't think I've ever been more sure of anything."

The absolute truth in my words arrows straight to my

heart. Despite the mess that surrounds us at this moment, I still have Donny. I still have my mom and dad. I have Jesse, Rory, and Maddie.

Family.

Family is everything.

"Callie and I would like to make the announcement tonight," Donny continues. "Are the two of you okay with that?"

Before my dad can answer, my mom zeroes in on my left hand and grabs it. "Callie! This is so beautiful. What kind of stone is that?"

"It's an orange sapphire," I say.

"I've never seen anything like it," Mom gushes.

"It matches her eyes, doesn't it?" Donny says.

Both my mom and my dad stare into my eyes—to the point where I'm almost uncomfortable.

"It does." Mom claps her hand to her mouth.

"No stone can hold a candle to Callie's beauty," Donny says.

My cheeks are blazing now. I'm sure they're bright candy apple red.

"Don," my father says, "you're damned right about that."

CHAPTER FORTY-FOUR

Donny

Uncle Ryan and Dad grab Callie and me while Dale and Ashley make sure everyone has a flute of Steel sparkling wine.

Then Jesse takes the microphone. "Hey, everyone! I need your attention up here on the stage, please."

Conversation lowers to a dull roar.

"We're going to start some music soon, but before we do, I want everyone to put your hands together for our host tonight, Talon Steel!"

Among the applause, Dad and Uncle Ryan take the stage. Dad walks slowly but almost looks like himself. His strength is returning, and that makes me ecstatic. The woman next to me has a little to do with that as well.

Uncle Ry, of course, takes the microphone. He's always the Steel spokesperson, because he has the most personality of all of us. Present company excluded.

"Thanks again for all of you being here," Uncle Ryan says. "We almost lost my brother a week ago, and we're all so grateful that he's going to make a full recovery. Talon, I love you, bro."

Dad takes the microphone then. "You all know me. I'm not like my brother here. I'm not gifted in the way of the word. I just want to thank you for all your support and for being here. I want to thank my lovely wife, Jade, and my lovely sister,

Marjorie, for putting together another one of their awesome parties. What would we do without them?"

More clapping.

"And my kids, Dale, Donny, Diana, Brianna, thank you for being my reasons along with your mother for getting up each morning. For loving my life."

More applause, and a few sniffles.

"But enough about me. Now I want you to put your hands together for my son, Donny. Come on up here, Donny. You too, Callie."

Callie and I walk up the four steps and onto the stage.

"I am absolutely proud to announce the engagement of my son Donny to this lovely lady, Callie Pike!"

Applause. And more than one gasp. I'm not surprised. The first of the Rake-a-teers to take the plunge.

I take the mic from Dad. "Hey, everyone. I can't thank you enough for being here to support my dad. Callie and I didn't want to rain on his parade, but he insisted that we make our announcement tonight."

Jesse, to the right of me, gives me an angry gaze. His brown eyes shoot darts. Poison darts.

"Before you try to kick my ass, Jesse," I say jovially, "I got your father's permission."

Laughter from the crowd as Jesse's cheeks turn slightly pink, but he grits out a smile. It's forced, sure, but at least he's trying. I didn't expect him to be thrilled. Hell, I wouldn't be thrilled if he married one of my sisters.

"I can't believe how lucky I am," I continue. "Callie and I haven't set a date yet, but you're all invited!"

I give the mic back to Uncle Ry, who introduces Dragonlock, and they take the stage.

"Let's go," I say to Callie.

"Go . . . where?"

"I don't know. Somewhere private. I need to talk to you."

She lifts her eyebrows. "Is everything okay?"

"Yeah. It's just . . . There's some shit I should have told you before you agreed to become my wife."

Before she can say another word, I take her hand and weave through the crowd, into the house, and to my bedroom, locking the door.

I open my mouth to speak, but she covers my lips with her fingers.

"It doesn't matter to me, Donny. Nothing matters. Not now and not ever. All that matters is that you love me and I love you."

"You have to know what you're getting into, Callie."

"I do. And you know what you're getting into with me. Together we'll figure this out. The operative word is *together*."

I believe her. Looking into her sparkling amber eyes, I believe her the way I've never believed anyone before.

Our love is strong enough to get through all of this. But still . . . I can't keep something that is so much a part of my life from the woman I love.

"You've probably wondered how I ended up at the Steel ranch."

She bites her lip. "I have. You said something a while back. When you were upset about everything that was happening and when you were faced with breaching your ethics."

I wrinkle my forehead.

"Don't you remember?" she asks.

"I don't know. What did I say?"

"You said, 'I feel like I'm back in a damned cage.'"

I close my eyes. Funny that I would use those words. How could I have said that? In front of Callie?

"It kills me, Donny," she says, "to think of you in pain. To think of you inside a cage."

"I suppose it wasn't really a cage in the literal sense. I mean, there weren't bars."

"You don't have to . . ."

I open my eyes. She's so beautiful. So full of love. How can I do this to her? How can I tell her about the hell that was those two months of my life?

"Donny . . ."

"I was seven years old. Dale was ten. They came for us after school at our home, when our mom wasn't there. They took us . . . I don't know. We must have been drugged. Somehow we ended up on an island in the Caribbean. That's where Dad found us. Dad and Uncle Ryan."

It pours out of me then. All of it. I don't cry, I just speak in a robotic tone as I tell her everything.

The pain, the torture, the humiliation.

The rapes. The beatings.

And through it all, my brother. Dale. My hero and my protector.

Everything he went through, some of which I only recently found out about, to shelter me. To save me.

Then . . . Dad and Uncle Ryan. Aunt Ruby. The dogs. Bo and Beauty.

And . . .

My attempt to end my own life.

Callie gasps at that one. She was being so good at trying not to look surprised. Trying not to look completely nauseated even when I know she is.

But that one got her.

"Donny, why?"

"I was a kid. A kid who had made a promise to his hero. Dale. That if either of us had a chance to end this miserable existence, we would."

"But you had been rescued."

"We had, but neither of us really knew that at the time. Sure, these people seemed nice, but we were still kids. Dale wasn't talking. I couldn't even get him to talk to me. So as far as I knew in my seven-year-old mind, our deal was still on. Thank God for Aunt Ruby."

"You owe her your life."

"I do. And I don't thank her enough. I seem to give all the credit to Dad and to Mom. But Uncle Ryan and Aunt Ruby—they have just as much to do with my salvation."

"I'm so sorry," Callie says.

I shake my head. "I didn't tell you this to get you to be sorry."

"I know that. But I can't help it. I can't even imagine what it must have been like."

"Please don't even try. I can't bear the thought of you experiencing even a tiny bit of it."

"If I could take it all away from you and bear it myself, I would."

"But that's exactly what I don't want. I wish I could bear *your* pain."

"I suppose neither of us can do that. But you don't have to bear it alone. I will always be here for you."

I reach toward her, let her soft hair sift through my fingers. "You're so beautiful, Callie. And I'm not even talking about this silky hair of yours, those amazing fiery eyes, that delectable ass that won't quit."

She smiles.

"I'm talking about everything inside you. Your good heart, your soul, everything about you."

"You're beautiful too," she says. "Your brilliance, everything."

I pull her toward me, inhale the sweet fragrance of her hair. "You know it all now. The good, the bad, and the ugly."

"If I could change it for you, I would," she says. "But you're the man I love, and everything you've been through has made you into that."

"I know exactly what you mean." I kiss the top of her head. "I'm sorry for everything you've been through too. But it's made you strong, Callie. Strong and brilliant and a force to be reckoned with. You're going to be a hell of a lawyer."

She stiffens then.

I pull back a bit. Raise my eyebrows.

"About law school..."

"What about it? You can go wherever you want. Money is no object anymore. You can start next semester, as you planned."

"But...you're the city attorney here now. Your mom is retiring. You can't leave Snow Creek, and there's no law school anywhere near here."

"I know, baby. I can't bear the thought of being apart from you either. I guess we're going to have to talk about online law school."

Her lips turn downward slightly. "I know. It's never been what I wanted, but it's a small sacrifice to make to be Mrs. Donovan Steel."

"You'll still be Mrs. Donovan Steel if you go to law school

in Denver. You can be here on the weekends."

She shakes her head vehemently. "Oh, no. You are not getting rid of me that easily. I can't be apart from you. And I'm not giving up law school. So online it will be."

"Thank God." Relief swells within me. "I would have supported you, but I can't stand the thought of being away from you."

She leans upward and brushes her lips across mine. "I know. That's why I love you, my beautiful, gorgeous man."

I grab her then, crush my mouth to hers.

Yeah . . . we're not going back to the party anytime soon.

CHAPTER FORTY-FIVE

Callie

As we kiss, Donny walks me backward toward his bed.

I push at him and break the passionate kiss. "Donny, the party. Your parents. *My* parents."

"The band just started," he says huskily. "Everyone's partying. They'll never miss us."

"Of course they will. We just announced our engagement. People will want to talk to us. We've already been gone almost a half hour."

"Don't care." His mouth comes down on mine once more, and he gives my ass a hard swat.

I jerk at the spank, but I don't break the kiss.

And oh, the kiss.

It's full of passion and . . . relief, almost.

I get it. I know everything now, everything about his past, and he's relieved. It's no longer bottled up inside him. In a way, he's free.

Just as I'm free.

Oh, there's still a lot of mystery to unravel, between his family secrets and my situation with Pat Lamone, but we're together, and we have no more secrets.

He breaks the kiss and turns me around to face the bed. In an instant, my denim skirt is hiked up and Donny rips off my cotton panties.

Seriously.

Rips.

Then—

Smack!

His palm on my bare ass.

Euphoria flows through me. Oh, it stings for sure, but the sting is also like a pathway to nirvana.

It swirls in and through me, and I gasp in a breath.

"Again," I say.

"You sure?"

I turn to face him, meet his beautiful hazel eyes that are blazing with fire. "Yes, I'm sure. It's not punishment, Donny. It's pleasure. Pure pleasure. And I love it."

"Fuck," he growls, kissing me again.

Our tongues tangle like two swords fighting for domination. But too soon, he pulls back once more, turns me around, and—

Slap!

Slap! Slap! Slap!

"This ass, Callie. So pink and perfect."

I'm reeling from the pleasure-pain of his palm on my tender flesh. I wait for another smack and am disappointed when it doesn't come.

I look over my shoulder.

Donny pulls something out of his drawer and then returns to me.

Slap!

I gasp.

Then—

Slap!

Slap!

Slap!

I fall against the bed, grab the covers, and wait.

Wait for more.

Wait to be sated.

But he flips me over so I'm staring up at him.

"You're so beautiful, my Callie," he groans.

"So are you."

He's wearing jeans, cowboy boots, and a white button-down that accents his naturally tan skin.

He slowly unbuttons his shirt, and I suck in a breath at each new inch of exposed flesh.

First his shirt.

Then his boots.

And last…

His jeans and underwear slide over his slim hips and perfect ass.

He's naked, and so am I from the waist down.

He moves toward me slowly, pulls my dress over my head, and removes my bra.

My breasts are already swollen and my nipples hard, but being naked in Donny's presence makes them jut out farther.

I gasp when Donny sucks one between his lips while he plays with my clit with his fingers.

I'm already soaking wet, of course. The kiss, the spanking… perfect recipe for a ripe pussy.

"Donny… please."

He drops the nipple.

"Inside me. Please."

"What about… something else?" he asks.

"What?"

He nibbles my nipple once more. I quiver.

"Your ass, baby. I want your ass."

I drop my lips into an O. Anal? He wants anal? Now? While a party's going on?

His gaze is pure seriousness, though.

In that moment, I want this more than anything in the world.

"Yes," I say. "Yes. Please."

"God, baby."

He squeezes some lubricant—that must have been what he got out of the dresser drawer—onto his fingers, and then he pushes my thighs forward.

His mouth finds my nipple once more, and I gasp when his slippery fingers begin working the forbidden place between my ass cheeks.

It's only a massage, but my God, it feels amazing, as if I'm about to explore something unknown and wonderful.

Donny switches to my other nipple and—

"Oh!"

He breaches the tight rim of my asshole with his finger.

"Easy. Breathe through it. Through the pain."

"No pain," I gasp out. "Feels . . . amazing. So good."

"That's what I like to hear. Good, baby. God, I love you." He tugs on my nipple with his teeth.

"I love you too. So much."

In and out. In and out. He fucks my ass with his finger as I go slowly insane with want and desire. Goose bumps prickle my flesh, and warmth flows through me. Wonder of all wonders, I feel everything—not only in my ass but in my pussy. In my clit. And in every other cell of my body.

This. This intimacy.

This pure trust.

This is what I have with Donny Steel.

"Please," I whisper.

He drops the nipple once more. "What, baby?"

"Please. Do it now. I need you. I need you inside that most private part of me."

He kisses my lips. "Are you sure?"

"Absolutely. I want this. I want *you*."

CHAPTER FORTY-SIX

Donny

I stand and push Callie's thighs forward.

I want to give her something—something I've never given another. I've had anal sex many times, but I've always taken from behind.

Not this time.

I'll look into Callie's blazing eyes as I breach her anal virginity.

Her beautiful body is pink with a warm flush.

Except . . . none of this is right.

As much as I yearn for this part of her—to take her virginity in this way—I can't do it now. Not when there's a party going on outside. My whole family is here. The whole damned town is here.

"Callie . . ."

She widens her eyes. "I don't like that tone."

"I can't do this. Not here. Not now. You deserve better."

"I want it. I want it now."

"But this is private. So private and intimate, and I—"

"Stop," she says. "Just stop it. You told me our first time that I didn't deserve a quick fuck but you were going to give me one anyway."

"This is different. You and I both know that."

"But is it? Sure, there might be pain. But this is us, Donny. This is what I love about us. We're quick. We're hard. We're fast. That's what makes us *us*."

"Anal can't be rushed," I say.

"Tell me you don't want me," she says. "Tell me you don't want my ass right now."

I close my eyes, let out a breath, and then open them. "I can't."

"Then you're wasting valuable time, babe. The whole town is out there, waiting to congratulate us, but we're not leaving this room until you fuck my ass."

My whole body erupts in a blazing inferno.

This woman. Caroline Pike. My woman. My God, I love her. I love her so much. She's one in a million. A billion. A fucking zillion.

No more talking. I was wrong. This is right. This is us.

My God, I can't control myself around her. It was almost torture to go slowly that night in Denver. I loved it and so did she, but she's right.

It's not us.

This is us.

I squeeze a touch more lube over my fingers and let it warm in my hand for a moment before I spread it between her gorgeous ass cheeks.

My cock is on fire, and I smooth it over her tight entrance, nudging the puckered hole just a touch.

"Please," she whimpers.

"Easy. I'm going to go in, and then wait a minute for you to get used to it. The toughest part is getting through the rim."

"Just do it!" she grits out.

So tempting...but I can't go all the way in on the first stroke.

I slowly nudge through the barrier. Callie sucks in a breath.

"Good?" I gasp out.

She nods. "Good. Please. All the way."

I rip the bandage off and thrust inside her tightness.

"Fuck," I growl. Instinct tells me to pull out and thrust back in. To fuck her and fuck her and fuck her. To be us.

I hold for a few seconds.

"Please," she says. "Please."

I draw in a breath, pull out, and plunge back inside her.

"Good?" I ask.

"Yes. Good. But different good."

"God, yes. Different. Even tighter. Damn, Callie. I love you."

"I love you too. So much."

I begin slowly but increase my speed as I massage her clit with my thumb. Her eyes close, and she clenches the bed linens. Moans escape her—soft and sexy moans—and I know I won't last much longer.

I increase the friction to her clit. *Come on, baby. You've got to come. Please.*

When she finally releases, I can feel the contractions even though I'm not in her pussy. And damn . . . Damn . . .

I close my eyes. Thrust harder, harder . . . Until—

"Damn, Callie," I groan as my cock pulsates into her.

I'm embedded so deep in her most private place, and the orgasm rocks through me like a tsunami.

Amazing.

Different.

And oh, so good.

Like nothing I've ever experienced before.

And I know . . .
I know for sure . . .
This is right.
This is *us*.

CHAPTER FORTY-SEVEN

Callie

We have to go back to the party.

I know this. I know it as I come down from the climax that propelled me to the moon.

I know it as Donny brings me a warm washcloth and takes care of me.

I know it as Donny and I dress.

And I know it as he kisses me hard and then whispers into my ear, "Thank you."

"Thank you," I whisper back.

He opens the door. "Shall we?"

"I suppose we don't have a choice. What are your parents going to think?"

"They won't think anything. Okay, maybe they will, but they won't say anything." He chuckles. "Okay, maybe they will. But they won't embarrass you. They'll just ask where we were, and I'll tell them…" His eyes widen. "I've got it. I'll tell them I took you into the office to show you the actual pumpkin diamond ring."

"Good," I say. "Except now I want to see the ring." I laugh.

"All right. Let's see if anyone's missing us, and then I'll take you to see it."

We head back out to the party through the kitchen, which,

mercifully, is empty. Everyone's outside. Jade and Marjorie are setting up the *Welcome home, Talon* cake.

"We should probably have some cake," I say.

Before Donny can respond, the vultures are on us, shaking our hands, offering congratulations.

Rory pulls me aside. "Where were you?"

My cheeks warm. "We've been here."

"Right. Is everything okay?"

"Everything's fine." That's all she'll get out of me. I'm not about to tell my sister what Donny and I were doing in his room. I can hear her now.

TMI, Cal. Geez.

"What have you been doing?"

"Singing, of course. You missed our first set."

"Sorry."

She laughs. "I'll bet you are. But I did something kind of stupid."

"What?"

"Right before the band went on, I made out with Brock."

"Brock Steel?"

"No, Brock O'Hurn."

"Who the heck is Brock O'Hurn?"

"That hot male model with long hair?" Rory rolls her eyes. "Of course it was Brock Steel."

"Well . . . how was it?"

"I didn't hate it," she says, her brown eyes sparkling.

"He's a Rake-a-teer," I warn.

"You're marrying the original Rake-a-teer," she chides.

"Touché," I say.

"It was nice," she says. "Just nice to fool around and know it doesn't mean anything."

"And . . . ?"

"And"—she grins—"he's a damned good kisser." She squeezes my arm. "Enjoy being queen for the evening. I'm going to get some cake."

Donny shoves a plate of cake into my hands. "Ready?"

"For cake? Always."

"To go see the ring."

"Oh. Yeah. Sure." I take a bite of cake and let it melt across my tongue. "My God, this is fabulous."

"Aunt Marj is great with cakes. She taught my mom to make a chocolate cake that's to die for. I'll make it for you sometime."

"Donny Steel in the kitchen?" I laugh. "That'll be the day."

"Yeah, not really my thing."

"Not mine either. Thank God for Trader Joe's."

He laughs as we walk back into the house, through the kitchen, and down the opposite hallway from where the bedrooms are. We pass the library, where we had our first time. Of course, then he left me stranded in the closet for an hour. Not Donny's finest moment, but he's more than made up for it since.

Donny stops in front of a closed door.

"My dad's office," he says before knocking.

"Who do you think's in there? Talon's outside."

"Just double-checking." He slides the door open.

The office is large and looks, well, like an office, with gorgeous wood furniture and a beautiful oil painting of a pure-black horse on the side wall. Donny walks toward the painting.

"The safe's under here."

He carefully removes the painting, and lo and behold, a safe appears. He turns the combination lock and—

He stops.

"What?" I ask.

"I've never opened this safe before."

"But you have the combination?"

"I do. Dad gave it to all of us when we turned eighteen."

"Then he won't mind, will he?"

"No. He won't. He says everything in here is our business. He wouldn't have given us the code otherwise."

"So what's the issue?"

"It's just . . . It feels weird. Like I'm about to see something I shouldn't."

"It's okay. I don't have to see the real ring." I hold out my left hand and let the orange sapphire dazzle in the artificial light of the office. "It can't be any more beautiful than this one."

"*You* make the ring beautiful, Cal." He brushes his lips over mine.

I warm, ready to melt into a puddle right here in Donny's father's office.

He turns back to the safe and finishes the combination. "I want you to see it," he says. "If I have it my way, it will be yours someday."

He opens the safe and pushes some papers out of the way.

Then he goes rigid.

"What's the matter?" I ask.

He pulls something out of the safe, but it's not a ring. Clasped between his fingers is an amber-colored feather.

"What's that?"

"A feather," he says, his tone robotic.

"Where's the ring?"

"It's not here."

My skin chills. "Did you move it? I mean, maybe your dad moved it."

"Yeah, maybe." His facial muscles relax a bit. He places the feather back inside the safe, closes it, and then replaces the painting.

"That's beautiful," I say.

"My dad's horse. His name was Phoenix."

"That's an unusual name."

"It made sense for him at the time. My dad . . . he . . . Let's just say he had some shit go down in his life."

I swallow. "You mean . . . similar to the shit you had?"

He nods. "Just between you and me . . . yeah."

My hand flies to my mouth. Talon Steel? Donny? Nausea climbs up my throat.

"Callie, it's okay. We're all okay."

I nod. I believe him.

But I still feel sick. We walk out of the office and back through the house to the kitchen, where I toss my half-eaten piece of cake into the wastebasket.

"You okay, Donny?" I ask.

He smiles, brushes his lips against mine. "I'm going to marry the most wonderful woman in the world. Why wouldn't I be okay?"

I smile weakly. "I love you."

"I love you too, Callie. Always and forever."

Rory clamors into the kitchen then. "Callie! There you are. I need to talk to you."

I look to Donny.

"Go ahead," he says. "I'll be out in a minute."

I follow Rory out onto the deck. She grabs my arm and pulls me over to a secluded part of the yard.

"Cal," she says, "I have an idea, and don't say anything until you hear me out."

CHAPTER FORTY-EIGHT

Donny

A feather.

No ring. A feather.

Dad must have taken the ring and put it somewhere safer. That's the explanation. It has to be.

My phone buzzes, and I pull it out of my pocket.

It's a junk text. I delete it quickly, but then another notification catches my eyes.

Voicemail.

I'm not sure how I didn't notice this before. Then I recall the phone call I got last evening from a number I didn't recognize. I get calls from numbers I don't recognize all the time. They're usually telemarketers who don't leave voicemails, so I never bothered to look until now.

I play the voicemail.

"Hello, Mr. Steel. My name is Janine Murray. I'm a nurse who worked on your father's case. I really need to talk to you. Please call me as soon as you can. Any time of the day or night is fine."

It's getting late, but if this concerns Dad, I need to know. I return the call quickly.

"Hello?"

"Hi, this is Donny Steel. You left me a message about my father."

"Yes." She clears her throat. "Mr. Steel, I got your number from your father's chart. I hope you don't mind me calling you."

"Not at all. What's the problem? Is there something new on my father's case?"

"Yes and no. I mean, your father is fine, obviously. I hope he's doing well at home."

Relief courses through me, though my heart is still pounding. "He is. Thank you for asking. But I get the feeling that's not why you called."

"No, it's not."

Nothing then.

Until I say, "What is it then, Ms. Murray?"

"I . . . I need to tell you something. And . . . I have to ask for your protection."

"Why would you need my protection?"

"Because I did something, Mr. Steel. I did something that I'm not proud of. I was coerced. No, that's the wrong word. I was *forced*."

"What in the hell are you talking about?"

"I need to see you in person," she says.

"All right." I'm supposed to go back to the property with Brock and Dale tomorrow, but meeting a nurse to talk about my father sounds infinitely more pleasurable than pulling down a roof and possibly finding decaying bodies.

"Where are you?" I ask. "Grand Junction?"

"Yes. I'm off tomorrow. Will that work?"

"I suppose so. May I bring my fiancée? Or my brother and cousin?"

"I don't know . . ."

"We're a very close family, Ms. Murray, and I have a feeling I'll need some moral support."

A pause. A long one. Finally, "Yes. That's fine. But I have to ask for discretion."

"You have it. I'll see you around two. Will that work?"

"Yes, but not at my house."

"Fine. You name the place."

"A coffee shop. I'll text you the address."

"Good enough."

"Thank you," she says. "And . . . I'm sorry."

"For what?"

"For . . . We'll talk soon." The call goes dead.

She's sorry? This can't lead to anything good.

I quickly text Dale and Brock that we're going to the city tomorrow afternoon.

Finding out who shot my father is more important than anything.

The missing ring and the feather will have to wait.

The secrets in the old barn will have to wait.

I close my eyes, inhale, exhale, inhale once more.

I should be high on life right now. I'm in love with the woman of my dreams. She knows all my secrets.

I inhale once more and then open my eyes against the images that want to invade my consciousness.

Good. That's good. I can deal with all of this. Callie and I together.

But inside my mind, inside my nose, I can still smell the sweetness of human decay.

I close my eyes and picture the black horse and the colorful bird for which he was named.

The phoenix—the bird that turns to ashes and rises again. A phoenix has feathers.

Ring. Feather. Barn. Safe-deposit box. A secret brother.

Liens everywhere.

Nauseating but sweet aroma.

Secrets.

Secrets and more secrets. Secrets and lies.

Spark turns to flame and flame turns to blaze.

Blaze turns to ashes—ashes from which we must attempt to rise again.

I swallow. My throat hurts. I know…

The ashes are coming.

CONTINUE THE STEEL BROTHERS SAGA
WITH BOOK TWENTY–TWO

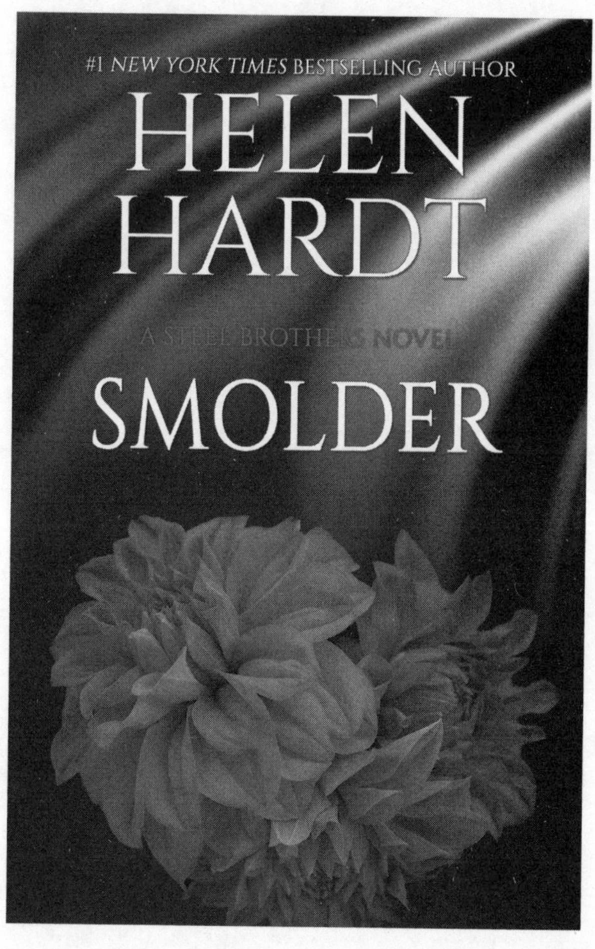

MESSAGE FROM HELEN HARDT

Dear Reader,

Thank you for reading *Blaze*. If you want to find out about my current backlist and future releases, please like my Facebook page and join my mailing list. I often do giveaways. If you're a fan and would like to join my street team to help spread the word about my books, please see the web addresses below. I regularly do awesome giveaways for my street team members.

If you enjoyed the story, please take the time to leave a review on a site like Amazon or Goodreads. I welcome all feedback. I wish you all the best!

Helen

Facebook
Facebook.com/HelenHardt

Newsletter
HelenHardt.com/SignUp

Street Team
Facebook.com/Groups/HardtAndSoul

MESSAGE FROM HELEN HARDT

ALSO BY HELEN HARDT

The Steel Brothers Saga:

Craving
Obsession
Possession
Melt
Burn
Surrender
Shattered
Twisted
Unraveled
Breathless
Ravenous
Insatiable
Fate
Legacy
Descent
Awakened
Cherished
Freed
Spark
Flame
Blaze
Smolder
Flare
Scorch

Blood Bond Saga:

Unchained
Unhinged
Undaunted
Unmasked
Undefeated

Misadventures Series:
Misadventures with a Rock Star
Misadventures of a Good Wife (with Meredith Wild)

The Temptation Saga:
Tempting Dusty
Teasing Annie
Taking Catie
Taming Angelina
Treasuring Amber
Trusting Sydney
Tantalizing Maria

The Sex and the Season Series:
Lily and the Duke
Rose in Bloom
Lady Alexandra's Lover
Sophie's Voice

Daughters of the Prairie:
The Outlaw's Angel
Lessons of the Heart
Song of the Raven

Cougar Chronicles:
The Cowboy and the Cougar
Calendar Boy

Anthologies Collection:
Destination Desire
Her Two Lovers

ACKNOWLEDGMENTS

And so another Steel trilogy comes to an end. Can you believe this is book twenty-one of the Steel Brothers Saga? Who knew, when I penned *Craving* six years ago, that it would spark a phenomenon! All of you readers made this possible, and I appreciate each and every one of you.

Huge thanks to the always brilliant team at Waterhouse Press: Jennifer Becker, Audrey Bobak, Haley Boudreaux, Keli Jo Chen, Yvonne Ellis, Jesse Kench, Robyn Lee, Jon Mac, Amber Maxwell, Dave McInerney, Michele Hamner Moore, Chrissie Saunders, Scott Saunders, Kurt Vachon, and Meredith Wild.

Thanks also to the women and men of Hardt and Soul. Your endless and unwavering support keeps me going.

To my family and friends, thank you for your encouragement. Special shout out to Dean—aka Mr. Hardt—and to our amazing sons, Eric and Grant.

Thank you most of all to my readers. Without you, none of this would be possible. I am grateful every day that I'm able to do what I love—write stories for you!

On to a new Steel couple… Can you guess who they'll be?

ABOUT THE AUTHOR

#1 *New York Times,* #1 *USA Today,* and #1 *Wall Street Journal* bestselling author Helen Hardt's passion for the written word began with the books her mother read to her at bedtime. She wrote her first story at age six and hasn't stopped since. In addition to being an award-winning author of romantic fiction, she's a mother, an attorney, a black belt in Taekwondo, a grammar geek, an appreciator of fine red wine, and a lover of Ben & Jerry's ice cream. She writes from her home in Colorado, where she lives with her family. Helen loves to hear from readers.

Visit her at HelenHardt.com